THE HEART OF HARTLEY MANSION

LINDA FAUSNET

My books contain steamy sex, bad words, and human beings of all sorts, include gay people. If you're not a fan of those things, you may want to stop reading now. If you're cool with that stuff, come take my hand and join me on this journey…

This book is a work of fiction. References to real people, events, establishments, organizations, or locales are intended only to provide a sense of authenticity and are used fictitiously. All other characters, and all incidents and dialogue, are drawn from the author's imagination and are not to be construed as real.

Published by Wannabe Pride 2025

Editing by Linda Hill

Cover Design by Chuck DeKett

FIRST EDITION.

French Translation Expert - Luc Peloquin

ISBN: 978-1-944043-85-8

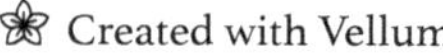 Created with Vellum

1

Cecily Rosewood could feel the ghosts of the past.

Walking slowly down the long, circular paved road that surrounded the large, lush lawn in front of the historic Hartley Mansion just after daybreak, she marveled that she got paid to tread the same ground as some of the earliest colonists in the United States. As the sun began to cast its light over the storied grounds, she drew in a deep breath. She could practically smell the ancient campfires lit by the early settlers as they huddled together to keep warm, cook meals, and tell stories.

It wasn't only her imagination. Olde Town district employees, or "Living History Interpreters," conducted daily demonstrations of cooking over campfires, and sometimes she caught a whiff of the remaining smoke in the air. It was all part of the atmosphere of the touristy area that showcased over four centuries of history, and Cecily found every bit of it thrilling.

She loved these quiet early mornings when she could take time to contemplate the magnitude of where she was. Though she had worked in the Olde Town historic district for two years, she still couldn't get over her good fortune that this was her job. The first mansion tour of the day wasn't until 9am, but she didn't care. Reveling in this quiet time and breathing in the fresh morning air made it worth waking up a bit early each day. That, and she could work on the book she was writing: *The Hartley Family: A History from 1634-1960.*

Upon entering the historic mansion, she punched in the code to disarm the security system discreetly hidden behind a small mirror. Though some modern advancements such as air conditioning were used in some of the historic buildings, the workers here did their best to preserve the old-fashioned decor for their guests. Once inside, she locked the door and headed toward her office.

The floorboards creaked beneath Cecily's feet as she stepped into the Great Hall. Walking down the light brown carpeted hallway, she could easily imagine being dressed in an elegant gown while attending a fancy party thrown by the Hartley family two hundred years ago. Two large chandeliers filled with candles hung from the ceiling, and the walls on either side were filled with large portraits of various Hartley men and women set in ornate gold frames. A huge, winding staircase to the right of the wide hall led to the many bedrooms upstairs. Heavy red velvet curtains adorned the two large windows toward the back of the hall, and a small stained-glass window decorated the top of the wooden door that led out to the vast gardens in the back. Silence filled the empty room, but in Cecily's imagination, she could hear the tinkling of dainty wineglasses, ripples of laughter, and sparkling conversation about politics and other events of the day.

At the end of the long hallway, Cecily turned right, passed through the grand Music Room, and headed to her office. Settling into her chair in front of her large wooden desk, she quickly became engrossed in her work, lost in the archives of the Hartleys circa 1750. She wasn't sure how much time had passed, but after a while she heard footsteps across the floorboards. Still holding the genealogy document she'd been studying, she paused to listen.

Creak ... creak ... creak ...

Hearing unexplained noises throughout the mansion wasn't unusual, considering the place was haunted.

Dr. Cecily Rosewood was a student of history, not the paranormal. A few years ago, she would have laughed at the idea of ghosts, but too many things had happened since she began working here to deny their existence. She frequently heard footsteps in the hallway, as well as the occasional faint sound of piano music coming from the Music Room. She had even seen lights flicker, and the antique chandelier was known to swing slowly back and forth on occasion. Once in a while, she'd catch a whiff of pipe smoke or the scent of a recently snuffed candle. Though she'd been terrified at first, she had gotten used to the strange occurrences. So far, she hadn't actually seen any apparitions, and the spirits didn't seem to want to cause her harm.

Cecily managed to block out the noise of the phantom footsteps and went back to work. At 8:30am her phone timer beeped to inform her that it was almost time for the first guided tour. She had learned the hard way that if she didn't set an alarm, she would get engrossed in her work and lose all track of time. A tourist knocking on the door or another tour guide with a group standing outside sending her a text telling her it was past time to unlock the door would be her only clue as to how late it was.

Having given hundreds of tours, it wasn't as if she needed time to prepare. Still, she liked to have half an hour to gather her thoughts before launching into the story of the Hartleys for paying customers. Plus, she needed a minute or two to slip into her "uniform" for the tour. Since the history of the mansion spanned more than two hundred years, she could choose from a variety of eras. The Olde Town Costume Design Center was responsible for ensuring the authenticity of historical costumes, and they had provided her with several different outfits she could wear on her tours. On any given day, she could choose from a large Victorian-era floor-length dress complete with an obnoxious number of petticoat layers, a simple cotton housedress, or a number of options in between. Today, as she so often did, she opted for the simple dress that a servant or poor farmgirl of the time might have worn. Not only was it more comfortable, but she could slip it on easily. The fancier dresses involved starting her workday in the main part of town to get help putting the dress on, driving back to the mansion ...

No thanks. When she wore her simple dress, she could spend the morning working on her book instead of getting her wardrobe prepared like some Hollywood star. Besides, the huge gowns were far more comfortable to wear in the wintertime than in the heat of summer.

She slipped out of her sundress and into her white servant gown, straightened her hair, and she was done. Easy peasy. After hanging her sundress in the closet in her office, she headed back out into the hallway.

The floorboards creaked again under her feet as she walked down the carpet of the Great Hall. A faint noise stopped her in her tracks. The sound of utensils clinking against china plates came from the dining room that was located on the other side of the wall.

"Good morning, George," Cecily called out before

continuing on her way. No sense in looking into the dining room because nothing would be there. Items might be moved around, but she wouldn't see anyone. She never did.

Cecily didn't really know that it was the ghost of George Hartley messing around in the dining room. It could be any number of people who had died in and around the house over the past several hundred years. From her research, she knew George had been quite fond of food, so it made sense that he might be haunting the room where food had been served all those years ago. It was nothing she could explain, but deep down she *felt* it was George. At any rate, it was nice to have a name to go with all the strange noises.

After checking her hair in the mirror, she headed toward the front of the mansion and opened the front door to peer outside. She often tried to size up the people on her tour before she began. Would they be the type to pay attention while she told the story of the Hartley family? Did the attendees include a bunch of children that would need to be watched carefully lest they touch anything valuable in the house? Truth be told, attempting to size up a crowd rarely did any good. She usually couldn't tell in advance how people would behave. Sometimes the kids were angels while the grownups were hell to deal with. It didn't really matter, she supposed. All Cecily hoped for was that people on the tour would learn a thing or two and maybe come away with the understanding that history didn't need to be dry and boring. Rather, it was filled with drama and pathos. Love and laughter. Life and death. No different than life now, really.

The tours she conducted were frequently filled to capacity since she only gave them Monday through Friday. The Hartley Mansion was normally closed to the public on weekends, except for special occasions like weddings or charity galas.

The day's first tour included seven people. A couple in their late sixties or so, a couple maybe in their early forties, and three kids. One girl and two boys; Cecily guessed them to be around five, eight, and twelve respectively. She always enjoyed having kids on the tour, and she relished the chance to get them excited about history.

After gathering the group together outside in front of the house and ensuring everyone was sporting their lanyards and badges showing they'd paid admission to the Olde Town tourist district, Cecily smiled at the visitors.

"Good morning, and welcome to the Hartley Mansion!"

The oldest boy rolled his eyes, bored already. That didn't bother Cecily much. She'd seen many an annoyed kid dragged along on a family vacation and forced to learn something.

"Just a few quick ground rules before we begin," she continued. "Please stay on the carpeted path as you make your way through the house, and of course, please don't touch anything.

The preteen boy grinned and stretched out his fingers as if to say *challenge accepted*. Cecily made a mental note to keep an eye on that one.

"You're welcome to take any pictures you like, just please don't use flash photography, and feel free to ask any questions along the way," she said. "Come on in."

Cecily led the group into the Great Hall and watched as the tourists looked around. The mother seemed particularly impressed as she gazed up at the fancy chandeliers and scanned the elaborate paintings of the Hartley family. Her expression darkened suddenly.

"Barry, for God's sake *get off that!*" the woman yelled,

startling Cecily. Sure enough, the oldest kid had already taken a seat in one of the velvet-covered chairs.

Barry jumped up, looking properly chastened. His father gave him a look that was enough to scare him into submission. These parents seemed willing to keep their kids in line. Sadly, that often wasn't the case; Cecily had seen quite a few obnoxious children with overly permissive parents.

Though she tried to focus on the interesting parts of the family's story rather than recite dry facts and figures, she had to provide some specific dates as background along with the more sordid details.

"The Hartley Mansion was built in 1783, but the Hartley family had been in possession of the grounds dating back to 1634," Cecily informed the group. "It's fascinating to think of all the people who have come and gone on these very grounds over the past nearly four hundred years."

It was fascinating to her, at least. Barry's eyes were glazing over again.

"For hundreds of years, people from all walks of life called the Hartley Mansion their home, though not all by choice. In addition to the wealthy Hartley family, there were also enslaved people, indentured servants, farmers, and other laborers who lived here."

Both the mom and dad nodded solemnly as they listened. Cecily was glad these kinds of tours had changed dramatically since she'd visited historic places as a child, when the enslaved people were barely mentioned. The focus had always been on the beauty and splendor of these large plantations and not on the dark history behind the glamour. The history of the Hartleys was dark indeed, considering the patriarch Oliver Hartley had raped at least one of the enslaved women and gotten her pregnant. As much as Cecily wished to tell the whole truth on these tours, it was delicate when there were children involved. The younger kids in attendance now were too young to understand what rape was, and she wasn't about to put their parents in a position to have to explain such a horrible thing.

"After arriving here in 1634 and being among the earliest colonists in the entire country, the Hartley family quickly began building up their wealth. But having already come from wealth in England, it was easier for them than for many others who arrived here at the same time. Over the years, the family got rich from various endeavors such as practicing law, buying and selling products, and farming the land for tobacco, grain, and anything else they could grow successfully. With the help of hundreds of enslaved people, of course, who ran the house and what was once a 25,000-acre plantation."

Oddly enough, the younger children on today's tour seemed more interested in Cecily's talk than the grandparents, who seemed bored out of their minds.

"You're standing in the Great Hall, where the Hartleys used to have all types of gatherings. Everything from fancy balls to weddings and funerals."

"Funerals? They actually had dead people in here?" Barry asked, wide-eyed.

Yep. That got people's attention every time.

"Oh yes, it was quite common to hold funerals in homes back in those days. They would lay the body out for viewing and everything," Cecily continued.

"Has anyone died in this house?" Barry asked, and his younger siblings perked up at the question.

Cecily smiled. It was one of the most common questions she got on this tour, especially from kids. The query was often followed up with *is this place haunted?*

"Yes," she answered cautiously, glancing at the other children. The younger the kids, the fewer details she provided where death and dying were concerned. "In fact, it was quite common for people to die at home back in those days. There were no hospitals close by, and when a person was sick and dying, they would usually be taken care of by family members until they passed away."

Barry nodded, and the younger kids stared wide-eyed. Cecily figured she should stay on the subject of death for the moment, since the topic had clearly caught the attention of her audience. Walking over to one of the large portraits on the wall, she said, "For example, Oliver Hartley died upstairs in his bed."

It figured that bastard lived to be seventy-two years old.

Cecily found it hard to hide her contempt as she glanced at the painting of the gray haired, dignified-looking man in a black coat with a white-collared shirt. Still, she managed to keep her expression neutral.

"Did anybody get murdered in this house?" Barry asked.

Cecily laughed softly. "Not that I'm aware of. But somebody did die out on the back lawn."

"Really?" he asked, eyes wide.

"Yes. He was riding his horse and was struck by lightning." A small stab of sorrow pierced her heart as she said the words. Poor George Hartley had only been twenty-seven years old at the time.

"Cool!"

Cecily let out a soft sigh. She understood the young boy's natural fascination with death, but she wasn't about to agree that the tragedy was "cool."

Whipping around to look at the portraits, Barry asked, "Which one is he?"

"We don't have a painting of George, unfortunately. I wish we did. I would love to know what he looked like."

She'd always felt a special affinity for George, though she wasn't sure why. She couldn't be certain that the ghostly presence in the house was him. Even if it was, for all she knew, the guy had been as big of a jerk as his father. And yet, something in her intuition told her the younger Hartley had been nothing like Oliver.

"If you will all follow me, we can tour the dining room and then head upstairs to see the bedrooms and Oliver Hartley's office."

The grandfather suddenly snapped to attention from his zoned-out state.

"Oliver Hardy? Like Laurel and Hardy?" the man asked, his eyes wide.

The old guy seemed very excited at the patently absurd idea that this house was once inhabited by a comedy team from the 1920s. Cecily had to bite her lip hard to keep from laughing before she responded.

"No, sorry. I said Oliver *Hartley*."

The man looked disappointed, and she suspected she had lost his attention for the rest of the tour. She decided to focus on getting the kids more interested.

"Upstairs, you'll get to see the room where Mr. Hartley died."

"Cool!" cried all three youngsters in unison.

Cecily continued the tour for the next thirty minutes, doing her best to keep the family engaged. The grandparents remained mentally checked out for the duration. The parents' attention ebbed and flowed, as did the children's. All in all, not her best tour, but not the worst either.

After ushering the family out the door upon her

concluding words, she heard the mother ask, "Did you guys have fun?"

"Nooo!" shouted the middle child.

Shaking her head, Cecily shut the door behind them. As always, she'd done her best. Still, she knew a brief tour of a historical house that wasn't owned by Thomas Jefferson or Elvis or Laurel and/or Hardy wouldn't be enough to turn resistant tourists into history buffs.

She gave two more tours before lunch, and those went slightly better. Those groups had given her a chance to field more interesting questions, and the last group before lunch consisted of only adults. That type of tour gave her the freedom to tell more of the unvarnished truth about the history of the Hartley Mansion, which made her feel like she was actually making a difference in educating people about the past.

After slipping back into her sundress and locking up the house for her lunch break, Cecily headed out into the bright June sunshine. The next tour didn't start for two hours, so she could take her time and walk to the main historical district. The Hartley Mansion was about a half mile from the main part of Olde Town, where most of the other historical buildings were located. Though many of the tourists chose to take the shuttle from the town to the mansion, Cecily preferred to walk if the weather permitted. She often reflected on what it must have been like for the enslaved people and other servants to walk the same route to gather supplies from the general store and other places in town. The wealthy Hartley family members would have traveled by horse and carriage most of the time. Cecily pictured George, as well as his parents, sitting up all prim and proper in their fancy horse-drawn carriage, making their way to town.

Olde Town, the historic tourist area within St. Mary's City, Maryland was always pretty, but there was really nothing like the gorgeous greens of summer. The lush trees blowing in the breeze and the gardens bursting with flowers made her smile every time she gazed upon them. She particularly enjoyed this time of early summer because she could eat her lunch outside in the picnic area in the center of town.

That all too familiar feeling of guilt swept through Cecily as she strolled the grounds of what had been only the fourth permanent settlement in the United States. She knew how utterly unfair it was that she got to work her dream job while so many others were stuck behind a desk at the mercy of their employers. Her family was extremely wealthy, not unlike the Hartleys. Both of her parents were rather famous technology moguls, so money was no object. Because of them, she had been a full-time student through college and while getting her PhD. So many others had to work hard to afford school, but her parents had paid for her education. Never having to work at a crappy retail job, she'd been able to focus entirely on her studies and hadn't been saddled with any student loans. How unbelievably lucky she was.

Cecily drew in a deep breath as she walked past the shimmering St. Mary's River. She often took the longer walk to town—really only an extra block—to see the *Ark* and the *Dove*, two ships that had first brought settlers here back in 1634. A gorgeous wooden replica of the *Dove* bobbed up and down in the breeze at its spot on the dock, awaiting the next round of tourists. The ship was so *tiny*. Cecily could scarcely imagine what it must have been like to travel all the way from the Isle of Wight in England to here. What a miserable trip that must have been.

"Hey, Dr. Rosewood," called a familiar voice.

Cecily turned her head to smile at Braydyn, a fellow historical tour guide. She always thought of him as "Braydyn spelled with a dyn" because that was how he'd first introduced himself. He was a sweet guy with his adorable slightly curly brown hair and inquisitive brown eyes. No matter how many times she'd told him to call her Cecily, he still addressed her as Dr. Rosewood. Braydyn was kind of a jack-of-all-trades historical reenactor who was a tour guide for the entire town, depending on the needs of the day. He frequently walked his tour groups over to the mansion, telling them facts about history along the way. He hung out inside the Hartley Mansion a lot, mainly to take advantage of the air conditioning when it was especially hot out. Many times, she would find him sitting on the bottom of the steps of the Great Hall, taking a break from the heat. She counted herself as quite fortunate to work in one of the buildings with A/C, and she never minded his friendly presence.

"Where are you off to today?" she asked.

"Today I'm pulling church tour duty," he said with a smile.

"Amen!" she said with a friendly salute as he passed her on the way to the churchyard.

Cecily kept walking and soon neared the picnic area, lost in her thoughts of the past. She often felt the spirits of the men and women who once walked these grounds. Walking through Olde Town, it was as if you could see the progression of human history from the 1600s through today. The historic town featured various buildings, either partial or total restorations, including a bakery, a church, a tavern, a theater, and much more. Tourist season was in full swing today as the streets were crowded with people, all sporting their daily, weekly, or even yearly Olde Town passes on lanyards.

Right now, of all the historical buildings in town, the theater was of tremendous interest to her, whether she wanted to admit it or not. And for once, her feelings had nothing to do with history.

Her current fascination with that particular building had to do with Ryan "Canuck" Armstrong, who was currently conducting a restoration project there. The owner of Armstrong Property Services, the guy could be seen all over the historical district working on all sorts of projects. A native of Montreal, he had the most delightful French Canadian accent. His coworkers loved to tease him about being from Canada, hence the nickname "Canuck." He never seemed to mind though, smiling good-naturedly when his friends teased him.

Cecily's breath caught in her throat when she spotted him working outside in the front yard of the theater. He looked especially delicious today, all sweaty with exertion, tight muscles rippling under his shirt. Ryan was *legendary* around here, and not just due to his chiseled jaw, dark brown hair, and soulful blue eyes—he was the quintessential tall, dark, and handsome man. But no, it wasn't just his good looks that got people's attention. The guy had once stopped a carjacking. He'd chased the perpetrator for four blocks, rescuing a woman and her two young children. The man was a *hero*.

And so, so out of her league. He was remarkably smart, seeing as he owned his own company and somehow understood complex electrical wiring, building construction, and could miraculously fix just about anything. Sadly, he didn't seem interested in her romantically. Around him, she always felt like a shy library nerd to his handsome jock. She knew for a fact he played hockey as a hobby, so he was definitely into sports. Her interests, which included reading history books and listening to classical music, would no doubt bore him senseless.

But then there was one time, about a year ago, when they'd seemed to really connect. Though she had seen him around Olde Town for a few months fixing this and that, that hot day in late August was the first time she'd actually spoken to the man. They'd been standing in a long line for ice cream at a popular sweets shop just outside the historic district and had struck up a conversation. Ryan had seemed genuinely impressed that she had a PhD in colonial history, and they'd had quite an entertaining chat. Prior to that conversation, she had assumed erroneously that a hot guy who worked in construction would have no interest in history. After talking to him for a few moments, she'd found he was fairly knowledgeable about colonial history and seemed as excited to work in Olde Town as she was. By the time they'd gotten their ice cream, Cecily was almost certain he was going to ask her out. After all, they'd really hit it off, having instantly fallen into a fascinating conversation despite barely knowing each other.

Alas, it was not to be. Once he'd gotten his ice cream cone, Ryan had bidden her adieu in his sexy French accent and gone back to work.

Cecily had been crushed. And then she'd felt stupid for thinking for even one moment that a guy like him could go for a woman like her.

Since that day last summer, Ryan had been filed strictly under the category of "you can look but not touch."

And yet, how wonderful it would be to touch him. Just once. Even with all her fancy education and degrees and advanced vocabulary, there was still only one word that could describe that delightful young Canadian buck.

Dreamy.

"Hey, Cecily," Ryan called, brightening her day considerably. The jolt of adrenaline that shot through her system at the sight of his smile did more to wake her up than the two cups of coffee she'd had this morning.

"Hey," she said, returning his wave as casually as she could. As much as she wished she could just stop and stare at him, she forced herself to walk the rest of the way to her destination.

Sighing as she sat down at a picnic table, she lamented that these brief encounters with the hunk of a man were never enough.

If only something major would break at Hartley Mansion. Something that would take months to fix.

The thought made her giggle to herself.

After lunch, she had three more tours booked. On the second to last tour of the day, she noticed it was starting to feel a bit warm inside the mansion. It was a hot day, so she didn't think too much of it until the tourists on the final tour of the day complained about the heat. Checking the thermostat, she found that the temperature was stuck at eighty degrees.

Damn.

If the system had stopped working earlier, she could have gotten maintenance to come and take a look and maybe even fix it right away. At this hour, all she could do was call in a repair request.

On the plus side, if she was *really* lucky, Ryan Armstrong would be the one to come to her rescue. Though it was certainly possible, he had lots of guys—and gals— working for him, and any one of them could come to the Hartley Mansion to fix the A/C. She'd just have to wait and see tomorrow.

As usual, she ended her night by glaring at the portrait of Oliver Hartley in the Great Hall and then heading over to the grand dining room.

She paused in the doorway before turning off the light.

"Goodnight, George," she said softly. "Rest well."

2

1835

George Hartley sat at the dining room table enjoying a sumptuous meal of pork with stewed apples. Dinah, one of the kitchen slaves, appeared behind him and placed a second helping on the table without him having to ask. Everyone knew how much he enjoyed his supper. It was a wonder he managed to stay trim, given his penchant for fine dining.

"How was your recent trip to New York?" his father Oliver asked, addressing Mr. Nathanial Taylor, a prominent lawyer and father of the woman George was expected to marry. No formal engagement had been made as of yet, but that was what dinners such as these were for. Getting both families together was important to make sure the arrangement would work.

Perhaps "arrangement" wasn't the right word, but George didn't know what else to call it. George was hardly in love with Victoria, not that he believed in such nonsense anyway. The long and short of it was that George's family was incredibly wealthy, Victoria's family was incredibly wealthy, and that was all that mattered to anyone. George supposed some couples actually did marry for love, but his parents certainly hadn't. Their marriage had worked out fine, and he figured his own would as well. Once he got all the marriage bother out of the way, he could get on with running the Hartley family business.

"Excellent," Mr. Taylor boomed in his loud, self-important voice. He went on to describe his various adventures in the big city while George concentrated on his savory meal.

"Such a dirty city," Victoria said, wrinkling her nose. Her light-colored curls bounced on the sides of her face as she spoke, her brown eyes squinting a bit.

She wasn't wrong. New York City might be an exciting, vibrant place, but it was also filthy. Trash filled the streets, and the air was thick with chimney smoke. It was noisy, too, with people shouting at one another and large carriages rattling around. Still, George found it a fascinating place to watch people. As he was expected to take over the family's various business holdings, he frequently accompanied his father on his journeys to other cities.

Victoria's eyes roamed around the elegant dining room with its bright blue painted walls, gold velvet curtains, and large ornate mirror attached to the wall. His family ate and drank only from the finest of china plates and crystal glassware. The dining room boasted extravagance everywhere one looked.

"I much prefer it here in Maryland," she said, glancing at George approvingly.

"I agree," he said with a nod and a smile in her direction.

Victoria giggled softly, demurely lowering her head. A slight blush bloomed on her cheeks, which was rather becoming. Her pale, delicate features combined with an impressive bosom were all points in her favor in becoming George's wife. Oh yes. She would do quite nicely.

As alluring as Victoria Taylor was, she couldn't quite compete for his attention once dessert had been served. George's eyes widened in delight at the slice of chunky apple cake that had been placed in front of him. Dripping with brown sugar sauce, the cake was one of his favorites.

"My boy has a fine head for finance, I assure you," Oliver said, grinning proudly in George's direction. "He's already proven himself indispensable when it comes to the family business."

The family business wasn't one venture in particular, as the Hartleys had their hand in all manner of industries. Their land was actively farmed for tobacco and grain, they bred and raced horses, invested in art, and even produced citrus fruit all year round via their Orangery building.

"Indeed, he takes after his father," said George's mother Penelope with a proud nod in his direction. No one was happier about his potential nuptials than she. As far as she was concerned, the sooner he worked on producing a male heir, the better. Penelope Hartley was quite concerned with the Hartley's wealth and reputation, and she was determined to add to the Hartley family tree.

George quickly lost interest in the mindless chatter once his dessert was gone and was pleased when everyone retired to the Music Room. He had become quite adept at playing the piano.

Victoria sat primly on one of the floral couches with her parents, while Penelope and Oliver sat together on the smaller love seat. George relished the opportunity to play the piano for guests, and he did so whenever the opportunity presented itself. He played one of his favorites; a bouncy little tune known as "Polonaise in D Major" by Richard Wagner. It was such a fun song to play, and it gave him an opportunity to show off his musical skills.

Upon playing the final note with a flourish, George earned a nice round of applause from his audience.

"That was quite impressive. Absolutely lovely!" Victoria said before bowing her head demurely and blushing.

"Thank you," George said with a smile, pleased that she enjoyed his performance. He truly loved music and relished sharing his passion with her.

Lifting her head slightly, Victoria's face held an expression of slight confusion. "But you know, you can always get one of your slaves to play the music for you."

Penelope laughed. "Thank you, Victoria! I can't tell you how many times I've told him that. There's no need for George to wear himself out when we could just as easily give piano lessons to one of the slaves."

George stifled a sigh. Leave it to his mother to dismiss his hard work and talent, not to mention the pleasure he derived from playing. How insulting it was to say that a mere slave could possibly learn to play the piano as well as he could. But he shouldn't have been surprised. Penelope Hartley was all about appearances, and she'd have much preferred using slave labor to flaunt their wealth in front of company rather than have her own son entertain their guests.

"It would be truly lovely if you could have one of them learn to play, George, so that you could sit by me as we listen together," Victoria said, fanning herself as if to ward off her blush.

George stifled another sigh. If Victoria and Penelope teamed up and had their way, he'd never be allowed to play the piano again. While Oliver was the official head of the family, of course, he frequently did as he was told by his wife behind closed doors. He did whatever was necessary to keep his mother happy. Perhaps "happy" was too strong of a word. Oliver did what he could to make Penelope less angry.

Without asking his audience if they'd like to hear another song, he plunked his fingers back onto the piano. He launched into another tune thinking he might as well seize his opportunity to play while he still could.

THE NEXT AFTERNOON, George found himself bored and craving something sweet to eat, so he decided he would ride into town and visit the general store to see if they had anything good. He rather enjoyed horseback riding, so that was his preferred mode of travel. However, Penelope did not approve. If he was to go into town, he was to use the horse-drawn carriage. His mother claimed to be concerned for his safety, which was ridiculous. George could race horses with the best of them, therefore a simple jaunt to town was hardly a challenge. The truth was Penelope would never waste an opportunity to show off the fact that the Hartleys were wealthy enough to own a carriage.

He grudgingly agreed to take the carriage, but only if he could drive it rather than have one of the slaves or other workers take him. He rather enjoyed solitude from time to time, and he would much prefer a solo trip to town. Springtime in Maryland could be quite lovely, and he was looking forward to getting some fresh air.

George pulled the string that was attached to the bell in the small hallway leading to the kitchen to summon Sam, his personal slave. Each member of the household, including his younger sisters, had their own slave to cater to them. Each bell had a different tone, which was quite convenient. Sam, a young man in his twenties, arrived quickly at George's side.

"Sam, my fine fellow," George said brightly. "Fetch me my hat and bring the carriage 'round, please."

George prided himself on being one of the good slave masters. He was always polite and kind to his slaves, unlike some other masters he'd met over the years.

He gazed out at the vast green lawn in front of the house, drawing in a deep breath of warm air. Once Sam brought the carriage around, the ride into the main part of St. Mary's City proved to be as lovely as he'd hoped. His favorite part was riding past the St. Mary's River, with its gentle, rippling waves shimmering in the sun. He arrived in town just as his stomach began to rumble.

The scent of sugary goodness greeted George's nose the moment he stepped inside Hawkins General Store.

"Oh, sweet heavens, what is that I'm smelling?" he asked.

Gene Hawkins, the slender, gray haired owner of the store, greeted him with a smile. "Mr. Hartley, it's nice to see you! You've come on a good day. We've got fresh-baked molasses cookies."

George glanced over at the brick fireplace to his right where, sure enough, he spotted the aforementioned cookies browning slightly on a cast iron paddle. A woman with her back to him was pulling the delicious-smelling treats out at that very moment.

The young woman turned around, and somehow George lost all interest in the cookies. For now.

Clad in a blue cotton dress with a white apron, the cookie lady smiled at George as she carefully placed the paddle on the wooden table.

Those eyes. They were absolutely *stunning*, the bluest of blues he'd ever seen, matching her dress perfectly. She wore a white bonnet, her pretty, loose blond curls bouncing slightly on her shoulders as she transferred the cookies to a plate.

"Anna, this is Mr. George Hartley," Gene said, gesturing toward him. "Mr. Hartley, this is my daughter, Anna."

Not typically one to be at a loss for words, it took George a moment to find his voice. "Charmed to meet you," he said at last.

Anna smiled warmly, a faint blush tinting her cheeks. Her shy expression was similar to Victoria's, and yet different somehow. He couldn't think of why or how. It was just ... different.

"Would you like to try a molasses cookie?" she asked, offering the plate to him.

I think I'm in love.

George damn near said the words out loud. After all, it wasn't every day a lovely young woman offered him fresh-baked sweets.

"Oh yes, I would. Yes, indeed," he exclaimed, selecting a cookie from the plate.

Anna smiled again, the joy reaching all the way to her eyes. Her cheeks bloomed with a slightly darker tinge of red, her smile still sweet and shy.

It's not fake. That's the difference.

The errant thought just popped into his mind. He wasn't sure where it had come from, but he realized the stray thought was right. When Victoria giggled shyly and lowered her head demurely, it didn't seem as real. Like she was putting on an act. It wasn't uncommon for women to go pale and faint at the slightest provocation, and he'd never real-ized how much Victoria really leaned into that helpless female act. In the first thirty seconds since meeting Anna, George could tell she was different. For one thing, the idea of Victoria cooking or baking anything herself was preposterous. She would never do such a thing, would no doubt insist that was what slaves were for.

He took a bite of the cookie, and the taste could only be described as heaven on earth. Closing his eyes, he moaned in delight. "This is delicious!"

Upon opening his eyes, he was greeted by another smile from Anna. "I'm so glad you like it."

"That's my girl," Gene said proudly. "She's a terrific baker. Anna can cook just about anything. Keeps me well fed, that's for sure."

"And why have I never seen this lovely woman in the store before now?" George asked.

"Welp, we used to have a lady work in the store with me, but we had to cut back a bit," Gene answered.

"I will certainly be bringing home a bunch of these cookies made by your daughter today," he said with a grin. He forced himself to tear his gaze away from the lovely Anna as he looked around the store. "What else have you got for me today, Gene?"

"Fresh-baked bread for one thing." He gestured at a table filled with various breads and biscuits.

"Did you bake these as well?" George asked, seizing the opportunity to look back at Anna.

"Yes, I did." She held her gaze on his in a way Victoria never would have done. He loved it.

"Then I'd better bring some bread home with me," he said. With a dramatic sigh, he added, "And I suppose I should be a good boy and bring something healthy back as well."

"Perhaps some apples and peaches?" Gene suggested hopefully.

"Sounds delightful."

Much to George's pleasure, Anna came to help him select his fruit. After all was said and done, he had an impressive amount of food to take home. Gene packed everything up neatly in apple boxes and, lucky for George, another customer came in needing assistance.

"I'll help him with his things," Anna told her father.

The notion of having just a few precious moments alone with her made him positively giddy.

Anna's gorgeous blue eyes flew open wide when she caught sight of the carriage outside the store.

"My goodness," she exclaimed. No doubt her reaction would have pleased his mother greatly.

Stacking the boxes in the carriage took no time at all. George, desperate to extend his time with Anna, thought of the perfect thing to say. He was quite curious to hear her reaction.

"Well, I'd best be going. I'd like to have some time this afternoon to practice the piano," he said as casually has he could.

"Oh, my," Anna exclaimed, her cheeks flushing with excitement. "Do you really have your own piano? And you know how to play?"

"Yes, I love to play."

"How lovely," Anna said. "My cousin has a piano, and I just love to hear him play it."

"You enjoy music?" he asked, even though he already had the answer. He just relished speaking about his passion with a pretty woman.

"Very much so."

"We have a harp in our Music Room as well," George said, hoping he didn't sound too pompous.

Anna shook her head in wonder. "Oh, I adore the sound of the harp! Years and years ago we were invited to a fancy party where they had a lady playing the harp. So lovely, it was. That must be what heaven sounds like. Oh, I hope it doesn't sound too stupid to say that."

She laughed at herself as she spoke. Now *that* was the sound of an angel in heaven. Once again, George enjoyed the flush of her cheeks. She wasn't playacting as she spoke. Everything she said was so genuine, and it made him realize how fake everyone around him was by comparison. The way his parents were always showing off their wealth and how Victoria was forever fanning herself and pretending to be shy. At least his younger sisters still laughed and played and behaved like actual human beings. For now, anyway.

"Not at all," George said. He allowed his eyes to linger on hers much longer than was appropriate, but he couldn't help himself. Anna was just so lovely in every possible way. "I wish I knew how to play it. Perhaps I should learn. We've had guests in our home come and play it, and yes, the harp does have a rather otherworldly sound I would say."

"Indeed," Anna said dreamily.

George nodded. He had run out of things to say, and they'd already spent more time together than was acceptable for an unmarried couple.

"I suppose I should be going." He didn't even try to hide the reluctance in his voice. "But I will be sure to come back for more cookies soon."

"Oh, please do," Anna said, still gazing into his eyes. In that moment, it was all too easy to forget that Victoria existed.

"Thank you so much for all of your help."

"It was my pleasure," she said softly.

With that, George took his leave, hoping she was watching him ride off into the distance in his family's carriage. Already, the seat next to him felt empty somehow. As if Anna Hawkins belonged there.

George rode home in a daze, hardly glancing at the river on his way home. Not long ago, he and his family attended a performance of *Romeo and Juliet* at the theater. As entertaining as the play had been, he'd dismissed the whole thing as melodramatic, romantic nonsense. He'd thought the notion of love at first sight was beyond ridiculous.

Now he wasn't so sure.

Throughout the rest of his day, especially while he was playing the piano, George's thoughts were utterly consumed by Anna.

He simply could not stop thinking about her.

3

R yan simply could not stop thinking about her. He adored Cecily Rosewood, even though he was sure he had no chance with her. She was just so friggin' *smart*. And he was not.

As he walked toward the Hartley Mansion to repair the air conditioning, he obsessed over what to say to Cecily. Nervous as he might be, he was still grateful there was finally something that needed fixing in the historical building where she did her tours. Lately, it seemed he worked everywhere in Olde Town *but* the mansion.

The idea that he, a high school dropout, could possibly date a woman with a PhD was ludicrous. But as they say, the heart wants what it wants. And his heart wanted her.

Ryan gazed out at the St. Mary's River as he strolled toward the mansion. He took a deep breath and tried to steady his nerves. He admired Cecily so much, but he had no idea how to tell her that. It was so cool how obsessed she was with studying history. Her doctorate was in colonial history, and she was currently writing a book on the Hartley family. And here he struggled just to *read* a book. Ryan's parents were right. He was just a dumb jock, and not even a good jock at that. Hockey was a lot of fun, but he wasn't exactly gonna make it to the NHL like his parents wanted. Such a stereotypical Canadian thing for his folks to expect him to play pro hockey, but they did.

Yeah. That was not gonna happen. He'd come to the United States to get away from all the pressure and drama from his parents. After he'd started his own construction and maintenance business, he never looked back.

Watching the rippling water in the evening sun, he contemplated the history here as he so often did. Damn, this was a cool place to work. Like Cecily, Ryan was fascinated by the people who had come here so long ago, building up this area from scratch. The old buildings, the cemetery, and the church in Olde Town were so rich with history and drama from the past. He loved learning, but he hated to read. Instead, he watched tons of videos and documentaries about history. In fact, he'd recently watched a lengthy YouTube series on cooking in the 1830s. Maybe he could somehow bring that up in conversation with Cecily without sounding like a complete idiot.

Ryan's stomach tingled with excitement and nerves when he reached the paved path that led to the Hartley Mansion. Since it was after 5pm, the tours would be finished for the day, giving him free rein to get his work done. It would also give him some precious one-on-one time with Cecily. Drawing in a deep breath, he turned the front doorknob.

His stomach sank. The door was locked.

Damn.

He had a key, so gaining entry was not the problem. A locked door probably meant Cecily had already left for the day.

Sighing heavily, he unlocked the door and went inside. He sighed again when he saw that the alarm was set. Cecily had *definitely* left for the day. As he punched in the alarm code, he thought about just coming back tomorrow to work on the repairs. Cecily often arrived early in the morning and stayed after hours in the evening to work on her book. Not tonight, apparently. Still, he'd made the trip here, so he might as well see if he could determine the problem with the A/C. He'd probably have to come back later with more tools anyway. The shed behind the Hartley Mansion had some supplies, but likely not everything he needed.

The mansion was eerily quiet, and he found the silence unsettling. His footsteps made the floor beneath him creak as he walked through the Great Hall toward the hidden thermostat on the wall. Olde Town tried to keep as much modern stuff hidden from the public as possible, which was why the thermostat had a flip cover over it that matched the wallpaper. Ryan tinkered with it for a few minutes to make sure it was in proper working order.

His muscles were tense as he worked. He couldn't help it. The mansion was beautiful, but it could be kinda creepy when there was nobody else around. He tried to ignore the growing dread in his stomach and concentrated on his work. The thermostat seemed to be working fine, but there was no denying it was hot as hell in this house. How did people survive way back when with no air conditioning and central heating?

The next thing he needed to check was the air filter to make sure it wasn't all dirty and clogged. An easy enough task. That was, for an ordinary house. Like most of the buildings around here, the Hartley Mansion was not ordinary. As much as he tried not to think about the strange occurrences he'd witnessed in Olde Town over the years, they were hard to ignore. Odd sounds, eerie footsteps, and sudden drafts of cold air.

He grudgingly made his way to the basement, which was the last place he wanted to be right now. Once again, he was tempted to just come back in the morning. That way he would not only get to see Cecily, he wouldn't be in this creepy house all by himself.

But that didn't sit right. Poor Cecily had to work in this house all day long, and he didn't want her to suffer with no A/C. The sooner he diagnosed the problem, the sooner he could get it fixed for her.

Ryan pulled the string to turn on the dingy lightbulb in the basement and headed down the stairs. There was no need to hide the electric lights since no tourists ever came down here. The air was cool and damp in the basement.

Like a tomb.

Why did he have to think that?

Because the walls are stone and the floor is dirt, that's why. Ugh.

He pulled out his flashlight and examined the air conditioning filter as quickly as he could. Though it wasn't exactly clean, it wasn't dirty enough to interfere with the system. He had just a moment to be relieved that he could leave the basement when he heard it.

The sound of faint piano music coming from upstairs.

A cold chill went through his body. His first instinct was to run, but he couldn't move.

He couldn't very well stay down here all night. Besides, the basement was even creepier than the upstairs. And for all he knew, whoever or whatever was playing the piano could come down here to get him.

Ryan's imagination ran wild; he was on the verge of a panic attack. He drew in several deep, cleansing breaths to steady himself before he forced his feet to move up the stairs to the main part of the house. The upper part of the house was slightly less scary. It was early evening, so it was still light out. Still, it was eerily quiet now, which was no better than hearing the creepy piano music.

At least that's what he had thought. Then the familiar tinkling of the piano started up again. The bolt of fear that shot through him suddenly turned to anger. Ryan did not enjoy being frightened. He dashed into the Music Room and found exactly what he had expected.

Nothing. No sound. Nothing to see.

He stared at the piano, an authentic piece he knew was several hundred years old. What if the ancient instrument was like one of the evil dolls in the movies that had some kind of malevolent spirit attached to it? His anger dissipated, and the fear returned.

Screw this.

The damned A/C repair could wait until morning. Ryan bolted out of the house.

The last thing he heard before slamming the front door was the faint sound of the harp from the Music Room.

AFTER A SOMEWHAT RESTLESS NIGHT, Ryan returned to the Hartley Mansion early in the morning. He felt guilty for not doing more to fix the air conditioning the night before, plus he wanted to make sure he got to see Cecily.

He unlocked the front door and checked to see if the security alarm was armed. It wasn't, so he headed toward Cecily's office. The house was just as quiet as it had been the night before, but nowhere near as creepy since Cecily was here. Thus far, he'd never had a ghostly encounter when there had been other *living* people around.

As always, his footsteps creaked across the floor of the Great Hall.

"Hello?" he called out, not wanting to startle Cecily with his presence.

After a few seconds, she appeared at the doorway of the hall like a vision. Her lovely, long dark hair flowed down her back, and her light brown eyes were gentle, radiating kindness. Cecily looked so soft and feminine in her light blue cotton sundress. She was rather petite, which always made him feel even taller when he was near her. She smiled as she fanned herself with her hand, and he felt even more guilty about the broken A/C. He felt bad because she was uncomfortable and because her sweaty face made him think of other activities that would make her sweat. Ryan couldn't help himself. With her under-stated beauty and her smarts, Dr. Rosewood was irresistible to him.

"Hey there," she said softly. "Come to fix the air condi-tioning?"

Ryan nodded, feeling a bit tongue-tied.

"You're my hero," she said.

Ryan usually felt uncomfortable when people called him a hero, which happened a lot ever since that carjacking incident when he'd helped that lady. But it sounded pretty good coming from her.

"I don't know how people used to live without air condi-tioning back in the old days," he said.

"Right?" Cecily's pretty brown eyes opened wide. She lit up every time someone brought up anything remotely historical, which was why he'd said it.

"I'm sorry the A/C is still broken. I did come over after

hours last night to take a look. Checked out the thermostat and the filter and all that."

"Thank you," she said, still fanning herself.

He hoped like hell there were no hidden security cameras in the house that caught his cowardice last night.

"Whoa, it's hot as hell in here," came a male voice that startled them both.

Ugh. Normally Ryan didn't mind talking with Braydyn. He was a nice guy who also liked to chat about history with him. Right now, though, he was intruding on Ryan's precious alone time with Cecily.

"What's up with the A/C?" he asked, fanning his face just like Cecily.

"Welp, in my experienced and professional opinion, I'd say it's broke," Ryan said. Cecily laughed, which made him less annoyed at Braydyn's presence. The guy was fun to banter with, and he felt slightly less nervous with him there as a buffer.

"Don't worry," she said. "Ryan will fix it. He can fix anything."

This was his chance to be her hero. Cool.

"For real, what did people *do* before air conditioning?" Braydyn said with annoyance.

"We were just saying that," Ryan said. Glancing up at the portrait of Oliver Hartley, he added, "I imagine ol' Oliver was a treat to be around in the summer."

Cecily laughed again and appeared delighted that Ryan had mentioned one of the Hartleys.

"Can you imagine?" She shook her head. "They say he had quite the temper sometimes."

"Yeah," Ryan agreed. "Not a good guy, and that's putting it mildly."

Cecily and Braydyn nodded. They all knew Oliver's

history, particularly about his track record of sexually assaulting the women he enslaved. It occurred to Ryan that maybe Oliver was the mystery musician haunting him last night. A scary thought, considering how evil the guy was in life.

"Yeah, yeah, yeah. The guy was an asshole. Less yappin', more fixin'!" Braydyn said.

"Listen, Braydyn with a 'dyn' ..." Ryan began.

"That's how I always think of him too," Cecily said, her pretty brown eyes twinkling with amusement.

"Such oddball names parents come up with these days," Ryan said.

Braydyn snorted. "*These days.* I'm what, five years younger than you, Canuck?"

Ryan pointed a finger at him. "Don't talk dat way to yer elders, eh?"

Cecily laughed heartily at that. He often affected a strong typically Canadian accent when people joked about him hailing from up north. His real accent was French Canadian, since he was born and raised in Quebec. But the regular Canadian accent was funnier.

"What brings you out here so bright and early anyway, Braydyn?" Ryan asked.

"Oh, right," he said. "Cecily, I wanted to ask if you had any openings left for your afternoon tours today. I was talking to a few people yesterday who said they might be interested."

"I think I'm technically all booked up, but if it's only two or three people, I don't mind squeezing them in. You can tell them to go to the Visitor's Center and let them know I said it's fine by me. If they try to book on the Olde Town app, the system won't let them if enough people already signed up."

"Okay, sounds good. I will let them know," Braydyn said.

"All right, I better get cracking on this A/C," Ryan said, cracking his knuckles.

"Finally!" Braydyn said with an eye roll.

"Don't you have tours to run yourself, young man?"

"Yeah, yeah. I'm goin', I'm goin'. The other places I gotta work today will probably be a lot cooler anyway. See ya 'round, Dr. Rosewood. And get to work, Canuck!"

Ryan laughed and shook his head.

"See ya later," Cecily said with a wave. Turning toward Ryan, she said, "Well, I better get back to work. Let me know if you need anything."

"Will do. Thanks." He allowed his gaze to linger on hers for a moment. She smiled gently, and he stifled a sigh. She was so damned sweet.

And she deserved to be comfortable, no matter how sexy she looked when she was all sweaty. He needed to fix the A/C quickly.

Fortunately, it didn't take long to find the problem now that he was no longer distracted by otherworldly creatures. He was glad he was able to get everything fixed before the first mansion tour of the day.

Ryan walked toward Cecily's office, trying to make his footsteps heavy enough that he wouldn't startle her. Her office door was open. She looked up when he appeared in the doorway.

"Got a minute?" he asked.

"Of course." She seemed unbothered by his interruption, even though she looked like she'd been hard at work.

Cecily followed him toward one of the air conditioning vents on the floor.

"Put your hand over it," he instructed.

She did as he asked, and her face broke into a pretty smile the moment she felt the cool air hit her hand.

"Yes! It's all fixed now?"

"Yup. I replaced the air filter and removed all the frost that was built up on the evaporator coils just in case, but really the problem was a simple blown fuse," he told her.

"Oh, that's so great. You really can fix anything," she said, sounding impressed.

Out of habit, he found his brain scanning her words for sarcasm. There was no need. Cecily would never make fun of him or talk down to him no matter how smart she was, but he couldn't help worrying about that sort of thing. He'd never been the best student growing up, and the smart kids had often mocked him for it. People often thought that only popular jocks were bullies, but it wasn't true. Mean girls and cruel guys came from all walks of life.

"Thank you so much," she said, and Ryan didn't doubt her sincerity. She sounded genuinely grateful. "I appreciate you coming in so early to take care of this."

"My pleasure," he said.

Cecily's gaze seemed to linger a bit longer than usual. It was probably just his overactive imagination.

But maybe it wasn't.

He could only hope that perhaps there was some kind of spark between them. Only time would tell, he supposed.

Ryan turned to leave, but then he hesitated for a moment.

"Something wrong?" she asked.

"No, nothing's wrong. It's just ..."

The sudden urge to just ask her out already overwhelmed him. If he didn't do it right this second, he would lose his nerve and he'd never get the courage again.

"Can I ask you something?"

"Of course," she said, leaning toward him encouragingly.

"Uh-um ... would ...I mean ... have you ever heard any strange noises in this house?" Ryan blurted out.

He'd not only lost his nerve, he'd come out with the only stupid thing he could think of to say. He wished like hell he could turn back time and just leave, the hero who fixed the A/C. Why did he have to go and screw it all up?

"Oh," Cecily said, seeming surprised at the question. "Do you mean like ... unexplained noises, as in like ghostly stuff?"

Ryan's face heated. He felt so stupid for asking such a thing.

"Never mind. Forget I asked. I—"

Cecily put her hand on his shoulder, surprising the hell out of him.

"No, no. I'm glad you asked. It's a good question." She dropped her hand from his shoulder. "Yes. I sure have. I don't talk about it much. I figure nobody will believe me, you know?"

He nodded, relieved she didn't think he was a total idiot.

"What did you hear?" she asked, eyes wide. "Like utensils scraping on plates?"

He shook his head. "No, not that. More strange music. Last night when I came to see what was wrong with the air conditioning."

"Piano music?" she asked.

Ryan nodded rapidly. "Yeah."

Cecily smiled. "I've heard that too."

"Wow," he said.

"Yeah. Pretty wild, huh?"

"I'll say. Well, I was just curious and thought I'd ask."

Ryan stood there for a moment, contemplating his next move. Just like their amazing chat at the ice cream shop last year, they'd found something in common. He had another chance to ask her out right now.

He didn't take it.

"Well, I guess I better get going," he said.

"Okay," she said softly. "Thanks again."

"Any time," he said, fighting to keep his expression neutral.

He turned to go. For real this time.

Shit.

4

———

George wandered aimlessly around the Hartley Mansion, reflecting over the events of the day. He chuckled to himself, remembering how Ryan had reacted to his ghostly presence last night. For the most part, he tried not to scare people, but sometimes boredom took over and he couldn't help himself. George found it amusing to see a big strong man like Ryan "Canuck" Armstrong get so scared over a few eerie sounds, especially considering his reputation as a hero. Funny how he could take on a real-life threat like a criminal attempting to carjack a woman but be terrified of a spirit he couldn't even see.

Though George couldn't help teasing Ryan a little, he had felt bad when he ran out of the house last night. Ryan was an affable fellow and didn't deserve that. Poor guy was only trying to fix the air conditioning.

George tried to imagine what air conditioning must feel like. What a delight it must be to have cool air blowing through the house during the hottest days of summer. No wonder people got used to that sort of thing and found it quite difficult to live without it.

As always, he enjoyed watching Cecily give tours, telling the story of his family. Impressive the way she got most of the facts right, despite having been born more than a hundred years after his immediate family had lived here. She was a sweet lady, and watching her and her tourists provided him with much-needed entertainment during the day.

Nighttime was another story. Bored out of his mind, George resisted the urge to vanish until morning. Vanishing was the ghost version of sleep. One was unconscious and unaware of one's surroundings. The ability to vanish was one of the few things that could keep a spirit from going completely out of their mind after existing in ghost form for hundreds of years. He could vanish until morning when there would be people like Cecily and her tourists to watch. The main difference between vanishing and sleep was that one could vanish indefinitely, even for hundreds of years. George knew this because sometimes he would encounter a "new" spirit, or at least one that was new to him. A ghost he'd met not long ago had been among the earliest settlers from way back in the 1600s.

Was that lady ever surprised to see the tourist trap St. Mary's City had become! The small town within St. Mary's City, Olde Town was deliberately named that because it sounded touristy. The name clearly worked, as the town enjoyed visitors year-round.

Rather than vanish, George continued roaming the house, lost in thought. When he reached the Music Room, he sighed heavily. Well, kind of sighed. It was rather difficult to do when there was no air in the lungs. His bodily functions may have ceased, but his emotions remained the same. The strongest of which was regret.

JULY 15, 1835

After that first meeting with Anna, George visited the general store as often as he could. Prior to that wonderful day when he'd found her baking the most delicious cookies, he hadn't even known Gene Hawkins had a daughter. And yet, from that day forward, he frequently found her there.

And she'd always seemed delighted to see him.

One glorious day in summer, he'd found Anna alone in the store. Her father had stepped away for a few hours to help a friend on his farm and left his lovely daughter in charge.

"George!" she cried when he opened the door, her beautiful blue eyes shining brightly. "Oh. I— I mean Mr. Hartley."

He smiled at her. "Anna, I think we've known each other long enough that you can call me George."

"George, then," she said softly. He noted the absence of a blush on her face. Victoria would have fanned her face and probably swooned if he'd had the same exchange with her when they'd first met. So melodramatic, that one.

Victoria.

Anna didn't even know she existed. Or at least she had no idea there was another woman in his life that he was expected to marry. It wasn't as if George had made any promises to Anna or anything. But he was clearly interested in her. Her father seemed to approve of his actions as well. Gene often smiled in his direction while he chatted with his little girl.

Like Anna, Gene seemed so *genuine.* So honest. Obviously, he knew about the Hartleys and their vast wealth, but he didn't seem to care. Rather, he seemed more concerned about his daughter's happiness than marrying her off to a rich man.

George didn't know what in the hell he was thinking, attempting to court another woman. He couldn't help himself. There was no denying he had fallen deeply in love with Anna. But to marry her would mean walking away from everything in his life. His parents, his wealth, his heritage, his *home.* The urge to do just that overwhelmed him sometimes. Sweep Anna Hawkins off her feet and marry her and run away and never look back.

Anna walked over to George and handed him a fresh-baked molasses cookie.

"You do know the way to a man's heart," he said, gazing lovingly at her so she would know he was talking about more than just feeding him well.

"I do my best," she said softly.

"How long will your father be out?"

"A few more hours, I suppose," she said, sounding breathless. It was a rare moment indeed for an unmarried man and woman to be left alone like this. Anyone could walk into the store at any time. And that made every single moment alone with her precious. He needed to make the most of the time he had.

"Your father is a good man. So kind."

"Yes, he is."

"May I ask ... is your mother still with us?"

George hated to be blunt, but there was so much he wanted to know about her and so little time to ask.

Anna fell silent for a moment. Tears formed in her eyes.

"Oh, I'm so sorry. I didn't mean to upset you." He touched her arm gently.

"No, it's all right. She ... passed two years ago. I miss her so much," she said, wiping her eyes.

George had no words, so he kept still and listened.

"I'm glad you asked, George. I want to talk about her. But my father ... it hurts too much. He won't even speak her name anymore. I'm sad too, but I don't want to pretend she never existed," Anna said, her voice filled with both heartbreak and anger.

"What was her name?"

"Caroline." She spoke her mother's name with deep reverence.

If we marry and have a girl, we will name the child after Anna's mother.

Speaking with Anna, touching her, the answer seemed so clear. Being with her would be worth anything he had to lose.

"I'm so angry at God for taking her away from me, from *us*." Her hands shook as she spoke. "You must think I'm terrible for saying such a thing."

"I don't think you're terrible, Anna. I think you're wonderful."

Gazing into his eyes, she said, "I think you're wonderful too, George Hartley."

He simply could not resist any longer. Pulling her to him, he kissed her madly, deeply, passionately. A dangerous kiss to be sure. Should anyone catch them, they would both be ruined. With Anna's lips on his and the sound of her soft moan, it was hard to give a damn.

George kissed the woman he loved for as long as he felt he could before reluctantly releasing her.

Breathing heavily, he said, "I would say I was sorry, but ..."

Anna laughed softly. "I'm not sorry either." She gasped

and took a quick step away from him. George realized why when the door swung open and a young mother and her two children entered the store.

Not missing a beat, George said casually, "You've reeled me in once again, Miss Hawkins. I surrender. I must take home at least a dozen of these incredible molasses cookies."

Anna laughed, relief in her eyes. "Of course, Mr. Hartley."

"Oooh, cookies!" cried the little boy who'd just come in. His mother heaved a sigh.

"Sorry," George said with a guilty shrug. "I have younger sisters myself, and I should have known better than to say c-o-o-k-i-e out loud."

The young mother laughed. "That's quite all right, Mr. Hartley. It happens."

George didn't recognize the woman, but most people in town knew the Hartley family. Most importantly, the lady didn't look suspicious at all. She'd likely been too busy with her brood to notice the two flushed and guilty faces before her.

"Please allow me to make you another fresh batch to take with you, Mr. Hartley," Anna said.

Clever girl. She'd thought of the perfect excuse to allow him to stay, hopefully long enough so they could be alone once again.

Alas, it was not to be. Though her father still had not returned, the store only grew busier the longer he waited. Eventually, he gave up and had to leave, forced to settle for a longing look between them instead of a goodbye kiss.

When he got home, George was dismayed to find Victoria sitting in the parlor waiting for him. His mother sat with her at the small wooden table where tea service had been set up.

"I'm glad you're finally back, George," Penelope said, her eyes narrowing. There was an edge to her voice, and she looked suspicious. He wondered how long they had been here. His mother was not a patient woman and did not like to be kept waiting. Plus, she would kill him if he did anything to jeopardize his impending marriage of convenience.

More the family's convenience than mine, it seems.

He supposed that might not be entirely fair. After all, his parents had no idea he'd gone and fallen in love with another woman. But he knew there was no way they would approve if they had known.

"So lovely to see you," Victoria said with a demure smile. She spoke softly and sweetly. So much like Anna, and yet so much *not* like her.

He had been euphoric after spending so much time with Anna today, alone with her and finally *kissing* her. And now, being here with Victoria was such a disappointment. He found it hard to imagine ever feeling about her the way he did about Anna, no matter how long they were married.

And that could be a long, long time.

Suddenly overwhelmed by the marriage decision he would have to make, and soon, George needed to get out, if only for a few moments.

"I look forward to joining you for tea," he said. "Allow me to wash up first. My trip was quite dirty."

George held up his hands as if to prove his filth, and both women nodded approvingly.

Hastily, he left the room. He headed past the dining room and into the kitchen to find a wash basin, figuring he might as well actually wash his hands while trying to gather his thoughts.

"Good afternoon, Mr. Hartley," Dinah said with a smile.

"Good afternoon." Though he wished to be alone, he decided not to dismiss her from the kitchen since he couldn't stay long anyway.

George walked to the window and looked out at the vast lawn and garden out back. He did this to make clear that he didn't want to talk. Dinah got the hint and went back to whatever she'd been doing.

He stared out at the perfectly tended garden, bursting in full bloom on this fine summer day. Gazing out at the acres and acres of land his family owned, the magnitude of what he would give up by running away with Anna struck him full force. When he was with her, the choice seemed so obvious. He *loved* her. He wanted to be with her forever.

However, back here at the Hartley Mansion, the choice wasn't so clear. His parents would hate him. They would abandon him. He'd be penniless and have to start his entire life over. Would he even be able to provide for Anna and any children they might have?

Worst of all, the selfish part of him didn't want to give up the opulence of his lifestyle. The Hartleys were wealthy beyond most people's imagination, and luxury was all he'd ever known. Could he really be happy living in some farmhouse far away from his home?

Sighing heavily, he knew he couldn't hide in the kitchen forever. Heaven forbid he kept his mother waiting any longer.

George turned around to see Dinah in the process of making molasses cookies, just as Anna had done this morning. He found himself transfixed by the motion of Dinah's hands. The way she rolled the dough out on a cast iron paddle and cut the shapes with a metal cutter. He watched her put the unbaked cookies into the woodfire oven in exactly the manner Anna had.

Strange.

He had always thought of slaves as different from people like him. He'd been taught they had limited mental capacity, and that wealthy people like the Hartleys were doing them a favor by taking them in and keeping them warm and safe. He found it odd that Dinah's movements were exactly the same as Anna's when they made cookies. Dinah was a slave and Anna was poor. It was almost as if there was little difference between them.

Maybe there was no difference.

Quite an unsettling thought, that was.

Dinah eyed him curiously. "Are you all right, Mr. Hartley?"

George looked into her eyes for a moment before she looked away. For the first time in his life, he *really* looked at her. He saw concern in her soft brown eyes, but also a hint of fear. Though he'd never been cruel to any of their slaves, George had the power to destroy her if he so chose. And they both knew it.

That was an even more unsettling thought.

He had the sudden urge to comfort Dinah. Assure her that he meant her no harm.

"Oh yes, quite all right," he said. "Looking forward to enjoying some of those delicious cookies is all."

Dinah laughed. "Of course. I might have known."

George laughed too. Everyone knew how much he enjoyed his sweets.

"Well, I best get back to Victoria and my mother."

She nodded and went back to work.

His mind whirled as he trudged toward the parlor. Though he'd known Anna such a short time, she'd made him question many things about himself and about life in general.

Perhaps I should vanish for the rest of the night.

George often did just that when the painful memories of the past proved too much for him. Floating aimlessly from room to room, his mind and heart were consumed with thoughts of his precious Anna Hawkins.

He found himself back in the Music Room. Gathering his strength, he managed to pluck a few keys on the piano. As a ghost, that was really all he could do. Oh, how he missed playing full songs. Anna had loved the piano and the harp so much.

A couple of times over the last hundred years in this house, he'd heard the strings of the harp play when he wasn't in the room. He'd often wondered, hoped that it was Anna. That perhaps her spirit had lingered too. But he'd never seen her in all these years; she was probably in heaven where she belonged.

Anna had loved music. And she had loved him.

God, how he missed her.

5

Cecily was excited as she arrived at the Hartley Mansion even earlier than normal. A treasure trove of new—technically very *old*—Hartley family documents had recently been found in the attic of a distant relative. As the foremost expert on the Hartleys, Cecily got first crack at cataloging the documents. She looked forward to perusing everything that had been found and label it before the items were turned over to the Olde Town museum. Dr. Adam Gallagher, Director of Education and Exhibition Planning for Olde Town, was going to bring over the documents for her this morning.

Her small office, tucked away behind the Music Room, had only a slightly more modern look than the rest of the house. Had she been allowed, she would have set up shop in Mr. Oliver Hartley's office to work. His workplace upstairs boasted a gorgeous dark wooden desk and matching ornately carved chair, not to mention a huge window that overlooked the grounds out back. Since it wasn't an option to work there and risk damaging historic property, Cecily had prepared her office to be the next best thing. Her small work area also featured a wooden desk and chair that she'd found at an antique shop. Though she wasn't sure how old the furniture was, at least she knew it wasn't some brand-new IKEA stuff. She'd also bought a couple of dark wood bookshelves, got an antique lamp that resembled an old lantern with a lightbulb inside, and she had a small window that overlooked the grounds. All in all, it was a pretty nifty place to work. It helped her get into the mood to delve deep into the past as she researched and wrote about the Hartley's family history.

Cecily found it hard to concentrate on her work this morning; she could hardly wait for Adam to arrive with the new documents. Her excitement over such a thing made her Queen of the Nerds, but she didn't care. She was happy to geek out over a bunch of brand-new—or new to her—documents about her favorite subject of study. Hopefully there was a lot of good stuff that she could include in the book she was writing.

For the next hour or so, she forced herself to get some writing done. After all, that was what she came in early for. Still, it was hard. For all she knew, the papers and letters and who knew what else Adam had could upend some of the information she thought she knew about the Hartleys. Sighing with impatience, she gazed out the window at the vast expanse of lawn. Sitting here in her office and listening to classical piano music, she could almost imagine living back in the 1830s. She took a moment once again to count her blessings that she was able to work in this magical place rather than being stuck in a mindless desk job she hated. As usual, she felt guilty about her good fortune but took comfort in the fact that she never took a moment of it for granted. She may have grown up wealthy, but she refused to become spoiled like so many others.

Like, for example, the Hartley family.

They'd loved being rich, that was for sure. Penelope and Oliver Hartley never missed an opportunity to show off their wealth. She'd found plenty of instances of that in her research over the years.

Speaking of research, where is Adam Gallagher?

The man wasn't really late, she was just impatient. In all the time she'd been working on her beloved pet project, no new documentation had ever come in. This was a big day indeed.

Out of nowhere, an image of Ryan Armstrong popped into her head. She wondered what he would think if he saw her nerding out over a bunch of documents. But that was a dumb thought for many reasons. For one, she shouldn't care what any man thought of her. And for another, oddly enough, she felt like he might actually understand her excitement. Though he wasn't a scholar like her, Ryan was genuinely interested in history. They'd had a few lively discussions about the history of Olde Town over the last year or so. That day at the ice cream shop had been the best, and when he came to fix the A/C they'd briefly bonded over their hatred of Oliver Hartley. Too bad nothing was broken in the Hartley Mansion today; she had a feeling Ryan would enjoy being here when the documents arrived.

Cecily reached over to the small speaker that sat on her desk to turn the volume off. She wanted to make sure she could hear Adam arrive.

And that's when she heard it. The faint sound of piano music still played in the house, and not from her speaker.

She sat still and listened. The music stopped.

In the past, Cecily had never been entirely sure she'd believed her ears. Having Ryan recently admit he'd heard things convinced her that it wasn't just her imagination.

"Knock, knock," called Dr. Adam Gallagher, announcing his presence. She'd left the door unlocked for him.

She practically leapt out of her seat to greet him.

"Adam! Good morning," she said as she stepped out into the Great Hall.

"Today's the big day," he said with a grin, holding up a large black canvas bag filled with the goods she'd been waiting for.

"Yay!" She clapped her hands like an excited child.

Adam laughed, his bright blue eyes gleaming. Not only was he Director of Education and Exhibition Planning for Olde Town, he was also an adjunct professor at St. Mary's College. With his longish dirty blond hair and those pretty eyes, Cecily couldn't help but admire his rugged good looks. None of her professors in school had ever looked like that. With his intelligence and handsomeness, he had a real Indiana Jones vibe going. But Adam had had a longtime girlfriend for as long as she'd known him, so she'd never thought of him as boyfriend material.

"Adam," she began hesitantly. "When you came in just now ... you didn't happen to hear any piano music, did you?"

Adam's head dropped. "Dr. Cecily Rosewood," he chided. "Don't start with that again."

"I know what I heard, Adam."

"Cecily," he said sternly.

"Adam," she said, matching his tone, but in jest.

"No, ma'am. I did not hear any such otherworldly sounds as a haunted piano playing by itself."

Dr. Gallagher was, to put it mildly, a non-believer. More than a non-believer, he actively *hated* the ghost talk that surrounded the area. As with most touristy historical areas, Olde Town ran highly popular ghost tours after dark. Cecily didn't mind them, and not just because she had a passing interest based on her own experiences. As far as she was concerned, anything that brought in more tourists was fine. Besides, visitors did get a chance to learn a little history while ghost hunting, so it was a win-win.

Adam didn't see it that way. He felt—strongly—that the ghost tours cheapened the historical significance of this place. He found the whole ghost trade distasteful and annoying, and he was not shy in saying so.

"You never know, Adam. The ghost of Oliver Hartley could be watching you ... right ... now," Cecily said, affecting the eeriest tone of voice she could summon.

"Oh, *plbbbb*," he said, blowing a huge raspberry.

"A very cogent argument, Dr. Gallagher."

He laughed, and so did she. Knowing his annoyance at anything supernatural, it was impossible not to tease him. And to his credit, he seemed to understand her temptation.

"Well, I've got to go open up the museum, so I better get moving," he said. "Take your time with everything. No rush, but let me know if you find anything especially interesting." With that, his eyes lit up. "Oh, by the way, there *is* something in there that you will love."

"Yeah?"

Adam nodded. "Oh yeah. There's a portrait of George Hartley in there. I know you've always said you wanted to know what he looked like."

"Oh my gosh, that's amazing!" More than amazing, Cecily wanted to scream with excitement.

"There ya go," Adam said with a light pat on her shoulder. He was kind enough not to bring up the reason she wanted to see George's face. He knew Cecily believed George was the one, or at least one of the ones, haunting the house.

"Enjoy, Cecily. See ya around," Adam said, tipping an imaginary hat to her on his way out.

"Thanks. Thanks so much!"

Heading to her office, she waited until Adam was out of earshot, or so she thought, to squeal with glee. She heard his good-natured chuckle just before he shut the door behind him.

Laughing to herself, she dropped into her chair to pore over the precious treasure trove before her. She had less than an hour before her first mansion tour of the day, so she had to be quick.

Cecily donned her gloves so she could sift through the documents without damaging anything. She pulled out some plastic sleeves from her drawer to put each document in a protective covering after she'd looked it over and labeled it.

"Oh wow," she said softly as she uncovered a letter written by Penelope Hartley herself. Cecily stared at the scripted handwriting, overwhelmed with the power of history to tell stories from the past.

She found more letters, some from Oliver and more from Penelope. There were a few drawings, perhaps done by the younger Hartley sisters as children.

Before she knew it, time had gotten away from her.

"Damn," Cecily muttered. It would soon be time to give the first tour of the day.

Ah, well. At least she had something to look forward to for later, as there were plenty more documents to go through.

But first things first. She wanted to find the portrait of George Hartley before she had to get changed for her tour.

She carefully flipped through the pages and gasped

when she saw the scripted handwriting that said George Hartley, 1835.

The year he died.

Cecily squealed again. This was it. The moment of truth. At last, she would have a face to go with the name she knew so well.

She flipped the paper over and stared at the sketched drawing.

It ... it made no sense.

It was impossible ... absolutely *not possible* that this could be George Hartley.

Those soulful eyes, the slightly curly dark hair, the familiar shape of the nose and chin. Familiar. *So familiar.*

The portrait of George Hartley was clearly, unmistakably ...

Braydyn, with a "dyn."

6

———————

Ryan stepped off the bottom rung of a ladder that leaned against the outside of the theater. He drew in a sharp breath when he caught sight of Cecily approaching the picnic area. For now, he was working on a project near the area where she usually ate her lunch. Rather than go off and eat with the guys, he tried to be around at lunchtime so he could see her. All too soon the work on the theater would be done and he'd have missed his chance with her. Considering the way he felt about Cecily, he'd be a coward if he didn't ask her out. Still, she intimidated him. Technically, *she* didn't intimidate him. She was kind and sweet and was nothing to fear. It was her *type* that intimidated him. The smart type. He was always afraid of saying something stupid around her.

As many times as he'd tried, never once had he approached Cecily during her lunch break. Usually, he tried to discreetly watch her as she headed over to the grassy area filled with picnic tables next to the theater. If he was lucky, some days she spoke to him as she walked past. Still, he never managed to seize those golden opportunities to ask her out to dinner already.

Funny how people around here thought of him as a superhero. Super *wuss* was more like it.

Ryan hadn't even realized he was staring at Cecily until she caught his eye.

Shit.

Hadn't even spoken a word to her and he was acting stupid already. She smiled at him uncertainly as she reached the sidewalk in front of the theater.

Great. I probably freaked her out by staring.

Just before he turned away to give her some space, she did something unexpected. She motioned him over.

Wiping his dirty hands on his jeans, he made his way to her. He reminded himself that the last time they'd been together when he'd fixed the A/C, he'd managed to not look like an idiot. He could do it again.

Maybe.

If only he could somehow recapture the magic of that day when he'd spoken to her in the ice cream line. At the time, he hadn't known her well enough to be so nervous. And, until that day, he hadn't realized she was *Dr.* Cecily Rosewood. Discovering that threw him off his game and made him worry about coming across as dumb.

"Hey, Ryan," she said, her brow furrowing with worry. "Can I talk to you about something?"

"Sure," he said, approaching her. "Are you okay?'

"Kind of. I'm not sure. Not really."

She began walking toward the picnic tables, and he fell into stride beside her.

After taking a seat at opposite ends of a table, he leaned forward and waited for her to elaborate. Cecily glanced down. He'd noticed she did that a lot when she was thinking hard. Or was worried about something.

"I guess I'm not really sure where to begin." She looked up to meet his gaze.

"Well, I'd like to help if there's anything I can do," Ryan said.

Cecily smiled, relief in her eyes. "Thanks. I appreciate that."

Once again, he waited. She didn't speak at first.

Finally, she sighed heavily. "It's, well, it's very hard to explain. It's better to show you, I guess. I hate to inconvenience you, but would you be able to come by the mansion after work?"

Are you kidding, woman? Try and stop me.

Doing his best to play it cool, he said, "Of course."

Though the prospect of seeing Cecily after work thrilled him, he was genuinely worried about her. "Are you all right? You're not in danger or anything, are you?"

She reached across the picnic table and grasped his hand, sending a bolt of electricity straight through his belly. He'd never had the chance to touch her before, and it was thrilling.

"Oh no, nothing like that." Cecily smiled, squeezing his hand once more before letting go. "Thanks again. See you soon."

She picked up her things and set off in the direction of the mansion, not having bothered to unpack her lunch, much less eat it. As much as Ryan wished he could have shared their lunch break together, being at the mansion later would probably be even better.

Of course, he spent the rest of the workday wondering what Cecily could possibly have to show him. Normally, when someone around Olde Town wanted to "show him" something, it was a clogged toilet, a broken window, or a burnt-out lightbulb. He'd seen everything from broken glass due to a crash-landed antique chandelier, to squirrels nesting in a heating unit. However, something told him that Cecily wasn't coming to him about a maintenance issue. Whatever it was seemed more personal.

What the hell could it possibly be? And why isn't it 5pm already?

When it finally *was* 5pm already, Ryan drove to the mansion rather than walk. Unlike most places in the historical district, the Hartley Mansion had a parking lot close to the building. It was still a little bit of a walk by design. The goal was to make sure no modern cars were visible anywhere near the mansion.

As much as Ryan wanted to run, he forced himself to play it cool and casually stroll over. For all he knew, Cecily was watching out the window, waiting for him.

At last, he made it to the front door and found it unlocked. He couldn't wait to see Cecily.

Ryan was about to announce his presence when she walked into the Great Hall from her office.

"Great, you made it," she said with a smile.

"Of course."

"Thanks for staying after work. I really appreciate it."

"Any time," he said.

Seriously. Name it. ANY TIME.

"Come on back to my office," she said, and he followed her down the hall.

Cecily did have a neat office with a wonderful old-timey feel. So different from other ones around here that looked like, well, offices. It was rather jarring sometimes to be in one of the buildings that was two hundred years old and filled with antiques and such and then walk into a hidden office inside with all modern light fixtures and furniture. Ryan loved how Cecily was determined to maintain the feel of the historic Hartley Mansion.

Once inside the room, Cecily sat down at her old-timey wooden desk and motioned for him to sit across from her. He gladly obliged.

She stared at him for a moment. "I'm sorry to involve you in all this. I just ... I didn't know who else to turn to."

"Well, whatever it is, I'm flattered that you came to me. You know, unless you need to hide a body or something."

Cecily's expression grew serious.

"Well," she said gravely. "Actually ..."

Ryan's stomach dropped. She burst out laughing.

Reaching over to touch him for the second time today, she squeezed his hand. "I'm kidding. Sorry, I couldn't resist."

He laughed along with her, his tension easing a little. "Fair enough, fair enough."

She met his gaze and smiled. She seemed to enjoy joking with him, and he relished every second.

"Okay," she began. "So, Adam Gallagher came by yesterday and brought over a whole slew of old documents from the Hartley family that were recently found in one of their descendant's attics."

"Oh wow!" Ryan exclaimed so loudly that it startled her. "That's amazing. That will be awesome for your book. You must be so excited."

Cecily seemed surprised and quite pleased by his reaction.

"Yes," she said with a gorgeous smile. "I still can't believe all the stuff we found. More than I ever dreamed of."

Ryan nodded enthusiastically. He was genuinely thrilled for her, and he also found the discovery quite exciting. After all, he spent a lot of time in this historical district, and he too was utterly fascinated by all the people who came before him.

"So there's one thing I found in all these papers that's quite ... disturbing," Cecily said, her brow furrowed with concern.

"Was it about Oliver Hartley?"

She laughed gently. "You'd think, right? No, it's just ... Well, it's this."

Cecily eyed Ryan nervously as she handed him a piece of paper. Some kind of sketched drawing, done in full color.

He stared at it.

"What is this, some kind of joke?" Ryan chuckled as he surveyed the drawing. "That's kind of hilarious. What, did Braydyn's family pay some artist to do an old-fashioned kind of drawing of him?"

"Good," Cecily said firmly. "So it's not just me. You see it too."

"See what?" Ryan looked up from the drawing he was still holding.

"Ryan. That's a picture of George Hartley."

He let those words, those impossible words, sink in.

"Flip it over."

He did as he was told, and found the words George Hartley, 1835 written on the back.

"1835. The year he died," she said.

"Died," Ryan repeated, not really understanding what was going on here. Or perhaps he didn't want to understand.

He flipped the paper back over to inspect the picture once more. That curly hair, those eyes ... This was *definitely* a picture of the young guy who worked in Olde Town who was constantly teasing him about being Canadian.

"This has gotta be a fake. I mean, just because Adam brought it over and said—"

"But it's not a fake," Cecily said, leaning forward. "That's the thing. I'm sure of it. Believe me, I've pored over and over it since it arrived yesterday. The watermark, the texture of the paper, the type of ink, and even the handwriting style … It's all consistent with that time period. It's real, Ryan."

Ryan stared at the portrait he held in his hand, his mind scrambling to make sense of what he saw and heard. The more he thought about it, the more freaked out he became. His hand began to shake, so he quickly put the paper down on the desk.

"I— I don't understand." Ryan realized too late that his voice was shaking as well.

"Me neither," Cecily said, her eyes wide. "I keep thinking about Braydyn and all the interactions I've had with him. I mean, he comes in here all the time, supposedly to cool off. I'm trying to remember if I've ever actually seen him sweat, you know?"

"Right, right," Ryan said, doing his damnedest to quell the panic that was rapidly rising within him. What was Cecily implying, exactly? That Braydyn, the lovable reen-actor they both joked around with all the time was the ghost of George Hartley? Was Braydyn actually … *dead*?

"I know," Cecily said softly, clearly reacting to his expression. He wasn't doing a great job of hiding his fear from her.

"This is all so crazy," he said, forcing his voice to remain steady. He could not have her thinking he was a coward. After all, she didn't seem afraid. More confused and perhaps a bit intrigued.

"It is. It really is. But like we talked about the other day, I've heard things in this house. Always have. Things like footsteps when there's nobody here. And sometimes I hear stuff like drinking glasses clinking and the sound of a fork on a plate, that kind of thing."

Ryan started to feel dizzy. Dear God, he'd better not pass out in front of Cecily.

He drew in a deep breath, determined to keep this conversation going.

"I *knew* I heard music in here," he managed to croak out.

"Yes!" Cecily shouted loud enough to help dispel some of his dizziness. "That's why I wanted to come to you with this. I knew you'd understand."

Ryan nodded. He was still conscious, so that was a plus.

"Oh, I'm so glad I could talk to you about this, Ryan," she said with a smile.

Hearing her say his name helped clear his head even more. Despite his fear, he was glad she'd come to him too.

Shaking her head, she added, "It's not like I could talk to Adam about all this."

Ryan laughed. "You're so right. Dr. Gallagher, not a fan of the ghosts."

He had chatted with the man at the museum once when there had been a problem with the plumbing. Some visitors had come in wanting to purchase ghost tour tickets. Adam could hardly hide his annoyance, which Ryan had found hilarious. Like Cecily, Adam was much, much smarter than he was. And yet he seemed like such a regular guy. The type you could grab a beer with.

Cecily laughed too. "It's funny, the whole ghost tour trade never bothered me. I figure whatever brings in more tourists, you know?"

"Oh, I agree. And all the tours happen after dark, so it's not like it affects us much. Other than occasionally having to work around them when making after-hours repairs, it's no big deal."

"Exactly," she said. "I don't know what his problem is."

Ryan didn't care what Adam Gallagher's problem was.

He was just glad Cecily hadn't gone to *him* about the Hartley sketch. Ryan might be straight, but he wasn't blind. Dr. Gallagher was gorgeous. Any student, or at least the ones who were attracted to men, would love to be in a class with a professor like that. It felt a bit unfair that a guy could be that good looking *and* smart. Good thing the man had a girlfriend. As much as he hated to admit it, Adam and Cecily would be a perfect match.

"It occurred to me that I don't think I've ever seen Braydyn in different clothes, you know?" Cecily said. "He always wears that dark frock coat over a white button-down shirt."

"Right," Ryan said, thinking back to all the times he'd seen Braydyn. Wracking his brain, he could not recall the guy ever sporting anything else, as much as he wanted to. "But don't all reenactors wear pretty much the same stuff every day?"

"Not exactly. They always wear period costumes, but they do have different ones they wear at different times. Like I usually wear a cotton dress when I'm working, but not the same one every day. Occasionally, I'll wear one of those bigger dresses. Still, I can't say I pay that close attention to the ones wandering around the main part of Olde Town. And I don't get too many of them here in the mansion. I mean, I do on occasion, but it's always for a planned demonstration or tour. I don't have them on the daily tours. For that, it's just me."

"Yeah," Ryan said.

It made sense. In the main part of town, there were lots of different buildings all right next to each other. The theater, the tavern, the general store, and the apothecary to name a few. The Hartley Mansion was a little distance away, and people could walk, drive, or take the shuttle to visit it.

That was why Cecily had scheduled tours in advance where she could speak to a group of people all at once. For the other buildings in town, tourists could wander in all day long and speak to a reenactor for a quick tour or to ask questions.

"Come to think of it," Ryan said. "Do you know what building he normally works in?"

Cecily thought for a minute. "I don't think he works in a specific building that I know of."

"That's kinda weird too, right?"

She nodded, looking uncertain. "Yeah. I mean, I guess I never asked him about it. He comes into the mansion and brings a bunch of tourists with him. He stays for a bit to get out of the sun and into the A/C. Or so he says."

"But then he could tell the air conditioning was broken when I came to fix it. Remember? He came in asking what was wrong with it."

"You're right. He did. Who knows? Maybe ghosts can feel stuff like that."

Ryan shuddered at Cecily's words. He couldn't help himself. That thought was creepy as hell. Who knew what ghosts were capable of?

Cecily laughed, and at first he thought she'd noticed his terror.

Shaking her head, she said, "I don't know. Maybe I'm being crazy here. For all I know, Braydyn is a distant relative of the Hartleys."

"Yes! That could be it."

Ryan's shoulders relaxed. He was relieved to have at least one possible rational explanation for all of this.

"I guess the best thing to do is to go find Braydyn and talk to him," she said.

He swallowed. "Yeah. I guess. I mean, that makes sense."

But it was the last thing he wanted to do. Braydyn had always seemed like a nice fellow, but now the mere thought of the guy terrified Ryan.

And he *hated* being terrified. It made him feel like such a coward. With his luck, he'd faint in front of Cecily the next time they saw the so-called reenactor.

"I'll see if I can find him on my lunch break. Are you guys still working on the theater reconstruction?"

Ryan nodded.

"Good. I'll see you around noon tomorrow then."

"Sounds good," Ryan said, forcing his enthusiasm.

"Thanks again," she said with a smile. "I really appreciate it."

"Any time." Despite his fear, he meant it.

He was grateful to step outside, where he hoped to clear his head. An awful lot of potential scenarios about Cecily's request to see him had run through his head throughout the day, but finding the ghost of George Hartley had certainly not been one of them.

The more he thought about this whole thing, the more freaked out he became. He tried to cling to the distant relative thing, but there was just no question that the guy in the drawing was a dead ringer for Braydyn.

Even the phrase "dead ringer" creeped him out. He had to get a grip on his fear if he was going to handle this odd situation alongside Cecily. If nothing else, it was a chance to get closer to her. After all, she had confided in him and not Adam Gallagher or anyone else. He could spend time with her without hitting on her and risking rejection. Instead, he could see how it all played out.

As he walked away from the Hartley Mansion, he found himself staring at a small signpost on the left-hand side of the pebbled path.

Hartley Cemetery.

Ryan knew several members of the Hartley family were buried just a short distance from the house, as was the custom in those days. At least it was the custom for wealthy families to have a family graveyard. On the spur of the moment, he gathered his courage to visit the cemetery. It was like aversion therapy. If he could face the graveyard alone, perhaps he'd be fine tomorrow if they encountered Braydyn.

Slowly, he made his way down the path. He'd been to graveyards before, and he reminded himself that this one was no different.

Except it felt different. The last time he'd been in a cemetery was years ago when his grandmother in Canada had died. That was before he'd moved here. Before he'd heard creepy, disembodied piano music in the empty mansion, and before he'd seen the portrait of George Hartley.

The rusty metal gate creaked as he opened it because of course it did. Anything to make this experience creepier. Older graveyards were, by their nature, scarier than new ones. The one in Canada had been downright cheery compared to this. The tombstones were more modern. Brighter and shinier, and many gravesites were simple flat metal plaques in the ground. The Hartley graveyard looked like something out of a horror movie with its ancient, weather-beaten headstones and over-grown weeds.

Sighing heavily, Ryan forced himself to look around. Many of the names on the stones he didn't recognize. After all, a lot of people had come and gone during the mansion's multi-century history. Finally, he saw headstones for names he did know. Penelope Hartley, beloved wife and mother,

1788-1852. Oliver Hartley, 1783-1855. Ryan noticed nobody had called him "beloved."

And then he saw it.

George Hartley, cherished son, 1808-1835.

A cold chill went through Ryan's body. His breath froze in his lungs. He'd always heard that people often felt a cold breeze when a spirit walked by. He had no idea if that was what he felt or if his fear was taking over. Either way, he was getting the hell out of here.

He forced himself to look at George's grave for a moment longer and then turned to slowly walk back toward civilization.

As much as he wanted to, he managed not to run.

7

____

1835

It was a typical Hartley party, stuffy and overdone, designed to impress so-called important people. George stood near the wall, hating every moment and avoiding Victoria at all costs. Ever since he'd met Anna, he'd been annoyed with Victoria's very presence. He could not help but compare everything she said or did with Anna, who was so completely and utterly different in every way. Victoria was forever playing up the whole delicate flower part of being a woman, damn near fainting at the slightest provocation. Anna was so much stronger. Indeed, she'd had to be. Having lost her mother, so much responsibility had fallen upon her shoulders. She doted upon her father and did her best to care for him. Just one of many things that made her so endearing.

"Are you quite all right?" Victoria asked, finally approaching him as he clearly wasn't going to go to her. Her eyes were filled with worry.

George suddenly felt terrible for all the things he'd been thinking about this poor woman. After all, she hadn't asked to be paired up with him. They'd both been thrust together by their overbearing families. And as far as the whole "shrinking violet" act, Victoria was only acting like a proper lady. She was doing what was expected of her and would likely be punished by her family and society as a whole if she didn't play that silly part. It was hardly her fault that her parents weren't as reasonable as Anna's father.

If he wasn't going to marry her, he should let her go.

His cowardly indecision was hurting both Victoria and Anna, and it was unfair to keep them both waiting while he pondered his choice. There was no question in his mind, or his heart, what he wanted. The issue was whether or not he actually had the courage to go after it.

Overwhelmed, George glanced around the crowded room. Some of the guests were strangers and some were people he'd known his whole life, but all of them seemed to be looking at the "happy couple" with approval. He found it difficult to breathe. He needed to step outside for a bit to clear his mind.

Pasting on a smile, he said, "Would you excuse me for a moment?"

"Of course." Victoria nodded, her curls bouncing slightly as she did. She still looked worried, and perhaps even a little scared. She wasn't stupid; she could tell his mind was occupied somewhere else. Hopefully she didn't realize that it was occupied by *someone* else.

George slipped outside as unobtrusively as he could. Drawing in a deep breath of night air made him feel slightly better. He wandered around outside the front of the mansion, lit only by a few lanterns, then walked down to the Orangery, a place of great pride for the Hartleys. Who else could boast that they could produce fresh citrus fruit in the dead of winter? Anna really enjoyed sweet fruits.

Anna would simply love it here.

Poor, sweet Anna and her dear, lovable father. Prior to getting to know them, he'd known poor people existed, but he'd never given them much thought. Penelope and Oliver had always insisted poor folks were simply lazy. That had always made sense to him. After all, his parents didn't do much, and they were drowning in wealth. Clearly, it wasn't very hard to make money. Or so he'd thought.

Knowing Gene and Anna Hawkins had changed so much about how he viewed the world. Those two worked so hard and had so little. Through them, he'd learned a simple truth; rich people stayed rich, and poor people stayed poor with little chance of ever improving their situation. That was the way of it most of the time.

And it had nothing to do with how hard anybody worked.

George longed to live with Anna in the Hartley Mansion. While she might feel a tad overwhelmed at first, no doubt she would come to love the place. Anna was the type of person who was grateful for everything she had because she had so little. But the notion of living at the Hartley Mansion with Anna was pure fantasy. It was clearly an either/or situation. Either he married Victoria and remained here, or he ran off with Anna and lived in poverty forever.

"What are you doing out here?" an angry female voice demanded.

George whirled around to find his mother right behind him, eyes ablaze. Penelope Hartley was certainly dressed for this all-important party, clad in a green silk dress layered with what seemed like hundreds of petticoats. As ever, not a hair was out of place.

"I simply needed a breath of fresh air," he said. "It's so stuffy in there."

In more ways than one.

"Your presence is required, George. You know that."

Yes. He knew that. For sure, he knew his job. Be seen by all of his parents' fancy friends. Most importantly, be seen courting Victoria properly so everyone would be happy when they got engaged. Well, not *everyone* would be happy.

"I'll be there in a minute, Mother."

"You need to propose to Victoria already," she hissed. "I don't know what in hell you're waiting for."

His mother's language shocked him. He knew she had a temper, but she was so good at keeping calm when others were around that he sometimes forgot how angry she could get. Penelope Hartley was all about image, but that facade was unnecessary when only her son was within earshot. With him she could be herself, and that was rarely a good thing.

George had no idea how to respond. He could only hold her off for so long before he had to make a decision. And not only her. His father, Victoria's family, and pretty much all of local society were waiting with bated breath for Oliver Hartley's son to marry and work on producing another heir. His chest felt tight again. Being out in the fresh air no longer helped. Not with his mother glaring icily at him.

Through clenched teeth, she said, "Get yourself in order, George. I mean it."

With that, her expression changed back to that of a calm, proper lady. The transformation was rather disturbing. Penelope's outward appearance was quite deceiving, and he wondered how many others in his social circle had similar abilities. It was impossible to know who to trust in this world.

George somehow survived the insufferable gathering in the Great Hall. The next day, he was all the more eager to visit his precious Anna. He craved not only her beauty and her touch, but also her sincerity. She led a simple life, and he found that type of existence increasingly more desirable. Deciding to forgo the damned carriage, he rode a horse into town instead. He rather enjoyed horseback riding, and he was annoyed at his mother. Not taking the carriage would please him and irritate Penelope, so he was happy with his decision.

"Hello!" he bellowed upon entering the store.

Gene Hawkins waved at him and smiled but didn't address him since he was busy with a customer. That was fine by George since it meant he could head straight over to Anna.

Her pretty blue eyes lit up at the sight of him. How he loved that she seemed as overjoyed to see him as he was to be here.

He handed her the bag he'd brought with him.

"Oh, thank you so much," she said, peering into it and squealing with delight when she saw what she'd known he would bring her.

"I know it's rather odd to bring you oranges instead of flowers, but I know what you like," he said.

"Yes, you certainly do."

They gazed at each other fondly, which was really all they could do in public. How he desperately craved some time alone with her.

The door behind him opened, and in walked yet another customer. Busy days at the store were the worst. Sometimes he barely got a chance to talk to Anna at all, and there was only so long he could stay without looking suspicious.

"So there you are, George. I wondered where you got to."

George froze. His mother was using that sickly-sweet tone that sounded perfectly nice to others but heralded danger for him. Anna looked alarmed at George's expression. She had never met Penelope as far as he knew, but she could tell by his face that something was wrong.

He turned to face her. Forcing to keep his voice even, he said, "Hello, Mother. What are you doing here?"

"I simply had to come and get some of those delicious molasses cookies you've brought home a few times," she said, meeting his gaze. She smiled, but he saw fire in her eyes.

"Oh, I make those," Anna said with a genuine smile.

"I might have known," Penelope muttered under her breath. She walked over to Anna and George had to fight the urge to tackle her to the ground. "I would love a dozen to take home. I'm lucky if I even get one or two when George brings them. Who knows how many he eats on his way home."

"Of course. I'll wrap some up for you," Anna said, busily getting to work.

Penelope eyed George icily but held her tongue until they were outside the store.

Naturally, the Hartley family carriage was waiting out front. Of course, that meant there was the driver to consider when she was dealing with her wayward son. After throwing the bag of cookies she would never eat onto the carriage seat, she pulled George out of earshot of the driver.

"So that's why you haven't proposed to Victoria yet," she said, glaring fiercely toward the store. "You have all the fun you want with your whore on the side, but you *will* marry the woman of proper breeding we've found for you. I will *not* have you besmirch our family name."

The family name. The most important thing in the whole world to his mother. Next to Anna's sweetness, such superficiality felt like a downright sin. It was ugly. So, so ugly. And so was the word his mother had called the woman he loved.

"Don't call her a whore," George said.

His mother laughed and shook her head in disgust. Penelope's utter disregard for his feelings and her insult should have thrown him into a ferocious rage.

Instead, it gave him an idea.

His mother calling Anna that awful name made him realize what a scandal it would be if, after having the honor and privilege of making love to Anna, he got her pregnant. Penelope could easily dismiss a poor girl in such a manner when that girl meant nothing to her and her precious family name. But Anna *would* matter to the Hartleys if she was carrying George's child. Then he would *have* to marry her, and they would *have* to live in the Hartley Mansion together. Either that or utterly ruin the Hartley's precious reputation.

Without a word, George got on his horse and rode away, leaving his mother sputtering in fury in his dust.

As madcap as his plan was, George was certain it would work. However, he would never deliberately seduce Anna and trick her into getting with child without her fully understanding what he wanted to accomplish. Women tended to be quite sheltered when it came to such delicate matters. He would only go through with this whole thing if Anna approved of it.

Which meant he had a difficult discussion ahead of him. Thus far, Anna had no idea that Victoria existed. He would first have to explain about the woman he was expected to wed before he could tell the woman he loved that he really wanted to marry *her*. Why was life so damned complicated?

If a man was fortunate enough to meet a woman and fall in love, he should be free to marry her without all this familial nonsense.

Anna had mentioned that her father was going to visit a friend on Sunday and would be gone all day. The store was closed on Sundays, which meant Anna would be at the farmhouse alone. The trouble was, he didn't know where the farmhouse was. At first, he worried that it would seem improper to ask someone in town where Anna lived. Then, laughing to himself, he realized that was actually a good thing. Penelope Hartley could not abide gossip about the family and would do anything to quell it. If rumors emerged of George's impropriety with a farmgirl, well then he'd best marry her. It was all so perfect.

George feared he'd frightened poor Anna when he approached the farmhouse. He saw her tentatively peer out the front door when she heard his horse nearing. Hand over her heart, she looked utterly terrified. But then he had the pleasure of seeing the recognition on her face when she realized it was him.

"George! My, what are you doing here? Is everything all right?"

"Oh yes. Everything is perfect. I simply had to steal away today to see you when I knew we could finally be alone."

Anna's lovely cheeks blushed as she bit her lip and smiled. Perhaps she was more worldly than he'd expected. Maybe before her untimely passing, her mother had gotten the chance to explain to her what happens on a woman's wedding night. When Anna was with child, George fervently hoped they would have a girl, both to name the baby after Anna's beloved mother and to vex his own mother. Unlike his parents, George wasn't concerned with producing a male heir. Any healthy children he might be blessed with would be good enough for him.

"Come in, come in," she said, eagerly ushering him into the sunny kitchen of her modest home.

George was immediately struck by the warmth and comfort of the place. The kitchen was tiny, especially compared to the one in his mansion, but it was so homey. He could easily envision Anna and her father sharing a cozy early-morning breakfast to start the day. The atmosphere was so different from where he came from.

She gestured for him to sit at the table.

"Would you like something to drink? Are you hungry?"

"Oh no, I'm fine. Thank you."

He knew how poor Anna was, and the last thing he wanted was to take any of her food. Best save it for her and her father. Besides, he knew there was no time to waste.

Anna eyed him curiously. No doubt she wondered what in the world had brought him here.

"I need to talk to you about something very important."

"Okay," she said nervously. She took a seat next to him.

George reached over and took her hand in his.

"Anna, I want to marry you."

She gasped, placing her hand on her heart. George gazed into her eyes, watching her process his words. Her eyes filled with tears and she nodded.

"I love you," he said.

"I love you too." Anna's voice was barely a whisper.

Before he continued, he allowed himself a few seconds to indulge in the sheer bliss of hearing those words from her lips.

"But there are complications ... things you should know."

Her face fell. She nodded again, but now she looked

worried. How he hated being forced to destroy the mood. He wanted to go back to the part where they professed their love for each other. Instead, he soldiered on.

"There's a woman that I'm expected to marry."

"Oh," Anna said, sounding as if her breath was caught in her throat.

"You have to know, I feel nothing for her. *Nothing.* But my family is very wealthy, and her family is very prominent. It's simply expected of me."

After a moment, Anna said in a very small voice, "I understand."

"What you need to understand is that I have no intention of marrying her. I plan to marry you."

George watched as the light of hope returned to her eyes.

"My parents would never allow it if I simply said I refuse to marry Victoria because I want to marry you. So, I came up with a plan. It's sort of ...well ... a bit mad."

Anna leaned in to listen as George struggled to find a tactful way to say what needed to be said. She was a modest young woman, and he was quite unsure of how she would react.

"But before I tell you, please understand that I want everything for you. I want you to live with me in my family's home with servants there to take care of you."

Though his family had both paid servants and slaves, lately the notion of having slaves work for free made him increasingly uncomfortable. For the moment, he chose simply to not address it, reasoning that once he took over the family business, he could figure out what to do with them then. First things first, however. He needed to secure his place, and his wife, in his home.

Anna nodded uncertainly, and he knew the notion of

having servants must seem so foreign to her. To be sure, she likely had more in common with the people who worked in his home than with his family. That was one of the many things he loved about her.

"And I want to make sure that your father is well taken care of," he said.

"Yes," she said with a relieved smile. "That would be wonderful."

Guilt gnawed at him. Though he had every intention of ensuring that Gene Hawkins never wanted for anything for the rest of his life, he'd only mentioned it to convince her to agree to his plan. He hated being manipulative, but he was desperate to sway Anna quickly, to secure their future. The clock was ticking, and her father would return to the house all too soon.

"Anna, if you were with child, my parents would be forced to let us marry," he blurted out.

"Oh!" She blushed a deep crimson.

He felt terrible for embarrassing her so, and opened his mouth to say as much. Before he could apologize, she gazed up at him with desire in her eyes. George was shocked and beyond pleased by her reaction.

She held her breath as their eyes locked. He could hardly contain his urge to sweep her into his arms and carry her to her bedroom. Not that he knew where her bedroom was, but he certainly hoped to find out as soon as possible.

He drew in a deep breath to steady himself. As much as he desired to be with her, it would not do to seduce an innocent girl without her full understanding of what she was agreeing to.

"I know I am asking a lot of you, and so quickly. But I just want to ensure our future together."

"I want that too," she said, her eyes filling with fresh tears.

George held his tongue for a moment to give Anna a chance to really think things over. The last thing he wished was for her to regret any of this.

"It's so strange," Anna said softly. "I guess I don't understand why you chose me over this other woman."

He saw the pain in her eyes when she mentioned "the other woman," and he understood completely. His heart would have broken to hear mention of another man in her life.

"So many reasons," he said, tenderly caressing her hands. "I love that the simple things make you happy. Things like greeting your customers when they come into the store. Making cookies for them. And for me!"

That made her smile, which in turn warmed his whole being.

"And you don't need fancy jewelry to brighten your day. All you need is a bag of oranges."

Anna laughed heartily at that. George couldn't remember what Victoria's laugh sounded like. The woman was hardly dour and humorless, but laughter didn't come as easily to her as it did to Anna. To be fair, Anna didn't have the burden of family the way Victoria did. Rather, her father would join in her laughter instead of insisting she act like a proper lady.

"What a wonderful mother you will be," George said gently.

That made her smile as well. He considered mentioning that he wanted to name their potential daughter after her mother, but he refrained. He didn't want to sway her any further. This vital, life-changing decision had to be her own.

"What wonderful parents *we* will be," she said,

squeezing his hands. Anna glanced toward the door, no doubt calculating how long they had until her father returned. Taking a deep breath, she said definitively, "I want to do this."

George's face immediately broke into a wide grin and his nether regions literally sprang into action.

"Wonderful. Wonderful! And just so you know, procreating is hardly the only reason I want to make love to you."

Anna blushed but held his gaze. "Oh, George," she said breathlessly.

Hearing her say his name in such a manner made him desperate to show her the pleasures of the marital bed. Doing so before marriage was even more exciting.

"Are you ready?" he asked, restraining himself from leaping out of his chair.

"Yes." She stood up, thus giving him permission to do the same.

Anna took his hand and led him up the stairs of the sunny farmhouse. Making love in the daylight also seemed naughtier, with the added plus that he would clearly see every precious inch of Anna's body.

Once inside her bedroom, Anna sat uncertainly on her bed. She looked up at him expectantly, and George felt reassured that she wasn't second-guessing her decision but was simply nervous the way any maiden would be. Despite the short time they had, he knew he must go slowly and take good care of her.

"Don't be afraid," he said gently. "Just think, we'll be well-prepared for our wedding night with all the practice we're getting."

Anna smiled and nodded. "You're right."

He sat next to her on the bed. Leaning toward her, he carefully pressed his lips to hers. The kiss began gentle and chaste but quickly transitioned to deep and passionate. To George's delight, she seemed as eager as he was. Anna's body went from tense to soft and relaxed as her apprehension shifted to desire.

George lifted his lips from hers, but only so he could remove her cotton dress. He tugged on it, and Anna stood up quickly so he could discard it. As much as he wanted to dispense with her underthings as fast as possible, he didn't want her feeling too vulnerable. He unbuttoned his shirt and tossed it aside.

"So handsome," Anna said, admiring his chest. "Just like I imagined."

"You've imagined me naked?"

"Oh yes. Many times," she said, and not shyly.

"Well then, it's time you experienced what you've thought of so often."

With that, he took off the rest of his clothes. He relished her admiring expression as he revealed himself to her.

"I wish we didn't have to hurry," she said, eventually lifting her eyes to his face after.

"Me too. But remember, this will be our first time of many."

"Yes," she said, that beautiful smile reaching all the way up to her eyes.

George couldn't help wondering what Victoria would have been like as a new bride. He nearly shuddered to think of having to put up with all the blushing, stammering, and maybe even fainting on their wedding night. Oh, how he adored Anna's eagerness to be bedded by him.

His desire spun dangerously out of control as he peeled off the rest of her clothes.

"In your case, not just as imagined. Better ... Even better than my wildest dreams."

The way Anna bit her lip was so lusciously seductive that he nearly lost all control.

Mind her maidenhood, he told himself. No matter how aroused he was, it would not do to harm his beloved.

Tenderly, he pushed her down onto the bed. She gasped, her blue eyes alight with desire and excitement.

"It may hurt a bit at first."

"I know," she said. "Just do it. Please."

The sound of her pleading was too much. The time to hesitate was over. As gently as he could, he slid himself inside of her. A deep, pleasured moan escaped his lips as a burst of sheer bliss rocked his body. He'd had sex a few times before, but that had been quite some time ago.

"Anna, my love ... oh God ..." he moaned. It would be a chore not to lose control too soon, but he was determined to make her first time memorable.

He glanced at her face only to see it was contorted with pain, but she didn't make a sound.

"Oh darling, I'm so sorry," he whispered.

"It's all right, my love. The worst has passed."

Anna breathed in and out a few times. "It's all right. Keep going, George. Make love to me."

George kissed down her neck, making her moan softly. What a relief to hear sounds of pleasure coming from her now. He intended to make those sounds grow louder. He moved in and out of her a few times, and she did cry out. Gazing into her eyes, he saw she no longer seemed to be in pain. In its place was a beautiful look of admiration and pleasure. As incredible as this was, he knew there was no time to lose.

Still, he wanted to make this experience one she would remember for the rest of her life.

He pulled out of her and bent to put his mouth between

her legs before she could protest. He swept his tongue across her most special place. Anna screamed with delight.

"Oh! Oh! G-g-g-eorge!"

Knowing she had never experienced anything like this in her life drove him mad with desire. He claimed her with his mouth, his body, and his whole heart. Anna writhed with pleasure on the bed, clutching the sheets with her hands. She was normally so soft-spoken, and he reveled in drawing screams of ecstasy from her lips as no other man ever had or ever would.

Gasping and moaning, she reached her peak, crying out one last time.

As he climbed back on top of her, George knew he would never forget the look of her flushed cheeks and her wide blue eyes—it was as if she hardly knew what he had just done to her. Until now, she probably hadn't known her body was capable of feeling so deeply pleasured.

George slid back into her with much more ease. She was slick and wet, and he pumped in and out of her. The notion that he was deliberately trying to impregnate her let loose a primal urge within him. He pounded her over and over again until he finally unleashed his hopefully life-giving seed inside the woman he loved.

"Oh, George," Anna said as he collapsed on top of her. The softness was back in her voice, but now it was out of exhaustion. He'd done his job.

He lifted his head to look into her eyes.

"George Hartley," she said, gazing back at him. "I never knew I could love anyone this much."

"I love you too. And I cannot wait to spend the rest of my life with you."

In that moment, George was sure they had done the right thing. The wonderful, beautiful, loving thing.

Only time would tell if he was right.

He rolled off of her, and they lay together in happy silence for a while. Eventually, Anna broke the silence as she stared up at the ceiling.

"Do you think I would fit in with your family?" she asked.

George turned on his side to look at her, unsure of how to answer. He thought of his mother and how angry she would be if he *had* to marry Anna instead of Victoria. He hoped she wouldn't take her fury out on Anna. George decided then and there that he would never allow that to happen.

"I think my sisters will absolutely adore you," he said honestly. His younger sisters were sweet and not yet jaded by his parents.

"And your mother?"

"She will learn to love you," he said reassuringly, hoping like hell it was true.

Anna smiled uncertainly.

"Are you troubled about this, darling?"

"A bit," she said. "I wonder what it will be like living in a mansion. It's difficult to imagine it."

"Oh, you will love it," George said, propping himself up on his arm. "You and your father will be well fed for the first time in your lives. You won't have to work so hard. And there will be time for you to learn how to play the harp."

Anna's face brightened at that, filling George with renewed hope. He would do everything in his power to make her every wish a reality.

"Sweetheart, I know it will seem strange at first. So different from what you're used to. But we'll be together, right? You'll never be alone. I will be at your side. Always."

Anna gazed lovingly at him. Her pretty eyes were still tinged with worry, but she smiled.

"Though I hate to cover up your lovely form," he went on, "I think we'd best get dressed. I wager we've pushed our luck far enough. No telling exactly when your father will return."

Anna nodded and got out of bed. George tenderly dressed her, his mind filled with happy images of her as his future wife. He imagined an emotional church wedding and then a big party in the Great Hall, or perhaps even in the garden out back.

George smiled to himself.

"What are you thinking about?" she asked.

"The future," he said. "Our future. Together."

She caressed his face tenderly with her palm. "Oh, how wonderful." He gazed into her eyes, gladly noting that the doubt had been replaced with a look of joy and hope. "How simply wonderful."

8
____

Cecily made the familiar early morning walk down the gravel path toward the Hartley Mansion. Since she'd come across that sketch of George or Braydyn or whoever he was, she'd been sleeping fitfully; her brain couldn't shut down long enough to rest. She simply couldn't wrap her head around it. The only way to get a clear answer was to find the guy and ask him what was going on.

What did it all mean? Was it possible that the young man she'd known casually for almost two years was a dead man? And not just any dead man, but George Hartley himself? The more she thought about it, the more she questioned her own sanity. She waffled between excitement over all the possibilities to feeling stupid for even thinking such a thing. People talked about the notion of doppelgangers. The idea that someone out there looked exactly like you. A person who not only physically resembled you but walked and talked the same as well. Cecily had read about this phenomenon somewhere. She recalled the word "doppelganger" was German, and it literally translated into "double walker."

She shuddered just thinking about that. How creepy. Over the last couple of years, she'd grown rather accustomed to the strange occurrences in the mansion, but this latest development was something else entirely.

For the first time ever, she hesitated to turn the key in the lock to the front door. Normally, she couldn't wait to get inside and start working on her book. This time, however, she'd managed to completely creep herself out on the way here.

Double walker. Dear God.

Cecily shakily gathered her courage, hating that she was afraid of what had been her favorite place. She walked along the creaky floor beneath the carpet in the Great Hall. Heading toward her office, she reminded herself that whatever ghosts or spirits she'd heard here had never tried to hurt her, and that nothing had changed. Still, she hoped she wouldn't hear any piano music or phantom footsteps.

Within an hour, her feelings had radically changed. She'd had time to calm herself, and her feelings of curiosity overrode her fears. The notion that she might get to meet—or had already met—the real George Hartley was an incredible opportunity that was too amazing to give up. As she pored over all her notes about the Hartley family, she grew more and more excited at the notion that Braydyn might actually be George Hartley. Naturally, she spent quite some time that morning staring at the picture of the mystery man.

All too soon, it was time to start the first tour of the day. She had two scheduled before lunch, and it would be a struggle to get through them. How could she concentrate on telling George's story to strangers when she would rather be out searching for the man himself? She planned to head to the main part of town the minute she wrapped up the second tour so she could look for Braydyn. Cecily mentally kicked herself for not searching there earlier this morning. The reenactor tour guides didn't begin their shifts until 9am. She realized too late that those hours applied only to *living* and *working* people. If Braydyn truly was a ghost, he wasn't bound to such rules. He could be anywhere around town at any time. After all, what else did he have to do?

Fortunately, the two morning tours went very well. They were both full of enthusiastic tourists who asked lots of interesting questions, which helped the time go faster. Cecily wrapped up the morning's tours and headed out toward the picnic tables in town.

As usual, she walked there since it was a nice summer day. Not only could she enjoy the weather, she could keep her eyes peeled for Braydyn/George. Out here in the daylight with so many people around, the whole situation seemed far less scary. After all, she'd spoken to this guy many times before. Nothing about him had ever seemed off or frightening. Now that she was out in public and not all alone in the mansion, searching for him felt more like an adventure. Cecily felt like a detective on the hunt for a suspicious person. The idea was exciting, and the more she thought about it, the more she desperately wanted to find him.

Cecily walked the grounds for a while, trying to cover all the spaces she recalled having run into him in the past. So far, there was no trace of him. She glanced over toward the bakery, both hoping to find Braydyn and contemplating buying some coffee and a little something sweet.

"Hey," came a male voice from just behind her.

Cecily let out a yelp of surprise and whirled around.

Ryan held up his hands. "Sorry, sorry. Didn't mean to startle you."

She put her hand on her heart. After catching her breath, she said, "It's okay. I'm kinda wound up, I guess. I've been looking all over for Braydyn."

"I figured. No sign of him yet, huh?"

Cecily shook her head.

"Have you eaten lunch yet?"

She thought for a moment and laughed. "No. Not only have I not eaten, but I was so focused on finding Braydyn, I forgot to bring a lunch. To my lunch break."

Ryan chuckled. "Would you like to go to the Cedar Tavern for lunch? My treat."

Her adrenaline surged at the idea of having lunch alone with Ryan. In that moment, it was easy to forget about Braydyn altogether.

"Oh, that would be so nice. Thank you!"

His smile got her heart thumping. The man was ridiculously handsome. He was the picture of masculinity, what with his dirty shirt and overall ruggedness. Cecily didn't care if it was stereotypical of her, but she simply loved that he worked with his hands and was the type of guy who could fix just about anything.

Walking beside him toward the restaurant, she reminded herself that Ryan was also the type who never gave her a second glance. At her high school, strong, sporty types like him had ignored her completely.

Like a gentleman, Ryan opened the door for her when they reached the restaurant. He smiled at the hostess and requested a table for two. That was certainly a good sign. Though this wasn't technically a date, she supposed, it was a start. It would give her a chance to get to know him better, and the way he treated the waitstaff would tell her a lot about him. Ryan had always been kind to others as far as she knew, but still. She'd been on more than one date with a guy who was rude to the servers. None of those jerks had gotten a second date.

The hostess informed them there would be a short wait for a table.

"That's fine," Ryan said. "Thanks."

Cecily smiled and nodded at the hostess.

She had also been on her share of dates with wealthy men, given the status of her own family. One guy had refused to take no for an answer when informed that the table wasn't ready yet. He'd begun by trying to pay off the hostess and ended with the "do you know who I am" line. Cecily cringed just thinking about it.

Ryan looked around the restaurant. "I've been here before, but it's been a while."

"Same with me. Funny how you can work here every day but sometimes forget all that Olde Town has to offer. I can definitely get stuck in a rut at the Hartley Mansion. Well, not *stuck*."

He laughed. "No, not stuck. I can tell how much you love it there."

"I do. I really do," she said, feeling absolutely giddy that he understood. Clearly, he knew she was a nerd, and he didn't mind. Whether he could actually go for a nerdy girl like her, well, that was to be determined.

"It smells so good in here," Ryan said.

"Right? I didn't realize how hungry I was until we walked in."

Indeed, the aroma in the tavern was nothing short of delectable. That unmistakable scent of smoked meat not only smelled delicious, it added to the old-timey feel of the place. Why *didn't* she come here more often?

In no time at all, Cecily and Ryan were seated at a cozy table near the back. It felt more and more like a date by the minute, but she had to get a grip on herself. For all she knew, Ryan had a girlfriend. She was fairly sure he didn't, though. She'd never seen him with a woman. Then again, it wasn't like you brought your significant other to work with you. But Ryan did seem like a standup guy, and it wasn't exactly appropriate to take another woman to lunch if you had a steady girlfriend.

If she was lucky, the subject might come up during lunch and she could find out for sure.

Cecily perused the menu. Everything looked so damned good. But then again, everything looked delicious when you were starving.

"Hard to decide," she said. "But I keep smelling that smoked ham, and that might be the winner."

"They do make a mean smoked ham and cheese sandwich," Ryan said.

"Okay, I'm sold," she said, closing her menu.

Ryan chuckled, a deep, throaty sound. So damned sexy. Too bad she wasn't funnier. She would try to make him laugh as much as possible. She remembered the way he'd joked around with Braydyn the last time they'd seen him. A sense of humor was definitely a desirable personality trait.

The server arrived and took their order. After she left, Cecily knew it was her chance to discuss this unique situation. Not that she knew where to start.

"Thanks for helping me deal with ... you know ... whatever this is," Cecily said.

"You're welcome," he said with a grin so sexy it sent shivers of delight down her spine. "It certainly spiced up an ordinary work week."

I'll say.

"I'm going out of my mind trying to figure this out," she said. "I wish I could track the guy down so I can ask him what's what."

Ryan nodded. "I don't even know what I would say if I did come across him now. Um, hey, dude ... weird question for ya. Are you still breathing?"

Cecily laughed. "I've gone over and over what I would say to him. But then it's like I don't know how I'll react when I do see him, you know?"

"Oh, I know," Ryan said with a slight grimace.

"Can you imagine if he really is George Hartley? Think of all the questions I could ask him about the family!"

Ryan opened his mouth to answer but waited as the server arrived with their drinks.

After she left them alone again, he said, "I hadn't thought much about that part. I guess I'm more focused on the whole 'talking to a dead guy' thing."

Ryan shifted in his seat. He kept scanning the room as if he expected a ghost to appear at any moment. Clearly, he was uncomfortable with the idea of speaking with the dead. That was fair, considering how frightened she'd been this morning.

"I'm so glad you don't think I'm crazy," she said.

"Honestly, if I hadn't seen the picture myself, I might have thought that. But damn. The resemblance is *uncanny*."

"Yeah. I mean, most blood relatives don't look that much alike, so it's hard to write this off as just a coincidence."

Ryan shrugged. "I dunno. Some people say there's such a thing as doppelgangers."

Cecily shuddered. "Yeah. I've heard that too. The idea of doppelgangers is kinda creepy."

"Creepier than a dead guy walking around?" Ryan asked in a hushed tone.

"Fair point," Cecily said. She glanced around the crowded restaurant, but nobody was paying any attention to their conversation. Still, they kept their voices down just in case. The last thing she wanted was to get a reputation for being a ghost hunter rather than a serious historian. Since there wasn't much more to say on the subject until they found Braydyn, she decided to change topics.

"So," she began nervously. "Tell me about you." She cringed inwardly, worrying that she was making their lunch seem like a date.

"I wish there was more to tell, but I'm pretty much a simple guy," he said with a modest shrug. He didn't elaborate, but Cecily really wanted to know more.

"Well, *Canuck*, what brought you to the United States?"

"I hate my parents."

Her eyes flew open wide, and Ryan winced.

"Okay, that came about way harsher than I'd expected." He paused a moment, as if his own words had surprised him. "I don't *hate* them. But we've never really gotten along. I came to the U.S. for a fresh start, I guess. I wanted to start my own business, so I moved here. Canada's a big country, so I could have stayed there and moved to another province maybe, but do you have any idea how friggin' cold it is there?"

Cecily laughed. "I've never been, but I've heard. I hear you. I can't stand the cold."

"You get used to it after a while. More or less. Like when it gets cold here, or what you Marylanders think is cold, it's not bad."

"So you're from Quebec, right?"

Ryan raised an eyebrow, impressed she knew that. "Yeah, Montreal to be specific. How'd you know?"

"The accent."

"That's so funny. I swear, I don't even hear it anymore."

"It's not strong, but it's there. Just on certain words," Cecily said, hoping she wasn't giving too much away by admitting how closely she listened to him. "So you speak French?"

With that, Ryan reached over and took her hands in his. Gazing into her eyes, he said, "J'aimerais que la bouffe arrive vite parce que je meurs de faim."

Mesmerized, she asked, "What does that mean?"

In the same gentle, dreamy voice he'd used while speaking French, he translated, "I wish the food would get here because I'm starving."

Cecily burst out laughing, drawing the attention of some of the other diners. Ryan laughed too and let go of her hands. Somehow, what he'd said was even better than if his words had been dreamy and romantic. She enjoyed how entertaining he was, and she loved how at ease she felt around him.

She scanned the dining room, seeing mostly tourists but also a few people who worked in the historical district. Notably, she saw Dr. Adam Gallagher sitting at a table alone with some papers spread out before him. He was a history addict just like her and tended to be a workaholic. He caught her eye and raised his eyebrow. Clearly, he was curious about what was going on between her and Ryan.

Your guess is as good as mine.

But she was dying to find out. She snapped out of her dreamy haze.

"So what's the deal with your parents?" she asked. His family situation sounded sad, which was a shame. Ryan deserved better. Her question was personal, but he was the one who had brought up the subject in the first place.

Ryan hesitated to answer, and she felt bad for asking.

"They thought I was stupid."

"What?" Cecily was horrified at the thought.

"Oh yeah. And they had no problem telling me that."

"Wow," she said softly.

The food arrived just then, and they both thanked the server. Ryan dug right into his sandwich.

"Sooo gooood," he moaned.

Cecily tried her ham and cheese sandwich and found it had the perfect mix of gooey cheesiness and salty ham goodness.

"There is nothing like delicious food when you're super hungry," she said.

"Exactly."

Once their hunger had been sated a bit, she said, "Your parents are idiots."

Ryan choked on his food, which made her laugh.

"Sorry, sorry. I'm not trying to kill you," she said.

"It's okay." He wiped his mouth with his napkin. "I just wasn't expecting you to say that."

"They'd have to be if they think you're dumb."

"I dunno. They may have been onto something."

"How can you say that?" It broke her heart to think he thought of himself as stupid. "I've always considered you to be very intelligent. We've talked about history a few times, and you've always struck me as very informed about it. You sound like one of the historical guides. If you weren't wearing your construction clothes, I would've assumed you were one of the reenactors."

"That's pretty cool. Thanks." Ryan sounded grateful but also seemed to be quite guarded as he spoke. "You should know ... I don't read much."

Cecily shrugged. "So? What does that have to do with anything?"

"A lot of what I learn about history comes from, like, YouTube and stuff."

"Nothing wrong with that. Like anything else you find on the internet, as long as it's from a reputable source, you can learn a ton online."

Ryan's eyes opened wide with enthusiasm. "I do learn a lot about history and everything else that catches my interest online. And yeah, I'm always careful to figure out the source and whether it's reliable or not."

"I'm sure you do," she said. "You don't strike me as the type of gullible person who believes everything they see on the web. That's part of what makes you an intelligent person. Which brings me back to my original point. Your parents are idiots."

Ryan chuckled. "Maybe. But it's not just that I don't like to read."

He stopped to take a bite of his sandwich as if he were stalling for time. Eventually, he spoke again. "It's like ... reading is hard for me."

She hated seeing how embarrassed he was to admit that part. He wouldn't even look her in the eye.

Without thinking, she blurted out, "You're probably dyslexic."

"What?"

"Sorry, sorry. That's not for me to say. I'm not a doctor. I mean, I am technically a doctor, but my PhD in colonial history hardly qualifies me to diagnose somebody with a learning problem."

"I'm not dyslexic," he said matter-of-factly. Fortunately, he didn't sound upset or offended by what she'd said. "I don't see letters or numbers as backward or anything."

Cecily munched on her potato chips for a moment,

forcing herself to slow down and think before she spoke. This was a delicate subject after all.

"That can be part of it. But it's more than that. Being dyslexic means you have trouble decoding words in your head. Like it can be tough for you to match letters with the sound they make."

Ryan slowly put down his sandwich. Cecily watched as the wheels turned in his head.

"Oh."

Clearly, she'd hit the nail on the head. Ryan was finally understanding a lifetime of struggle. A flash of fury rocked through her system on his behalf.

"Ridiculous," she muttered angrily.

"You think I'm ridiculous?" he asked, sounding horrified.

"No, no! God, no. Ugh, it's just that a long time ago, when people didn't understand dyslexia or learning disabilities, teachers and parents thought some kids were just unintelligent. It was the same thing with kids who were left-handed. For a long time, people thought there was something wrong with them. But in this day and age, there's no excuse for your parents and teachers not to have realized what your issue was."

"Oh," he said quietly.

"Look, like I said, I'm not a specialist or anything. So I can't say for sure, but for God's sake, stop beating yourself up and thinking you're stupid, okay?"

Ryan smiled. "I'll try. Well, whatever the reason, that's why I ended up doing construction. Since I'm not so much with the book-learnin', I picked a job that any idiot can do."

Cecily burst out laughing. "Oh my God, Ryan. You really think any idiot can do what you do?"

Ryan shrugged.

His parents really did a number on him.

She sighed heavily. He'd confessed a lot of personal things today, and she knew it was her turn. "Okay. I'm gonna out myself right now as a stereotypical dumb girl when it comes to repairing stuff, building stuff, you name it. I'm not proud of it, but things like electrical wires absolutely mystify me."

He smiled, and she could tell he felt more at ease. That made her confession sting a bit less.

"I feel so bad about it. Like I should be a modern woman and know how to change the oil in my car, or at least know how to change a tire. But I don't. I'm the kind of person who when the repair guy comes to fix the water heater, I can't even tell him where it is."

Ryan laughed gently, no trace of mocking in his voice. She was grateful that he didn't seem to think less of her now.

"You have to be very intelligent to do what you do, Ryan. I'm not kidding. There's a lot more to life than book smarts, which you do have too, by the way. Just not from actual books."

"I guess," he said with a shrug.

"And education isn't everything. Consider all the physical work you and your crew do every day. I can't imagine how hard that work must be and how grueling in the heat of summer and the cold of winter. And think about it. What happens if I don't do my job? Not much. But without guys like you, the whole world would fall apart."

"That's a bit dramatic," he said with a laugh. "But thanks."

"And thanks for not judging me for being so clueless about so many things." Cecily sighed. "I really should take some time and learn more about how my car works, as well as the stuff in the house that needs fixing."

"You said you got a PhD, right?"

"Yeah."

"You know plenty, Cecily. You shouldn't feel like you need to know *everything*. So why don't *you* stop beating *your*self up."

Cecily smiled warmly at him. "Thanks. I'll try. "

After they'd finished eating, she sat back in her seat. "This was really nice."

"Yeah. It was." Ryan's eyes lingered on her for a moment, and then the server arrived to see if they needed anything. Ryan glanced over at Cecily and she shook her head.

"Just the check, then," Ryan said. "Thanks." He sighed. "Back to the grind, I guess."

"Yup. "

Once they got outside, it was time to part ways.

"Thanks again for lunch." She couldn't help wondering if perhaps he would have kissed her if they weren't out in such a public place in the middle of the day. A public place that also happened to be where they both worked.

"Any time," he said with a grin.

I will definitely take you up on that.

Glancing around, he added, "Let me know if you see any sign of you know who."

"Oh, I will. I definitely will."

Cecily turned to leave, but then she turned back.

"You need something?" he asked.

"Yeah. Your cell number."

"What?" Ryan looked quite surprised.

"I— I mean, you know, in case I find him."

"Oh. Right. Sure," he said.

She took out her phone and entered his number into her contacts as he read off the numbers. "Thanks. I'll keep you posted."

Cecily headed back toward the Hartley Mansion. While she did keep a lookout for Braydyn, she was more than a bit distracted by her lunch with Ryan. Despite knowing him for a while, she'd spent more time with him in the last few days than the rest of the time combined. Now she knew not only was he ridiculously handsome, she was at ease around him. Like something clicked between them. And yet, she felt some hesitation from him. Like he was holding back. If he was interested in her romantically, he wasn't in a hurry to do anything about it.

She managed to get through the last tours of the day, but it wasn't easy. Cecily was antsy, with too much on her mind. Unlike this morning, these tours dragged on. The tourists were polite but didn't seem particularly interested in anything she had to say. Some tours were like that, but she still had to get through them.

Once she was finally done, she headed back to her office to work on her book a little more. It wasn't long before exhaustion set in. She was tired from not sleeping well lately, and today had been such a rollercoaster of emotions. She'd gone from being afraid of finding Braydyn to being excited about the idea, and of course, her lunch with Ryan had brought up a new swell of emotions. Now, she was well and truly worn out. She decided to knock off a bit earlier than usual.

Wearily, she picked up her purse and headed into the Great Hall.

And that's when she heard it.

The scraping of a plate coming from the dining room. The sound was faint at first but soon grew louder. She stopped dead in her tracks to listen. The noises stopped.

This very same thing had happened many times before. She would hear noises coming from the dining room, but when she went to check, there had been nothing there. Something told her today would be different.

Her pulse rate soared as her exhaustion evaporated, replaced by pure adrenaline. Both excited and terrified by what she might find, she drew in a deep breath and forced herself to rush to the dining room. She knew if she hesitated for even one second, she would lose her nerve and run out the front door.

Muscles tight, she peered in the doorway.

There, sitting in one of the chairs at the table facing her, was Braydyn. Or whoever he really was.

Cecily's breath caught in her throat. She tried to speak, but no words came out.

Braydyn smiled. "You know who I am, don't you."

She nodded. "Y-y-y-yes. At least I think so."

"It's true. I'm George Hartley. Nice to officially meet you."

Cecily stared at him, willing her brain to comprehend the incomprehensible.

"It's okay," he said softly. "You don't have to be afraid. It's still me. Well, kinda. The guy you've seen wandering around the historical district all this time."

She thought back to all the times she had spoken to him in the past, thinking he was an employee. And all the times he'd "escaped from the heat" here in the air-conditioned mansion. He'd always been kind and funny. If he'd wanted to hurt her, he'd have done it by now.

"Take your time," he said. "I know this is a lot to deal with. When you're ready, you can sit across from me if you like." Braydyn—or George officially, now—gestured to the dining room chair on the opposite side of the table. "I won't make any sudden moves. I promise."

Indeed, George kept quite still for fear of scaring her away.

After a moment, he spoke again. "I apologize for eavesdropping, but I was there when you and Ryan were talking about my picture. I get bored, so people-watching is something of a hobby of mine. Don't worry. I never do anything creepy like follow you to the bathroom or anything."

Cecily nodded. Hearing him speak calmed her down a little. He seemed so *normal*. No wonder she'd never noticed anything unusual about him before. She carefully pulled out the chair and sat down across from him. He smiled warmly, putting her even more at ease.

"You doing okay Dr. Rosewood?" he asked.

"Yes, I think so." Laughing softly, she added, "I've told you a million times to call me Cecily."

He laughed too. "I know. I just come from a time when women weren't exactly respected for their intelligence. You must have worked awfully hard to earn your doctorate, so I wanted to show you the proper respect."

"That's so sweet. I appreciate that. But we're friends, right?"

"Right. Okay, from now on I shall call you Cecily."

"And I have to remember to call you George and not Braydyn. Where did you get that fake name, anyway?"

George laughed. "I've heard a lot of wacky names from tourists over the years, so I picked the most modern name I could to throw you all off track."

"It worked."

"I know," he said with a grin.

"I just ... wow," she said, her mind going over all the interactions she'd ever had with the man. "How did I not know you were ... I mean, you brought tours over here all the time."

"Yeah. They were never actually *my* tours. When I heard people talking about heading here for a tour of the mansion, I would tell them I'd just wrapped up one of my tours and had time to walk them over." George shrugged. "It was like a free mini tour for them because I could answer most of the questions they had about Olde Town and its history. Nobody ever questioned it."

"That's quite clever," Cecily said.

"I've had a lot of time to think of things like that."

Cecily shook her head in wonder. "So ... you're dead. Like really, actually dead."

"I sure am."

"Wow. What's it like to be dead?"

George looked as if he sighed, but of course there was no breath. Fascinating.

"Boring. So very boring. That's why I am incredibly fortunate to have died in the middle of a tourist district. Or what is now a tourist district. Other dead folks can't exactly walk around in the clothes from the time period where they died without arousing suspicion. You've known me for years and you never noticed that I always wore the exact same thing."

She glanced at his black frock coat and white-collared shirt. "You're right. I never even thought about it until I saw that sketch of you. So, was that you every time I've heard noises in this house?" she asked.

"Maybe. Though I'm not sure," George said, looking around the dining room. "Lots of people have died here over the years. It's hard to imagine that I'm the only one still here."

Cecily contemplated that for a moment. It was all so hard to wrap her head around.

"I've never seen anyone else. Not here in the house, I mean. There are lots of other ghosts around town."

"Are you serious?"

"Oh yeah. Are you kidding?" George smiled with amusement. "This place has been inhabited for almost four hundred years. *Lots* of ghosts around here."

"Amazing," she said. Cecily was far more excited than afraid by the thought of so many old souls wandering the grounds. The things she could learn from them!

She laughed suddenly.

"What?"

"I was just thinking Adam Gallagher would be awfully surprised to know that."

George laughed as well. "That is for *sure*. The man is as stubborn as all hell. Easily dismisses any strange sounds as nothing."

"So you've tried haunting him?"

"Yes. It's kinda fun to mess with him."

"I'm sure it is. Gives you something to do, right?"

"Exactly."

Cecily eyed him curiously, wondering if it was possible to see through him. She found it wasn't. He appeared as solid as he always had while pretending to be Tour Guide Braydyn.

"Do you just hang around here all the time?"

"I can, but I don't have to."

"You mean you can travel to other places?"

Shaking his head sadly, George said, "Oh, how I wish I could. I just meant that I don't have to stay conscious all the time. It's a mercy, really. Wandering aimlessly for over a century could drive a man mad. I have the option to vanish at will. Vanishing is like disappearing, but when you vanish, you're not conscious."

"It's like sleep for a ghost," she observed.

She stared at him in wonder, doing her best to take in everything he was saying. It was all so strange. Perhaps the oddest part was how utterly *normal* he seemed. This was like chatting with an old friend.

"Exactly right. It's different from simply disappearing, which just means living people can't see me. I can disappear at will, too. See?"

With that, George's image completely faded from view and then reappeared before her eyes. She gasped, making him wince.

"Sorry. Maybe you weren't ready for that yet."

"No, no. It's okay. It just took me by surprise. Anyway, that was proof positive that I'm talking to a ghost."

He smiled a bit sadly. "Yes. Hard to argue with that kind of proof."

"You could just do that to Adam Gallagher, and then he'd believe."

"He would, but teasing him subtly is more fun."

Cecily laughed. "Fair enough."

There were so many things she wanted to ask him—her mind whirred with the possibilities, yet it was hard to come up with specific questions.

"So you just hang around here being invisible all the time? I assume you can't feel anything. You knew the air conditioning was broken because you heard us talking about it?"

"Yes. I can see and hear but cannot smell or feel anything physical. For the most part, anyway. I can touch some things."

"Like a knife and fork, and perhaps a piano?"

"Yes," he said with a smile. "I can touch things sometimes if I work hard and concentrate. It's very difficult, but I've spent considerable time practicing. Practice makes you better. I suppose that goes for anything in life ... and beyond. Many ghosts I know cannot touch a thing. Me? I've worked on it. I can only do it for a short time. For example tonight, had I scraped the plates much longer to get your attention, I would have disappeared from view."

"But not vanished."

"Right. I would still be sitting here, but I wouldn't have had the strength to appear visible to you. Normally, it's not hard to stay visible, but I've found most ghosts prefer to be left alone, so they prefer to be unseen. If I don't sap my strength by touching things, I could stay visible all the time if I wanted."

"Fascinating. So much to learn about ghost life. Or should I say, ghost existence."

"I'm happy to answer any questions you have."

"There's so much I want to know! But I'm coming up blank right now."

"That's okay. I have all the time in the world."

"Yes, I suppose you do," she said.

George seemed so sad.

"Do you know why you're still stuck here?"

"I have my suspicions."

Cecily nodded but didn't want to pry.

"Well, I'm glad to officially know you, George."

"Me too, Dr.— I mean, Cecily. Why don't you go home and get some rest? You've had a long day, what with looking for me and having lunch with Canuck."

"You know about that?"

"Yes," he said sheepishly. "I promise you I don't normally follow you around like that, but I knew you were searching for me. Please understand, I didn't stand there and listen to your whole lunch conversation. Mind you, I have no problem doing that with strangers that I'll never see again, but not with you. That's different."

Cecily could see the truth in George's eyes. He seemed to be a man of honor.

"That makes sense."

"We'll talk again soon. I promise."

"I sincerely hope so."

George nodded and then faded away.

"My God," Cecily whispered softly.

After sitting in the dining room for a few moments gathering her thoughts, she finally left for the night.

9

Ryan woke up the next morning to an alarming text message from Cecily: *I FOUND HIM!!*

He sat up in bed, no longer groggy. Nothing like a creepy message about a ghost still wandering the earth to really get you going in the morning.

Ryan: *Are u serious?*

Cecily: *Yes. He was waiting for me last night in the mansion after hours.*

Ryan sucked in a deep breath. The idea of being confronted by Braydyn in the huge house with no one else around was terrifying.

Cecily: *We had a long talk, and he is fascinating. I can't wait for you to meet him! You know, again lol.*

Apparently, Cecily wasn't the least bit frightened. Throughout this whole thing, she'd seemed way more intrigued than scared, so he wasn't really surprised. Still, thinking you're okay with meeting a ghost was one thing. Actually being confronted with one was quite another. As for him, he already knew he was *not okay* with meeting George. And yet, he had no choice. Not only was he in too deep with this adventure, he also could not have Cecily think he was a wuss. Which he totally was, at least when it came to this.

He hesitated, unsure of how to respond. If nothing else, he could at least act brave in text form.

Ryan: *That would be awsome! I can't wait to talk to him.*

Cecily: *I should have set something up with him yesterday. I just didn't think of it. I was a little overwhelmed.*

Ryan: *Well, yeah. I guess so lol. I'm sure he could squeze in a quick meeting with us during his busy shedule.*

Cecily: *Haha, you're right. How about you come over to the mansion after work? Hopefully I can find him again and ask him to stick around and talk with you.*

Ryan: *Sounds good.*

Cecily: *Perfect. See you then!*

Ryan put down his phone and groaned as he got out of bed. If nothing else, at least he would get to see Cecily again today. And maybe with any luck Braydyn wouldn't show up and he could just be alone with her.

Not Braydyn. George.

That would take some getting used to.

That was a worry for later. Right now, he really needed to concentrate on his job. He needed to pay close attention to what he was doing to avoid hurting himself or someone else.

Mornings were often the busiest time. As the owner of Armstrong Property Services, he took on lots of roles— project manager, property manager, construction worker, and all-around fixer. His company was quite successful and growing by the minute. Truth be told, he really didn't have to get his hands dirty and do the actual grunt work anymore, but he wasn't quite ready to let go of that type of work just yet. Earning the respect of his employees meant a lot to him, so he didn't want to be some out-of-touch over-seer type who had no idea how hard his guys worked. For the time being, he liked being in the trenches with them.

Dispatching the work for the day, which involved figuring out who was needed for what and where, gave him a break from freaking out about all things ghostly for a bit. Though the Olde Town historical district was by far his biggest client, he also had some contracts with a few smaller properties. There was a small apartment complex and a medical office building as well.

Scanning the laptop he had perched on the hood of his truck, Ryan double-checked the schedule for the day. He smiled as he recalled Cecily's words about his business and how she thought you had to be pretty smart to do what he did for a living. He also considered her theory that he was dyslexic. If she was right, it would certainly explain a lot. Ryan had always thought of himself as not that bright because he struggled to read and wasn't great with spelling, but what if it had been a learning disability all along? Even if it wasn't, Cecily didn't seem to think less of him for watching videos online to study history instead of reading. She had the attitude that learning was learning, and who cared how you did it?

Cecily was even cooler than he'd thought. But though he felt more comfortable around her since lunch yesterday, he was still intimidated by her intelligence. Back in high school, the smart girls made fun of him for struggling to read. Even after all these years, he winced when he thought about how they'd all giggled when the teacher forced him to read passages from a book out loud. Though he knew Cecily would never laugh at him, it was hard to imagine she could really be into a guy like him. Adam Gallagher, the hot professor, was undoubtedly a much better fit.

As it drew close to quitting time, Ryan was a jangled mess of nervous energy, and not because of Cecily. The real concern was hiding his terror of the ghostly George Hartley.

It would be daylight after work, and it wasn't as if he would be alone with the guy, but still. Part of him held out hope that Cecily wouldn't find George today, but another part of him knew it was better to get this over with. He was tired of stressing out about this meeting. Sooner or later, it was going to have to happen.

Just as he was wrapping up for the day, Ryan's phone buzzed in his pocket.

Cecily: *He's here!*

He suddenly felt dizzy. His hand trembled as he held his phone, and he nearly dropped it. Good God. He had to get control of himself.

Ryan: *That's great!!!*

He laughed ruefully at himself. As if three exclamation points would show how brave he was.

Cecily: *We are out back in the garden.*

Ryan: *Okay, be there soon!!*

"You okay?"

Ryan spun around, heart racing.

"Dude, what's wrong with you?" Charlie, his coworker and buddy looked at him as if he was nuts.

Ryan forced a laugh. "Sorry. Just kinda out of it today for some reason."

"So I've noticed," Charlie said dryly.

"Didn't sleep well. I'll be better tomorrow." He slapped his friend on the shoulder. "Have a good night."

"You too." Fortunately, Charlie seemed to accept Ryan's weak explanation for his oddness and headed off.

Nothing left to do now but walk over to the Hartley

Mansion garden. He was grateful to have a few moments to himself to gather his courage.

It was so frustrating because he wasn't the type to scare easily. Horror movies never bothered him—they were all fake. They weren't his favorite thing since he found jump scares annoying, but it was nothing he couldn't handle. He wasn't afraid to walk alone at night, that kind of thing. But this? This was completely uncharted territory. Until now, he'd never had strong feelings or fears about ghosts. Before all this happened, he wasn't sure if they were real or not, but he figured he was unlikely to ever encounter any ghosts, so he'd never given it much thought. Normally, Ryan didn't mind a challenge, but to have to face one like this in front of the woman he so desperately wanted to impress seemed unfair.

Once he arrived, Ryan stared up at the formidable Hartley Mansion. He couldn't help wondering if George was the only spirit haunting the place. A chill went through him when he remembered the phantom piano music he'd heard when he was all alone in the house.

He shook his head as if to ward off these frightening thoughts. Freaking himself out was no good. Somehow, he had to keep it together in front of Cecily. Ryan trudged his way to the back of the house, trying not to think of the graveyard that was located not too far away.

Sure enough, Cecily and George were seated on two wrought iron benches across from one another on the gravel path that wound around the garden. Strange how George appeared to be sitting on the bench like a normal person. He looked so solid, which made Ryan question everything for a moment. Could this be some sort of elaborate prank on Braydyn's part? Did Cecily have any proof that he was George Hartley?

Doubting that Braydyn was actually a ghost should have made him feel better, but it didn't. This whole thing was still so damned creepy.

"Ryan!" Cecily called to him cheerfully.

She certainly didn't sound afraid. It looked as if she and her buddy "George" were having a grand old time.

Swallowing hard, he made his way over. He tried to concentrate on Cecily as he took a seat beside her.

Beaming with excitement, Cecily said, "Ryan, I want to formally introduce you to George Hartley."

The man grinned at him. "What's up, Canuck?"

He sounded like the same jokester who had always teased him about being from Canada.

Ryan fought hard to keep his voice steady. "Nice to meet you, George. If that's really you."

He wanted to make sure, once and for all, what they were actually dealing with.

The guy smirked. "You don't believe me?"

"I'm not sure."

Without missing a beat, George swiped his hand down onto the armrest of the bench. *His hand went right through it.*

Dizziness overwhelmed Ryan. He was petrified he would pass out.

"Proof enough for you?" George asked.

Ryan nodded rapidly, unable to speak.

"You okay?" Cecily asked, looking worried. "I know this is a lot to take in."

He nodded again, still silent.

"It's still me, you know," George said. "I mean, kind of. I'm the same guy you've always known. Just with a different name."

If you say so.

"You can ask him questions if you want," Cecily said

encouragingly. She smiled at George and he grinned back. They seemed to have developed a rapport already.

"Ummm, it's hard to think of anything at the moment," Ryan said. His voice sounded high and squeaky, which made him afraid to say another word.

"I get that," George said. "Take your time."

Ryan breathed in deeply. The smell of the flowers around him helped clear his head. He looked around at the Hartley garden. The place was enormous. He'd never paid much attention to it before, but it was quite lovely. Everything was lush and blooming right now, and he found himself wishing he were alone with Cecily. Ryan would have loved to walk with her down the gravel path that weaved in and out all through the expansive gardens. No wonder people often held their weddings here.

He was quiet for an uncomfortable amount of time, but it was tough to think of something to ask a ghost.

"I ... I don't even know where to start," he said at last. At least his voice wasn't so squeaky anymore.

"I know what you mean," Cecily said. "I still have so much I want to ask him. Yesterday, all I could think of was to ask him what it's like being dead."

Ryan shuddered involuntarily.

Turning toward George, Cecily said, "I'm writing a book about the Hartley family."

George smirked. "I'm aware."

"Really?" she asked.

"Sure. I've even read over your shoulder sometimes."

Cecily didn't look too thrilled about that.

"Sorry. Like I told you, I get bored. Sometimes I just check in on what you're working on, that's all."

She nodded, looking uncomfortable.

"Look, I promise I won't do that anymore. I won't hang around when you can't see me, okay?"

"Okay," she said with a relieved smile.

"I will say, though, your work on the Hartley family is impressive. You got most of the stuff right."

"Oh, that's great. Good to know," she said, her eyes lighting up.

Ryan stared at George. He looked and sounded so normal, so real. Just when he began to relax a little, his mind drifted back to the cemetery nearby. George's corpse was there, underground, rotting for all eternity. Those morbid thoughts made him lightheaded all over again.

"You found out some things I didn't even know about my family," George said.

"You're kidding," she said, leaning forward with interest.

"Nope." George shook his head sadly. "I didn't ... It wasn't until I saw what you were writing that I found out about my father and that slave woman."

"Oh," she said softly. "Wow."

"Yeah. I mean, I guess I shouldn't have been surprised. I think I always suspected that he slept with some of the female slaves, but I didn't know he raped one. Or possibly more. We only know about the one for sure because she got pregnant."

"Well," Cecily began. Ryan watched as she took time to form her words. "Technically, it was always rape if it involved a master and an enslaved person. I mean, there's really no such thing as consent when there's a power dynamic like that."

"You're right," George said, nodding sadly.

"Do you mind if I ask ..." Cecily continued cautiously. "How did you feel about owning slaves?"

George leaned forward on the bench, and Ryan jumped

in his seat. He couldn't help it. Cecily glanced at Ryan, but didn't comment on his reaction.

This is all so weird.

He tried to concentrate on the gravity of this important conversation, but it was tough. He wondered if he could ever get used to speaking with a dead man.

"That's a fair question," George said thoughtfully. "The answer is I feel very differently now than I did back then. Well really, things started to change not long before I died."

Ryan shuddered again.

No. He would *never* get used to talking to a dead man. George's mention of his death made Ryan think once again about the graveyard. And the fact that George must have had a funeral. This was all so bizarre.

"Something happened that made me question a lot of things."

"What happened?" Cecily asked.

"I met someone that made me feel differently." George sounded quite sad as he spoke. "And now? I've had an awful lot of time to think about everything. I used to think of my father as this admirable, respectable businessman. A man who was passionate about horse racing, running all his business dealings, and who appreciated the finer things in life."

He paused as he spoke, taking a moment to gaze around at the garden. In that moment of silence, Ryan became aware of the chirping of the birds and the gentle rustle of the leaves on the trees. His body started to relax a bit—he wasn't quite so on edge.

"After all this time, you realize none of that shit matters," George said, a sharp edge in his tone. Then he added, "Sorry for the language."

"It's all right," Cecily said. "It's nothing I haven't heard—or said—before."

George smiled ruefully. "Then I saw all that stuff my father had written in his daily journal you have in your office. About Dinah, and what he'd done to her. He wasn't sorry. Only angry that she got pregnant."

"I know," Cecily said.

"Dinah was really sweet. She didn't deserve that. I mean, no one does."

Both Ryan and Cecily nodded.

"That probably wasn't even her real name," George said sharply. "Dinah. And my personal slave was named Sam."

Ryan noticed the way George winced when he mentioned that he'd had his own slave. It made Ryan respect him more. Though it wouldn't change the past, it was still good to learn from your mistakes.

"No way that was his real name either." George laughed bitterly. "They all had names like Sarah, Jane, Mary, Joe, and John. I mean, come on. Those were all names given to them by their ignorant white masters."

"Right," Cecily said, nodding sadly.

"Sam," George said softly. "I wish I'd known his real name."

"I wonder if there's a way to find out what his birth name was," Ryan said.

Both Cecily and George turned to look at him, and he realized he hadn't spoken in quite some time. It was hard not to completely freak out when George looked at him.

"I-I-I mean, like maybe there's some record of him somewhere? Like where he was born and stuff?"

"I wish," Cecily said. "Unfortunately, so much of the history of enslaved people has been lost because they weren't considered important enough to document."

"Pretty much," George agreed somberly. "I do know his parents were originally from West Africa."

"That's a start," Cecily said. "Maybe you can give him a name. An African name."

George stared at Cecily for a moment, and then said, "I would love that."

She smiled. "Let's see, I do know some African names. It's funny, there are several very old African names that you still hear today. Ones like Denzel, Dewayne, Kadeem, LeBron, Kofi, Latoya, and even Ludacris."

"No way," Ryan said. "Really?"

Cecily nodded enthusiastically. He loved how smart she was. It was so damned sexy.

"Let me think ... other African male names ... Duante, Kyan, Luister, Ebi, Dembe, Lado, Sika—"

"Dembe," George said firmly. "I don't know why, but I feel like Sam was really a Dembe."

"Cool." Cecily smiled. "It's never too late, you know. To honor them. To remember them."

"Thank you," George said, his voice barely a whisper.

"I hope you don't mind my grilling you about your past, George."

"I don't, Dr.— I mean, Cecily. I really don't. It's nice to have people to talk to." George glanced at Ryan as he spoke. Ryan's muscles tensed. He felt guilty about it, but it was out of his control.

"I have lots more questions, you know," she said.

"I know," he said with a laugh.

The man might be dead, but he was a damned good sport.

"You guys have got to be tired from working all day," George said, looking at Ryan and then back at Cecily. "You should probably go home and get some rest."

Ryan breathed out a sigh of relief, but at least he had the presence of mind to do so quietly.

"Yes. I guess so," Cecily said reluctantly.

"Don't look so sad," George said. "We have plenty of time to talk about whatever you want. We'll talk again soon."

"Okay." She got up from the bench. "I'm really glad to know you, George."

"You too," he said.

I wish I could say the same, Ryan thought. Perhaps he would get there at some point.

But not yet.

10

———

Thus far, it had been an uneventful morning at the mansion. Cecily ran her tours as usual; the crowds were getting slightly larger now that all the schools were out for the summer. She hadn't seen George yet today. She wondered if he was here and was just invisible.

When she finally got a break in between tours, she texted Ryan.

Cecily: *Hey there. I was wondering if maybe you'd like to go for a walk during your lunch break. It's such a nice day out.*

She held her breath and hit send. Texting him felt a bit forward for her comfort, but she really wanted to see him and didn't have the patience to wait and see if he would ever ask her out. That, and she was rather worried that if she didn't make some kind of move, perhaps he never would. Did that make her seem desperate?

Ryan: *Just us, or will there be a dead guy there?*

She laughed. That was a fair question. She wanted to meet up with Ryan partly because she got the feeling he was quite nervous around George. He hadn't said much to

George yesterday, whereas Cecily thought she'd never run out of things to ask him. Since she'd been the one to drag Ryan into this madness, she wanted to make sure he was okay. If he didn't like to be around the ghost formerly known as Braydyn anymore, she would understand. She'd be disappointed because she loved sharing this strange adventure with him, but she would respect his feelings.

Cecily: *Lol. Just us.*

Once again, she worried about sounding too forward. Meeting up with George had been the perfect excuse to hang out with Ryan, but this was different.

Ryan: *I would love that. Meet at the usual place? Noonish?*

She let out a deep sigh of relief.

Cecily: *Okay cool. See you soon!*

She spent the rest of the morning nervously watching the weather. Storm clouds had gathered, and she worried they would have to postpone their stroll. By lunchtime, the clouds were still there but not a drop of rain had fallen yet. She was more than willing to risk it if Ryan was.

As she made her way toward the main town square, it even *smelled* like rain. With any luck, they'd be able to squeeze in a quick walk before the heavens opened up.

Thinking of the heavens made her wonder about George and why he was still here. She'd always heard that restless spirits wandered the earth because they had unfinished business. Something they needed to fix before they could cross over. With everyone George ever knew long dead, it was hard to imagine what he could possibly do to fix anything anymore. There was still so much to ask him, and she wanted Ryan to be with her when she did. But it wasn't fair to force him along on this wild ride if he was an unwilling participant.

The crowds had thinned out a bit with the threat of rain,

and Cecily spotted Ryan easily as she approached the main part of Olde Town. He sat on a park bench, arms spread out on the back of it, showing off his muscles. She had the pleasure of gawking at him for a moment before he noticed her. His face visibly brightened, giving her a glimmer of hope for what the future might hold for the two of them.

Ryan got up and headed toward her.

"Hey there," he said with a smile that made her stomach quiver with anticipation. She enjoyed just being close to him. "I've been hoping the rain would hold off. So far, so good."

"Yep," she said.

They set off in the same direction without coordinating out loud. Such a simple thing, but it made Cecily feel like they were naturally in sync. They walked through the heart of the Olde Town district where most of the touristy activities took place. A few streets over from the St. Mary's River, this was where most of the old buildings were located.

Cecily breathed in deeply as they walked past the Stonehouse Bakery. "There is nothing like the smell of delicious coffee. I don't know what it is about Stonehouse or what they do differently, but their coffee is the best. Everything they make there is amazing. I love that place."

Ryan glanced at the bakery. "Me too. Unfortunately, I have quite the sweet tooth."

She nodded. "Same here. I can't get enough of their molasses cookies. For real, I can't buy them. If I do, I'll eat the whole package in one sitting."

He chuckled. "Been there."

Cecily discreetly watched Ryan as he gazed at the historical buildings. He looked at them almost as if seeing them for the first time, which was the same way she viewed them.

"What are you thinking about?" she blurted out. It

wasn't like her to be so impulsive. She usually thought before she spoke, but she couldn't help herself. She genuinely wanted to know what was going through his mind.

He smiled. "I was just thinking how cool it is to work here. I mean, this isn't the only place where Armstrong Property Services does business, but our contract here keeps us busy most of the time. I feel really lucky to spend most of my workdays here."

"I feel exactly the same way."

Without looking at her, Ryan said, "I know you do."

She followed his gaze as he looked over at Hawkins General Store.

"It's wild to think of all the people who have been here over the years," he said. "I mean ... the *history* here. It's mind boggling. To think people have been wandering this piece of land for nearly four hundred years. The place is young compared to the rest of the world, but still."

"Yeah." A shiver of delight ran down Cecily's spine being in the presence of someone who felt the same way she did about Olde Town. And about history in general. Lately, being with Ryan, she felt less like a boring nerd. He seemed to enjoy talking with her about all things colonial.

"I know not all the buildings have been here the whole time. But the ones that are still standing, and even the ones that are reconstructions built on the same spot where the originals stood all those years ago, those are the coolest." He paused. "I hope that doesn't sound dumb. Calling them 'the coolest' probably isn't the smartest way to say what I mean."

"It's not dumb at all," she said. "I know exactly what you mean. It's so wild that people are going into Hawkins General Store and buying souvenirs in the same spot where people bought vegetables and home goods several hundred years ago."

They walked for a little ways in a comfortable silence. Once they got outside of the main part of the historical limits, she asked, "Want to go down by the water?"

"Sure, that would be nice," he said.

Together, they turned the corner and headed down toward the St. Mary's River.

"Can I ask you something?" Cecily ventured nervously.

"Of course," he responded with a smile.

"About George ... He scares you, doesn't he?"

Ryan let out a deep sigh. He hung his head slightly.

"I understand, Ryan. I really do. For what it's worth, I don't think less of you for it."

"Well, I think less of me," he said gruffly.

"Oh, I wish you wouldn't," she said, trying to find the right words to reassure him.

As they got down to the banks of the river, she could feel the cooler breeze coming off the water. Cecily watched the water rippling for a moment before she spoke again.

"This whole situation is so bizarre. I'm glad you've been here to witness it with me, otherwise I would be questioning my sanity. And honestly, I don't know why talking with a ghost doesn't scare me. It should. I don't know. George just seems so normal, so human when you talk to him, you know?"

Ryan nodded. "That is true. There were a few times yesterday when for a few seconds, I would forget that he was dead."

He shuddered exaggeratedly on the word "dead," which made her laugh.

"Yeah. The thing is, every once in a while when I would hear something ghostly in the house like footsteps, or plates moving around, or the sound of the piano, I always had this feeling that it was George Hartley. Not Penelope, not Oliver or anyone else who lived and may have died there, but George. And somehow, I just knew he was friendly. That he was nothing to be afraid of."

"That's pretty cool. And it seems you were right. Not only was it him, but he does seem nice enough. If he wanted to hurt us, he'd have done it by now."

Cecily could still hear the uneasiness in his voice, and he looked embarrassed. She felt bad for him and wondered if it would help to make herself equally vulnerable.

"I think you're one of the bravest people I know," she said.

Ryan turned to look at her, which made her blush.

"Really? How do you figure that?"

"Ryan, you chased down a carjacker and saved a woman's life. And her children's life!"

He chuckled. "Oh. That. That was different."

"Sure, it was different. The George thing just means you're creeped out by ghosts. The carjacking was a real, life-threatening situation, and you were a true hero."

He shrugged modestly, which made him the sexiest man alive in her eyes. Other men would have bragged about such a feat. Ryan seemed embarrassed by the attention.

Cecily laughed. "You are *such* a Canadian, Canuck. Shying away from attention that you deserve."

Ryan laughed too. She watched his eyes as he looked out at the vast river.

"It's so pretty out here," he said.

"Yeah. It really is. Even when it's raining. I just felt a drop." The breeze had picked up, sending ripples through the leaves of the trees.

"Me too," he said, glancing skyward and then blinking when the rain got in his eye.

Fortunately, it was just a few sprinkles. For now.

They kept walking, and Cecily wanted this stroll to last forever. The dark clouds above and the waves on the surface of the river didn't feel negative or foreboding. Not when she was with Ryan. With him, it was like two lovers taking a walk along the beach. Trouble was, she had no clue if he felt the same way.

They soon approached an ancient church located right by the water with a very old cemetery out back. Cecily reflected that it was a truly lovely area to have one's final resting place.

"Now *that* place gives me the willies." He turned toward her and pointed his finger at her. "The *willies*, I tell you!"

Cecily burst out laughing, and Ryan chuckled as well. She adored how self-deprecating he could be sometimes. Other men would have put on a brave front, refusing to admit their fears.

"Not only is there a creepy old cemetery out back here, but there's bodies inside that church. You know that, right?"

"Yes. I know that."

"Of course you do," he said with a smile.

There wasn't much she didn't know about the history of Olde Town. She was well aware that the bodies of several early colonists had been found on the grounds many years ago. They were subsequently laid to rest in their very old caskets and displayed in the sanctuary. Though Cecily had always found such a display in Olde Town fascinating, she could hardly fault Ryan for thinking it was creepy.

She stopped walking for a moment and Ryan did the same. She gazed out at the water.

"It's really okay if you don't want to talk to George anymore. I would understand."

Cecily truly did understand, but she still found it impossible to hide the disappointment in her voice. Though she hated that Ryan was scared, she wanted him by her side.

Ryan sighed and waited a bit before answering. "I admit he creeps me out. I can't help it. He just does. But then I think ... what a waste of an opportunity if I avoid him. I mean, he's not just some random dead guy. He's George Hartley. Of the famed Hartleys. So much of this town's history traces back to them."

"Yeah. It's wild to think about." Cecily blinked as she felt the rain start to pick up.

"Damn," Ryan said, putting his hand out to feel the drops. "We'd better get back."

"We can try to grab the shuttle before we get completely drenched."

"Good idea," he said, and they jogged toward the closest shuttle stop. With their work ID badges, they could ride for free.

"Did you ... get anything to eat yet?" Ryan asked, slightly out of breath from running.

"Nope. I figured I'd ... grab something ... from the shopping district," she answered. The shopping district was the more modern area with a huge gift shop run by the National Park Service, as well as a bunch of restaurants and other shops to visit. Located just past the historical area, it was open to the public with no badges required.

Ryan nodded. "Same here. I've got a hankering for Mexican food, so I'm gonna grab something to go from Texy Mexy."

"Sounds good to me."

Fortunately, they were able to catch a shuttle that wasn't

too full yet. Cecily figured most people had seen the rain approaching and had already settled somewhere dry before the storm hit. Unexpected showers were more likely to make available seats hard to come by.

"Hey there, Carl," Ryan said to the driver when the door opened. He gestured for Cecily to go in first.

Carl waved hello before shooting a curious look at them. He must have seen them walking or jogging together.

Cecily smiled to herself. Between Adam Gallagher catching them having lunch together and Carl's curious looks, there was bound to be talk about the two of them being an item.

She wasn't mad about it.

After they grabbed takeout at the Tex-Mex place, she and Ryan said their goodbyes. Ryan got off the shuttle at the historical district, and Cecily rode the bus back to the Hartley Mansion since it was still raining. Though there had been zero chance of a kiss goodbye in public, she settled for what she considered a lingering look from Ryan upon his departure.

Yes. Unless she was completely imagining things, there was definitely something between them.

Cecily sat in the formal dining room of the Hartley Mansion to eat her lunch. She wasn't supposed to bring food in there; it hadn't been used as a real dining room for decades. As long as she cleaned up thoroughly, no one would be the wiser. Cecily ate her lunch in silence, hoping that George would show up to join her.

He didn't.

She wondered if perhaps he was there in the house and was just invisible at the moment. When she finished eating her lunch, she sat still for a few minutes. Cecily closed her eyes to concentrate, attempting to feel any ghostly presence.

She had often heard of people who were naturally sensitive to the paranormal. When they visited battlefields like those in Gettysburg, they could feel the spirits of the past. Cecily seemed to have no such gift, but she wondered if it was possible to develop that kind of ability. As a hardcore believer in ghosts now, maybe she could train herself to feel when they were nearby.

At least that way I could give Ryan some advanced warning.

She opened her eyes and sighed. Still no sign of George.

Thinking back to her conversation with Ryan, she realized she hadn't gotten a clear answer from him about seeing George again. If nothing else, bringing Ryan into this whole ghost adventure had given her an excuse to spend time with him and to get to know him better. Even if he wanted to avoid future conversations with dead people, maybe they could still hang out together and see what happened. She couldn't help worrying that if Ryan was interested in her, he would have made a move by now.

Cecily stood up, taking care to remove any trace of her having spent her lunch break in the dining room. As she straightened out the china dishes and fancy silverware on the tablecloth, she thought about what it must have been like back in the 1830s. She could easily picture George seated at the table with Penelope, Oliver, and his sisters. She wondered what they would have talked about, and what their family dynamic was. From everything she had read, there had been a lot of pressure on George to take over the family business.

And then George had died suddenly.

So many things she wanted to ask him. She was disappointed that she hadn't seen him yet today, but it was just as well. Cecily had three more tours to run this afternoon, and there wouldn't have been much time to chat.

The rest of the day went by quickly. The tourists were fairly attentive to her storytelling, and they all seemed grateful to be in out of the rain. Fortunately, the weather improved significantly as it neared quitting time.

After the last of the guests had left for the day, Cecily wandered around the mansion for a bit. There was still no sign of George.

"George," she called out to what may or may not have been an empty house. "If you're here, I'd really like to see you."

Sighing deeply, she walked up the large staircase that led from the Great Hall and into one of the upstairs bedrooms. Nothing but silence greeted her. Once again, she closed her eyes and tried to feel any kind of presence.

Suddenly, her eyes flew open. Perhaps it was her imagination, but for a second she thought she felt an entity nearby.

"George? Are you here?"

She strained her ears, hoping for a hint of piano music or phantom footsteps. Cecily walked back to the top of the staircase.

She looked to her left and to her right, hoping to catch a glimpse of him.

Then she had a bizarre feeling of complete weightlessness.

Everything went black.

11

———

Ryan spent the rest of the day thinking about Cecily. There was absolutely no question that he was falling for her. *Hard.* He berated himself for not being more forward. For not just going for it already. He knew he couldn't exactly kiss her in public in front of not only a bunch of strangers, but in front of people they both worked with. Still, there was zero excuse for not asking her out on a proper dinner date. From what he could tell, she did seem interested in him.

And yet, he was still afraid. Cecily said she'd thought he was brave, but how wrong she was. The worst-case scenario was she would shoot him down. Say she wasn't interested. He should be able to deal with that. But he still could not get the image of all those smart girls in high school out of his head. The ones who had mocked him mercilessly and rejected him because he was dumb. Or at least they'd thought he was dumb. Maybe he really was dyslexic and not a moron after all. Who knew?

Either way, he *was* being stupid when it came to Cecily,

but he wasn't sure how to get up the nerve to ask her out officially.

The rain finally stopped toward the end of the day, which just figured. He'd gotten some work done on the inside of the theater reconstruction, but he'd really wanted to finish the roof. With any luck, tomorrow's weather would be better.

As he finished putting away all his tools and got ready to walk to the parking lot, he saw something out of the corner of his eye just to the left of the theater building. He turned to see someone running toward him. A surge of pure terror shot through his body when he saw it was George.

Ghosts can run. I can't believe ghosts can run.

The wild look in George's eye terrified him further. That, and it was so bizarre, so otherworldly that he wasn't out of breath.

Because he doesn't breathe anymore. He's dead.

When George was a few feet away from him, he recoiled in horror.

"Ryan!" he snapped. "I know you're scared of me, but get it together. You've got to help me."

He was so freaked out that he could hardly think straight. "Wh-what? What?"

"It's Cecily. She's hurt."

Ryan blinked and shook his head, trying to get control of himself and focus on what George was saying. He already felt off-kilter being near George and seeing him running toward him full force and scaring the hell out of him.

"What do you mean she's hurt?" he asked, finally wrapping his head around what this man was telling him.

"I— I don't know what happened. I didn't see it. I was in the house and I heard a crash and then I found her at the bottom of the stairs." Lifting up his useless, ghostly hands, he said, "I— I can't touch her. I can't help her."

Ryan's eyes flew wide open.

George's face was filled with terror as he added, "Ryan, I don't know if she's breathing."

"Oh God." Fear and adrenaline surged through his body, far stronger than when all he'd done was see a ghost.

He had to get to Cecily.

"I'll meet you there!" George said somewhere behind Ryan as he ran for his truck.

Ryan jumped in his pickup truck and gunned the engine. Sweating the whole way, he sped toward the Hartley Mansion, doing his best not to let himself think the worst. Though the tourist crowd had thinned a bit at this hour, there were still enough people around to get in his way. He could barely keep from yelling expletives out his window to get them to move faster.

Please be okay please be okay please be okay.

Picturing Cecily Rosewood lying crumpled at the bottom of that giant staircase was unbearable. He jammed his truck into a parking spot at the mansion and sprinted for the house. Hands sweating and heart pounding, he fumbled with his key. He figured with the amount of adrenaline coursing through his system that he could have kicked the door down in one shot. Finally, he got it unlocked.

Racing down the hallway, he found George kneeling over Cecily, looking stricken.

Oh God, it's too late.

"Her chest is moving. She's breathing. That's all I know."

Ryan thought he remembered hearing that you're not supposed to move someone who was injured, but he couldn't help himself. Acting on instinct, he sat down next to her and pulled her gently into his arms.

He quickly confirmed that she was breathing, and her color seemed good. Ryan wished he could tell George to call an ambulance, but clearly that wasn't an option. Holding Cecily in the crook of his arm, he managed to reach into his back pocket and get his phone.

No sooner than he'd grabbed it, it slipped out of his hand and clattered to the floor.

"Dammit!" he roared.

As he tried to stretch out and reach his phone, Cecily stirred slightly.

"Cecily? Cecily?" Ryan shook her gently, even though he knew that was probably a bad idea. He was desperate to see those beautiful brown eyes open and reassure him that she was all right.

And then, they did flutter open.

He breathed out a sigh of relief.

"Thank God. Thank God!" George jumped to his feet.

"Ry—Ryan?" she asked uncertainly, looking around. "What— What happened?"

Ryan looked over at George, who shook his head.

"I'm not sure," Ryan said. "I think you fell down the stairs."

"I did?" she asked, looking up at him.

"I wasn't here when it happened. George rushed into town to find me to come help."

"Oh," she said. Cecily struggled to sit up a bit, and Ryan tenderly helped her.

"Are you all right?" Ryan asked. His surging adrenaline had finally eased a bit. The worst of the crisis had passed, and he was able to breathe easier.

George was pacing back and forth. Now, he was the one who seemed utterly freaked out.

"I think so," she said, managing to sit all the way up.

Reluctantly, he let go of her. "My head hurts a little, but I think I'm okay. It's so freaky, though. To black out like that and not know what happened."

She sounded so frightened that Ryan couldn't help reaching out to hold her again. She leaned into his arms.

Rubbing her back gently, he said, "It's all right. You're okay now."

"Thank you," she whispered, allowing him to hold her for a bit before she let go.

"You want to try to stand up?" he asked.

Cecily nodded. He stood first so he could help her up. She staggered a little but seemed steady for the most part.

"You don't remember anything about what happened?" he asked.

Cecily paused for a moment. "Actually, I think maybe I do."

"Really?" George asked, stopping dead in his tracks.

Glancing up to the top of the staircase, she said, "Yeah ... I— I was upstairs ..." She paused to laugh softly. "Looking for you, actually."

George nodded sadly.

"And I'm not totally sure, but I feel like ... I think I was *pushed* down the stairs."

"What?" Ryan asked in horror. "By who?"

Or what, he couldn't help thinking.

Cecily leaned back against the wall next to the stairs.

"I'm trying to remember. I didn't see anything. There was nobody up there with me. I don't think ... but it kind of felt like something might have been up there with me. And it was like I felt two hands on my back, and they shoved me down the stairs." She shivered as she spoke, probably more from fear than from a chill.

"Stay here," Ryan ordered. "I need to go upstairs and check it out."

Though he was scared to find whatever was up there, his anger over Cecily being injured took precedence. He had no clue what he would do if he did come across some kind of ghostly entity, but he had to at least see if he could find the culprit. He glared up at the top of the stairs before stomping down on the first step.

"I'll come with you," George said.

"How do I know you weren't the one who pushed her?" Ryan asked sharply.

"If I was the one that hurt her, why would I come and get you to help her?" George asked.

His words made sense, but that wasn't what convinced Ryan that he was innocent. George looked utterly spooked, which was saying something because he was a ghost. He looked genuinely terrified about what had happened, and he seemed devastated about Cecily getting hurt. Ryan wondered if George had feelings for Cecily similar to his own. Whatever the reason, he knew deep in his bones that he could trust him.

Ryan simply nodded, and the two of them headed upstairs.

"Be careful!" Cecily called out.

Ryan worried a little about leaving her alone downstairs, but he reasoned that at least she was within shouting distance if anything happened.

Oddly enough, Ryan didn't feel at all creeped out by the fact that George was walking right beside him on the stairs. He did seem like a good guy, and in these scary circumstances, it was kind of nice to have him close by. It still struck him as a tad eerie that, while Ryan's footsteps made the old stairs creak,

George's steps were soundless. And yet Cecily had often heard phantom footsteps when George had been around. There was so much he didn't understand about the paranormal.

Once they reached the top of the stairs, Ryan turned to George.

"Does anyone else haunt the mansion?"

"I don't know," George said. He sounded frustrated and angry. "Not that I know of. I've never seen anyone else here, but I'm not always around. There have been times when I've vanished for a long time. For decades. It's hard to imagine there's no one else but me. But I just don't know."

Ryan nodded. He began searching upstairs, peering into all of the rooms to the left of the staircase. There were a lot of bedrooms. More than a dozen by his count. Rather than simply look inside, he walked all the way into Oliver Hartley's office. He'd been a horrible man in life, and Ryan wouldn't put it past him to push Cecily.

"You in here, Ollie, you bastard?" Ryan called out. Silence. He waited a moment to be sure and then walked back out into the hallway. George was walking in the other direction, which was probably a good idea. They could cover more ground that way. Ryan watched him for a moment, noticing that he still walked normally. As a ghost, George probably had the ability to float or even fly for all he knew. But during all the time Ryan had spent with him, he'd never done anything freaky like that.

Which Ryan greatly appreciated.

Nothing but eerie silence greeted them both. How strange it was to be up here. He'd only come up here once or twice before to make simple repairs. As he walked around, the floorboards creaking beneath him, he wondered how many people had died in this house. Perhaps women had died in childbirth in some of these many bedrooms. No doubt illness had taken many others in these rooms—it wasn't as if people went to hospitals in those days. People had lived in this area for nearly four hundred years. For all he knew, hundreds of people had died on the grounds where the mansion now stood. What were the odds that George Hartley was the only spirit left behind?

And sweet Cecily might have been attacked by any one of them.

His anger flared again. Why her? Who the hell would want to push her down the stairs, potentially killing her?

Ryan heard the anger in his own footsteps as he stalked down the hallway. He no longer feared running into any ghosts. He *wanted* to confront whoever or whatever had caused harm to Cecily.

He started to worry about how long he had left Cecily alone downstairs. Eventually he met up with George again.

"Anything?" Ryan asked.

George held up his empty hands in frustration. "Nothing. If it was a ghost that hurt her, he or she is probably long gone by now. It's all too easy to just slip away when you want to. However, if the ghost is still hanging around here but chooses to be invisible, I'll be able to see him or her, but you can't."

"Really?"

"Yes. A ghost can make himself invisible to the living, but other dead people like him can still see him. Now, if a ghost *vanishes*, he's actually faded from consciousness and even I can't see him."

Ryan stared at him.

George shrugged. "I don't make the rules."

Ryan nodded, then he gazed out the window at the lush garden out back, spanning several acres. What did he expect? He'd see some apparition floating around outside in broad daylight? George was right. Ghosts were downright slippery bastards who could come and go as they pleased. How in the hell could he possibly keep Cecily safe here?

Growling deep in his throat, he grudgingly trudged downstairs, hating that he'd come up empty-handed.

"Sorry to say we didn't find anything," he told Cecily once he'd reached the bottom of the stairs where she stood, looking worried.

"That's okay," Cecily said with a grateful smile. "I really appreciate you guys searching anyway."

She'd said "you guys," but she looked only at Ryan. She seemed truly thankful, and he got the feeling she was impressed with him for going up there. As much as he hated that she knew he'd been afraid of George, at least he showed his bravery by searching for other ghosts in the house.

"How are you feeling?" Ryan asked.

Touching the back of her head, she said, "Okay, I think."

"You need to take her to the hospital," George said firmly. He eyed Cecily with great concern. "Just because she feels okay, doesn't mean she is. She could have a concussion."

"How do you know what a concussion is?" Ryan asked curiously. He figured that as a dude from the 1830s, all he knew about medical care was cocaine and leeches.

"I've been around for almost two hundred years. You think this is the first accident I've seen?"

"Fair enough."

"I'm a lot older and wiser than you, young man," George said with a smirk.

It occurred to Ryan that "Braydyn's" dry personality wasn't an act. That was how George Hartley talked.

"He's right," Ryan said, turning toward Cecily. "I should take you to get looked at."

She shook her head, wincing slightly as she did. "I can't ask you to take me to the hospital."

"You're not asking me. Mr. Hartley here is ordering me to."

"Damn right," George affirmed.

"I'll be fine. Really," she insisted.

"I don't want to risk it," Ryan said. "I would feel a lot better if you let me take you. Just in case."

He gazed into her eyes, hoping that the prospect of spending some time alone with him was a selling point. It certainly was for him. That, and he was genuinely worried about her.

Cecily sighed softly, but she didn't take her eyes off him.

"You're probably right. It's best to be sure."

"Yeah," he agreed, trying his best not to grin like an idiot. Even a trip to the hospital would be fun if it was with her. "I'll go bring the truck up. You wait here."

"Thank you," she said with a smile.

"I'll go with you," George said.

For once, Ryan didn't mind having George around. After what had happened this evening, his fear of the guy had vanished. There might be ghosts to be feared, but he wasn't one of them. His caring for Cecily had made all the difference. That, and Ryan had spent enough time with George now to feel comfortable with him. He seemed so *normal*, like a regular dude. Who just happened to be dead.

Ryan no longer shuddered when thinking about that. George's body was lying underground in an old, moss-covered grave, but his spirit was alive and well. And Ryan found he rather liked that spirit.

They both walked out the front door normally, with once again no ghostly theatrics like walking through walls from George. Once the heavy door of the mansion was shut, George spoke freely.

"You've got a thing for her," he said simply as they walked toward the parking lot.

"What?" Ryan asked.

"Don't play dumb with me," he said good-naturedly. In a sing-song voice, he said, "You like Dr. Rosewood, you like Dr. Roooosewoooood."

Ryan laughed despite himself.

"I feel bad," George said. "Had I known earlier, I never would have teased you so much."

"What do you mean?"

"I mean I wouldn't have tried to scare you when you were in the house. Tinkering with the piano and all that."

"Oh," Ryan said with a laugh.

"Truly," he said, sounding somber. "I know you want to look brave in front of her, and I didn't mean to mess you up."

George sighed with a sound but not an actual breath.

"I just get so bored sometimes," he continued. "And I knew you were actually very brave, what with saving the woman and her kids and all. So it was kind of fun to try to get a rise out of you."

"Fair enough."

"I am sorry. Or as the kids say today"—George tapped his chest soundlessly with his hand twice—"my bad."

Ryan cracked up at that, and George joined in.

"It's okay. No harm done."

"I used to haunt Cecily, too, sometimes. But she never really got scared. She was more curious than anything else. And it was wild—she knew it was me. Before she'd ever seen me, and out of all the people who could have been haunting the mansion, she would always say 'Hello, George' and 'Goodnight, George.' I don't know how she knew. She just did."

"That is wild," Ryan said as they approached his truck.

"Thanks for taking her to the doctor," George said. That spooked look was back on his face. He seemed quite worried about Cecily's health. "Take good care of her."

"I will."

George nodded and then disappeared.

Ryan stared at the spot where George had just been standing as clear as day. So odd how that kind of thing didn't freak him out anymore.

He drove to the mansion and found Cecily waiting outside for him. He jumped out of the truck so he could rush over and open the door for her.

"Thanks so much for doing this," she said as she climbed inside. "I hope I'm not keeping you from anything."

"Nope. I didn't have any plans for tonight anyway."

After making sure she was settled in the passenger seat, he headed to the driver's side.

Being a Friday night, he hoped his comment would make it clear that he wasn't currently seeing anyone else. He glanced over to gauge her reaction. She nodded thoughtfully.

Gesturing at the truck radio, she asked, "What kind of music do you like?"

"I'll show you," he said. He turned on the radio to the station he'd last been listening to, featuring loud metal music.

She winced, and he turned it down.

"Sorry," he said, chuckling. "As if your head didn't hurt already."

Cecily laughed and waved her hand. "No, no it's fine."

Glancing at her discreetly from the side, he could see

her warm smile. Clearly, she was not a fan of heavy metal music, but she didn't seem to mind that he was.

"What kind of music do you like?" he asked.

She laughed. "Now I don't wanna say."

"What? Come on, you can be honest."

"You're gonna think I'm a nerrrrd," she said.

Ryan shot her a wry look.

"That ship has sailed, hasn't it?" she said with a laugh. He didn't answer, which made her laugh again. "Classical. I like classical music. I mean, not only that kind of music. I try to listen to a little bit of everything to see what's out there. But classical is my favorite."

"That's cool."

"I actually got to hear Brahms and Stravinsky performed at the New York Philharmonic."

"Ummm," he said. "I saw Saliva perform at the county fair."

Cecily laughed, and so did he. She obviously had much more refined tastes, yet it didn't feel like she was talking down to him. She totally got his wry humor.

The hospital wasn't too far away, so their conversation was cut shorter than he would have liked. They got Cecily checked in and then headed to the waiting room. At first they didn't talk much, but that was okay. They bonded over laughing at the goofy sitcoms playing on the waiting room television.

Eventually, she turned to him and said, "I hope this doesn't take too long. I hate to hold you hostage all night."

"It's fine. I don't mind at all," he said.

Maybe he was imagining things, but he thought he saw a glimmer of hope in her eyes. Did she want him to be interested in her?

He watched as she turned her head to look at the other

people in the waiting room. There was an elderly lady in a wheelchair who had nodded off, a woman in her twenties or so holding an ice pack to her wrist, and an older gentleman who kept coughing. Fortunately, the coughing guy was seated fairly far away and was wearing a hospital-issued mask. Cecily frowned, and he wondered what she was thinking.

"You have good insurance, I hope? Hospital bills can be pretty scary," he said.

"Yeah. I don't have to worry about stuff like that."

"Why, are you a secret billionaire or something?"

She stared at him wordlessly.

"Shit, are you?" he asked incredulously.

Cecily laughed, putting him at ease. She'd really had him going there.

"No, no, no. I'm not a billionaire. But my parents are."

Ryan laughed, but Cecily only nodded.

"Wait ... seriously?"

"Yep," she said. She didn't sound thrilled about the idea, which confused him.

"RozamSoft."

His eyes grew wide. RozamSoft was an incredibly popular and well-known software. Companies all over the world used it.

Cecily sighed. "Rosewood ... Zamecki ... hence RozamSoft."

"Your parents are Samuel Rosewood and Emily Zamecki?" he asked in a voice that was far too loud for a hospital waiting room.

She looked around uncomfortably. For whatever reason, she didn't seem to want people to know her family was rich. And famous, for that matter.

"Yes," she said, still looking ill at ease. He wished he

understood, but he didn't. "I want you to know it's not like I let them pay all my bills or anything. I mean, not anymore. But let's just say I got an amazing head start in life because of them. Like they bought my car for me for one thing. I pay for my own groceries and for my rent, but I have, you know, a good savings account for anything else that comes up."

Ryan studied her curiously. In all the time he had known her, nothing about her had suggested wealth of any kind. She'd always been so unassuming. Though she wore some jewelry, it was nothing fancy. Not that he knew from jewelry exactly, but she wasn't dripping with diamonds.

"In case you ever wondered how I could afford to get a PhD and have no school loans, now you know." Cecily sounded guilty. Ryan still didn't understand. Her parents were loaded. What was there to feel bad about?

"Actually, I was sitting here wondering why you bothered to work at all when you don't have to."

That made her smile for some reason.

"I never thought of it that way."

Ryan shook his head. "I never would have guessed this in a million years."

"Good. The last thing I want is people thinking I'm some spoiled little rich girl."

That made sense, he supposed. Unlike a lot of people, Ryan had always felt a bit sorry for the nepo babies of the world. Sure, being related to a celebrity or high-powered CEO would get you a foot in the door, but after that it was like no matter what you did, people would dismiss all your accomplishments. The child of a famous or wealthy person could become the best singer or dancer or business mogul in the world, but their talent and hard work were often written off by many as just the result of being born into it. And that would suck.

"I get that," Ryan said.

She smiled gratefully.

He didn't want to pry, but he had so many questions. And she seemed to know it.

"What?" she asked.

"Just thinking."

"About what?" she pressed. "Come on. What do you want to know?"

"Were you always rich? Like, I'm trying to remember when RozamSoft first came out."

"Before I was born. My parents weren't even married yet when they teamed up."

"Huh," Ryan said.

"So, yes. I was born rich. Been rich all my life."

"Cool, cool, cool." He was trying to *play* it cool, but inside he was screaming. This was all so unexpected.

Cecily looked at Ryan uncertainly before she turned to watch the television again. It gave him some time to process this new information.

The more he thought about it, the more he realized this revelation was not a good thing. It might be great for Cecily and her family, but not for his romantic prospects for her.

Talk about out of my league.

Cecily Rosewood was the child of billionaires. She had grown up wealthy, and Ryan's mind reeled just thinking about what that meant. Fancy private schools, lavish vacations, hobnobbing with other rich people. She inhabited a world he knew nothing about. Even if by some miracle he managed to get the chance to date her, would she be embarrassed to introduce him to her family? Knowing that she was both smart *and* rich was beyond intimidating.

Ryan was saved for now from further obsessive thinking when a nurse finally called Cecily's name. He went with her to sit and wait in the little triage area where they made small talk for a bit. Eventually, she was led off to get some medical scans to check the extent of her injuries. So far, she'd had no outward signs of a concussion, but these tests would make sure.

Once she was taken away by the nurse, Ryan had the chance to drop his "I'm pretending I'm cool with the billionaire thing" act.

"Good God," he muttered aloud, holding his head in his hands.

Now he was glad he hadn't made a move on Cecily. He was more unsure than ever that she was into him. He'd thought he had felt a spark between them, but this unbelievably wide status gap had him second-guessing himself. Again.

Fortunately, Cecily got the all-clear from the doctor. No permanent damage done. The only prescriptions were rest and over-the-counter pain medicine as needed.

Ryan breathed a sigh of relief. He'd been so bent out of shape over the wealth revelation that he'd almost forgotten to worry about Cecily's injuries. Still, he was grateful that she was okay.

Cecily thanked him profusely for his time on the truck ride back to the mansion. She certainly didn't sound like a rich girl used to being chauffeured by limo all over the place. In fact, upon arriving at the Hartley Mansion parking lot, he saw that Cecily drove a simple Toyota. No doubt her parents would have bought her anything she liked, but still, she hadn't gone for a flashy Porsche. He supposed that counted for something.

Before getting out of the truck, Cecily turned to face him. "Thanks again. So much."

"You're very welcome. Again. I'm just glad you're all right."

She gazed into his eyes. If ever there was a moment to kiss her, it was now.

He hesitated. Visions of her billionaire life filled his head, and he froze.

She waited long enough to give him the perfect opportunity, but the moment grew awkward when he didn't make a move.

"Well ... good night," she said. Then she got out of the truck.

Damn.

12

As usual, Cecily arrived early in the morning at the Hartley Mansion. But this time she was afraid. Since last night, she'd had plenty of time to think back on what had happened to her. The more she thought about it, the more she was convinced that she'd been pushed. Nobody just fell down the stairs for no reason. She certainly hadn't been running around up there and not paying attention to where she was stepping, and she was quite sure she hadn't stumbled.

No. She distinctly remembered feeling two hands pushing on her back, sending her violently tumbling down the stairs.

Shakily, she made her way through the Great Hall toward her office. She hated being afraid of the place she loved.

"Hey there," came a voice from just behind her.

Cecily screamed, dropping her purse on the floor.

"Sorry, sorry! I'm so sorry. I didn't mean to scare you," Ryan said, holding his hands in the air in a display of innocence.

She clutched her chest, her heart pounding. It took her a while before she could speak.

"It's okay," she said once her bodily fight-or-flight response began to ease. "Normally I hear you come in. I guess I was distracted."

"Understandably," Ryan said, looking concerned.

She smiled weakly at him. Since last night, she'd also had time to ruminate over her current situation with Ryan. She was fairly certain he had romantic feelings for her. He'd given plenty of subtle signs and, unless she was completely off base, there was something between them. But still Ryan was holding back for some reason. He always seemed on the verge of making a move, and then he would pull back.

Cecily decided it was probably best to bide her time. Perhaps he'd had his heart broken in the past. For all she knew, he could be a widower. She also realized that telling him she came from a family of billionaires probably hadn't helped matters. The good news was that Ryan was clearly not a gold-digger. The bad news was that her family's wealth could intimidate anyone, especially a blue-collar business owner like him.

Though Cecily didn't give a damn about anyone's background, wealth, or pedigree these days, that hadn't always been the case. She wasn't proud of it, but there had been a time in her life when she would have looked down on someone like Ryan Armstrong. Now, she couldn't have admired him more.

"Are you all right?" he asked, those deep blue eyes filled with worry.

"I think so," she said wearily. She self-consciously touched the bruise on her head. Fortunately, her hair covered a lot of it. The part that remained was dark and ugly. "I hate being scared in this house now."

"I get that," he said grimly.

"It's funny. The paranormal stuff never used to bother me because I figured they were ghosts and couldn't harm me, but I guess I was wrong."

"You really think it was some kind of spirit that hurt you?" he asked.

"I do. I know it sounds crazy, but there was nobody up there with me that I could see, and I definitely felt like I was shoved."

"I believe you."

Touching his shoulder gently, she said, "Thank you so much for going up there to check things out for me. I know it must've been scary, but we really need to try to figure out what we're dealing with."

"Got that right," came another voice from behind them.

Both Ryan and Cecily yelped in surprise.

"Sorry, sorry," George said, holding his hands up the same way Ryan had just done. "Thought you guys saw me walk in."

"It's all right," Cecily said, clutching her chest once more. "I guess we're all really on edge."

"I'm sure you are," George said. "Are you okay? How are you feeling? What did the doctor say?"

"I'm fine, really. I got all checked out, and nothing is wrong."

"Very glad to know that," George said.

For a ghost, George had seemed quite spooked by what happened yesterday. She recalled he looked positively traumatized when she had gotten hurt. Cecily wondered what his story was and why he was so rattled by something like this. During his centuries of existence, he must have seen it all.

"Are *you* okay?" she asked. "You seem pretty upset by all of this."

"I was thinking the same thing," Ryan said.

"Yes," George said wearily. "I have my reasons for this"—he gestured toward the staircase—"hitting me so hard."

"Really?" Cecily asked, intensely curious.

He nodded but didn't elaborate.

"I've been wanting to know so much about you, George," she said. "I'm trying not to pry, but it's hard. And it's not just because of my interest in the Hartley family history. I'm interested in *you*. I want to know why you're still here, and I want to figure out if maybe there's a way we can set you free. Get you to move on or cross over or whatever you might call it. To the next realm, or to heaven."

George's eyes lit up slightly at that, and Cecily held out hope that she could get him to open up about his life. And death.

Then he scoffed bitterly. "You're assuming that I deserve to go to heaven."

"Yes. Yes, I am. I'm sure you do," she said.

"Because you don't really know me. You don't know my life and what I've done."

"I want to know, George. So much. Maybe it would help you to talk about it?"

Cecily held her breath as she watched George consider her words.

"Perhaps ... perhaps it would. I've told my sob story to other ghosts over the years." He laughed softly. "Spirits tend to commiserate over such things. But I've never told a living person about my life."

"I would love to hear about it," she said.

"So would I," Ryan offered.

George seemed a bit unsure. "You would?"

"Of course." Ryan gave him an encouraging smile.

"Do you two have time now?"

Ryan checked his watch. "I do, actually. Got here early to check on Cecily, so I've got some time before I have to get to work."

George nodded. Then he looked around at the walls of the Great Hall.

"Would it be okay if we walked around outside while we talked?" he asked.

"Sure," Cecily responded.

The three of them headed outside into the early morning sunshine. They walked together down the large circular road outside of the mansion.

Cecily drew in a deep breath of morning air. "I love the smell outside when the weather is warm. But I guess you can't smell anything anymore."

George shook his head.

"I'm sorry," she said. George simply shrugged with resignation.

The trio walked in silence for a bit.

"There's so much to tell," he said at last. "It's hard to know where to start."

"How old were you when you died?" Ryan asked.

"Twenty-seven," George and Cecily responded in unison.

"Sorry," she said. "I should just let you talk."

"It's okay," George said with a smile. "So you know how I died."

"I don't," Ryan said.

Cecily held her tongue, wanting to allow George to tell his own story, but George looked to her to answer.

"He was struck by lightning while riding his horse."

"Oh wow," Ryan said. "I'm so sorry."

"Yeah," George said. "You know how I died, Cecily, but I assume you don't know exactly how it happened? What led up to it?"

She shook her head. "I always thought it was a tragic accident."

"And I always thought I got what I deserved," he said bitterly.

It broke Cecily's heart to hear him say such a thing. Nobody deserved that.

The breeze rippled quietly through the leaves on the trees. Taking in another breath, Cecily resolved never to take her sense of smell for granted again. The scent of fresh-cut grass, the smell of the earth in warm weather. Simple things, yet still so important. The smells of rebirth, of starting fresh after a long winter. One of the many things she hadn't appreciated as much as she should have.

George stepped off the paved path and began walking across the grass, and Cecily realized he was heading toward the slaves' quarters that were located a short distance from the main house. George paused when they reached the outbuildings where the enslaved people had lived. Cramped wooden shacks with only the bare necessities for survival. They were reconstructions of course, but very much based on the reality that those men and women had experienced. The tiny dwellings weren't much better than doghouses, and Cecily couldn't even fathom what it must have been like to live in them.

"I've had a lot of time to think since my death. So much time," George said somberly as he gazed at the outbuildings. "We kidnapped human beings and held them prisoner. The whole notion is mind boggling to me now. For all I know, that's why I'm still here."

"Lots of people had slaves back in those days," Ryan

said. "I'm not saying it was right, but if having slaves kept you earthbound after you died, there would be hundreds of rich white bastards still floating around."

George cracked a smile at Ryan's honest words.

"Exactly," Cecily said. "By that logic, your father should still be trapped here. He not only held slaves captive, he sexually assaulted them."

"That he did," George said. "Like I told you before, I didn't know that at the time. I wonder who else knew. Did my mother know?"

Cecily shrugged. "I don't know."

"Maybe Oliver is still floating around here somewhere," Ryan said. "Or maybe he went down *south* where he belongs!"

With that, Ryan looked down at the ground and stomped on it, making both Cecily and George laugh.

"Remember when I mentioned I met somebody who made me change my mind about slavery?"

Both Ryan and Cecily nodded.

"I need to tell you about her," he said.

Cecily watched as he gathered the emotional energy to tell his story. Clearly it wouldn't be easy, but she hoped he might feel better once he got it all out of his system.

"Do you know about Victoria Taylor?" he asked Cecily.

"Yes! She was the woman you were supposed to marry."

"Right. Well, it wasn't her that changed my mind. I'm afraid she was just another innocent victim in my story."

Cecily nodded, but she was confused. From what she knew, after George died, Victoria went on to marry someone else, had kids, and lived to a decent age. No tragedy had befallen her that she was aware of. Still, she knew dusty historical papers with dry facts didn't always tell the whole story.

"I was supposed to marry her, but I fell in love with someone else. Someone my parents didn't approve of."

"I bet she was poor, then," Cecily said dryly.

"Exactly," George said. "She wasn't worthy of the prestigious Hartley name, according to Oliver and Penelope Hartley."

"What was her name?" she asked.

"Anna Hawkins," he replied with deep reverence. "Wow. I can't remember the last time I spoke her name out loud. Yes, it was Anna Hawkins. Her father owned the general store."

"Hawkins General Store!" Ryan said. "The one in town. It's still there. Or maybe it's one of the reconstructed buildings."

"It has undergone renovations over the years," Cecily said. "But it stands on the same spot where the original store was. At least I'm pretty sure it does."

She looked to George for confirmation, and he nodded.

"Very good. Yes, that is the same spot. And it looks very much the same as it did when I was alive."

He sounded so wistful as he spoke. Cecily was dying to know what happened, but she could see how difficult it was for him to talk about everything. She needed to be patient and not make this any harder than it already was.

"That's where I met Anna."

She noticed that he enjoyed saying her name as much as possible.

George walked away from the slave outbuildings, so Cecily and Ryan followed. They made their way around the huge circular path around the mansion.

"Anna worked there sometimes, helping out her father. They owned a farm not far away, and she helped out there, too. She worked very hard. Not like me. Not like me at all." George gazed toward the mansion as he spoke.

Cecily could relate to that for sure.

George turned back to look at the buildings for the enslaved people again as he walked.

"For the longest time, I never gave a second thought to owning slaves." He winced as he spoke. "*Owning* slaves. *Owning* people. The whole concept is so foreign to me now."

"Because you've grown. You've changed. That's a good thing," Cecily said encouragingly.

"Doesn't make any difference now, though, does it? Those people are long dead, and they never got a chance to live a free life."

"I suppose they're free now," she said.

George glanced skyward. "I hope so." To Cecily, he said, "It was her hands. Anna's hands. I loved her so, so much. And I remember watching her hands as they made cookies for the store. The way she mixed the flour and the sugar and the butter, and the way she rolled out the dough. Put the raw cookies in the oven to bake. And then I came home and watched Dinah, one of our slaves, in the kitchen. I watched her hands. I watched as she did the exact same thing as Anna did. It just hit me."

Chuckling softly, he added, "Like a bolt of lightning, you might say."

Ryan laughed, clearly appreciating George's gallows humor.

"I suddenly realized there was no difference between Anna and Dinah, save for the color of their skin. I'd always been taught that Black people were beneath me. That they weren't as intelligent and weren't capable of thoughts and feelings like white people. But in that moment, I realized I'd never seen proof of that. Not in my entire life. These people laughed and loved and had children and families. Sure, they spoke differently because they didn't have the education that we did, but that didn't make them stupid."

Cecily nodded, unsure of what to say. He sounded so disgusted with himself.

"I came to realize that the slaves loved each other just like I love Anna. And yet people like me, like my parents, ripped them away from their families and—"

"It's okay, George."

He blinked, looking confused. "What?"

"I'm not saying slavery is okay. Of course not. I'm just saying that beating yourself up for something that you truly, deeply regret isn't helping you or anyone else. If you could go back in time and fix it, you would. But that's not an option."

"I guess," he said wearily.

Cecily never thought it was possible to feel bad for a former slave owner, but somehow, she did. She supposed part of it was that kind of connection she'd always felt with George Hartley, even before she officially met him. In the same way she'd always had a deep hatred for his father. She wondered if Oliver Hartley, wherever he might have wound up in the afterlife, was sorry for what he had done.

A few moments ago, Cecily wasn't sure what to say to make George feel better. Now she had an idea, but she wasn't sure if she could go through with it. Not with Ryan standing right there.

She decided she needed to do the right thing.

"George, my family is wealthy too. Just like your family was."

"Really?" he asked, looking quite surprised. "I never would have guessed that in a million years."

"I take that as a compliment."

"As well you should," George said with a smile. "So, how wealthy are we talking?"

"My parents are billionaires."

George's eyes and mouth flew open wide.

"Pretty sure that's the face I made when I found out," Ryan said with a laugh. "I had no idea either. And now that she's told me, I can say I've actually heard of her parents. Pretty much everyone has these days."

"Who are they?" George asked.

"Samuel Rosewood and Emily Zamecki," Cecily said.

"The computer software people," George exclaimed.

Both Cecily and Ryan laughed in surprise.

"Damn, I guess pretty much everyone has heard of them," Ryan said.

"Oh yes. You learn things when you hear people talking all day long. Almost everybody that works on a computer around here uses RozamSoft."

"They sure do," Cecily said. "Half the free world uses it. It's incredibly popular. The point is, I grew up really rich and spoiled, and I know where you're coming from. Money skews your perspective greatly. You don't have a real understanding of what it's like to have to survive in the real world."

"I guess that's true," George said.

"In the end, I think we all have to take responsibility for our actions, but the way you were brought up can make you view the world a certain way."

Cecily sighed, not wanting to continue. But her desire to help George won out. She glanced back at the mansion, contemplating all the ways that her family was similar to the Hartleys. Rich. Spoiled. Lacking compassion for those who had less.

"My parents always told me that hard work equals

success. Seems so simple, right?"

George nodded, and she got the feeling he would understand everything she had to say. Ryan, however, was another matter. But she shouldn't be concerned about that now. Helping George deal with his past was her top priority, no matter what happened. If Ryan thought less of her, she would just have to accept it.

"And my parents did work hard," she continued. "They met when they were pretty young. In college. They were both very smart."

"Must be where you get it from," Ryan said charitably.

"Maybe," she said with a smile. "Like wealth or good looks, intelligence can be something you're born into as well. Sure, what you do with it matters, but people are born with all kinds of limitations. Mental health issues, learning disabilities, that kind of thing. Things they have no control over, but that can limit their success in life. Through no fault of their own."

"I guess," Ryan said.

"So they were smart, but they did work very hard. My mom and dad got good grades and worked tirelessly to develop the software that made them rich beyond most people's wildest dreams. And because of that, they felt they deserved everything they got."

George nodded grimly. Yes. He understood.

Cecily concentrated on George as she spoke. She watched as his gaze drifted over to the Orangery building located on the opposite side of the house to where the slave quarters were. Having that type of greenhouse building in those days was the height of opulence.

"My parents had this idea that if you work hard, you will be rewarded. That had been their experience, so they assumed that's the way things are in the world. Obviously it's the way things should work, but it isn't. You were born into a wealthy family, while so many enslaved people were born into bondage."

"And God knows they worked hard. Not that they had a choice," George said bitterly. "And where did it get them?"

"Right," Cecily said. "I remember … I used to look at our housekeeper and landscapers and think they didn't have much money because they didn't work enough. My God, it sounds so ridiculous now as I say it out loud."

She refused to look in Ryan's direction. She just couldn't do it.

Instead, she took a seat on an iron bench near the front of the house. Ryan sat down next to her while George remained standing, still attentive to her story.

"Of course, most of the people I grew up with were wealthy too. Lots of business owners, corporate CEOs, that kind of thing. It took me a long time to learn that just because the head honcho of a company was rich, didn't mean they worked the hardest. Not by a long shot."

"That's the truth," Ryan said.

Cecily figured Ryan had been at the mercy of a jerk boss at least once in his life. Most people had.

"Then one day I went to visit a friend's house. I knew her from a local softball rec team, but she didn't go to my fancy school. We were hanging out on a Saturday. I must have been, I don't know, sixteen years old or so. We were starving, and they had very little food in the house. My friend Kayla shrugged and said her dad didn't get another paycheck until the following Tuesday, so they would be light on food and snacks and stuff until then. That was my first introduction to what living paycheck to paycheck meant."

George nodded, seeming to understand what she was saying.

She risked a glance over at Ryan. He nodded. She couldn't discern any sense of judgment from him, but she had no doubt that he'd always been aware of the paycheck-to-paycheck concept.

"I remember trying to make sense of it. I thought to myself that Kayla's parents must not have worked hard enough. They must have been lazy, and that was why they had no money. And yet here it was, a Saturday and both parents were at work." She shook her head at the memory. "I was such an idiot."

"You were young," Ryan said.

He smiled warmly, exuding understanding. Cecily's tense muscles relaxed a little.

"I wish I could say I totally changed my mind after that, but it still took some time. Then something else happened. This time, it was a friend of mine that I'd known since childhood. Like me, Susie grew up wealthy, and that existence was all she knew. Her father had started a company that had once been quite profitable, but something happened and he lost the business. I think that was the first time I realized working hard wasn't a guarantee of anything. First, it scared me to think that everything could be taken away in the blink of an eye. And second, I realized that not every business takes off in the first place. You can work incredibly hard, take out a business loan or whatever, and do the best you can but still not make it. In fact, far more businesses fail than succeed. I know that now."

"That is true." Ryan said with a firm nod.

"That's one of the things I admire about you, Ryan. You came here from another country and managed to start up a business from scratch."

"Thanks," he said, pride twinkling in his eyes. "Believe me, I don't take any of it for granted."

"I know you don't." Cecily sighed wearily. "So, there's those experiences that I had. And eventually I also realized that not everybody begins at the same point. In my parents' case, they didn't start out with much. They did have to take out a business loan, but a lot of my rich friends were rich from birth. They'd take Mommy and Daddy's money to start up a business and then brag about how successful they were. Some of them even hired other people to take charge, and they had little to do with running the actual business. They'd call themselves Presidents or CEOs or whatever, but they didn't really do anything."

"I can believe that," George said. "I saw that happen even in my day."

Cecily smiled at him, and then she looked over at the paved road, the one that so many wealthy people had trod over the years. "Well, there you have it. Those were my 'Anna's hands' moments."

George grinned widely. "I like that. And I feel like Anna would like that. You know, there's this song that you play in your office sometimes that makes me think of her."

"Really? Which one?"

"'Simple Gifts.'"

"Oh yes," Cecily said, putting her hand over her heart. "That is a beautiful song."

Though she played mostly classical instrumental music while she worked, there were a few quietly sung tunes on her playlist that didn't distract her too much from her writing.

"I don't know that one," Ryan said.

"That's because it's not heavy metal and there's nobody screaming," Cecily quipped.

Ryan chuckled. "Fair enough. How does it go?"

He looked at Cecily, who shook her head. "You do not

want me to sing. Believe me."

"You really don't," George said with a grimace.

Cecily laughed. "Stalker much? How much time did you spend watching me?"

"Not that much, Cecily. Honestly," he said, looking worried that she might be offended. "Mostly I can hear your music when I'm wandering around, feeling super bored."

"Okay then." Turning to Ryan, she said, "The lyrics basically say that it's a gift to be simple, as in appreciating the simple things in life."

"Yes," George said. "That was Anna."

George gazed back sadly toward the slave dwellings in the distance. "It took me a long time—too long—to realize how awful it was to have slaves so we could enjoy a wealthy lifestyle."

"I know my experience isn't quite the same as yours," Cecily said. "But I do understand how the way you are brought up can seriously mess up your life view. Being taught that you—or anybody—deserves to have such an obscene amount of money can be a real mind fuck."

Both men's heads snapped in her direction, shocked by her language.

"Sorry. Pardon my French."

"Tu es pardonné," Ryan responded.

Cecily laughed. "You sound so sexy when you speak French."

George looked at Cecily curiously but didn't comment. She hoped Ryan hadn't noticed her blush.

"I'm just saying I get where you're coming from," Cecily said, turning her attention to George.

"Well, good for you for figuring all this stuff out while you're still alive," George said grimly. "While you still have time to change the way you treat people."

Cecily watched as George's gaze kept wandering over to the slave shacks.

"Let's take a walk around back," she said, standing up from the bench. She led the two men toward the back of the house where they could enjoy the garden. As they strolled down the path, flowers blooming all around them, she asked, "Will you tell us about Anna?"

He smiled just hearing her name. "She was so beautiful. Pretty blond hair, with the sweetest light blue eyes. She really did appreciate the simple things in life. She loved oranges, and she was so excited about our Orangery."

"That place is pretty cool," Ryan said.

The Orangery still stood on the grounds. It was essentially a greenhouse where the fruit trees could flourish all year long.

"Yeah. I never really thought about it much until I saw how happy it made Anna."

"I think about things like that a lot," Cecily said. "In an odd way, I can almost feel sorry for rich people."

"Really ..." Ryan said wryly. With that smirk, he looked more amused than offended.

"I know, I know. It sounds odd, but think of it this way. When rich people go on a fancy vacation or visit an expensive restaurant, it's like no big deal. But when a poorer person saves up for a long time to do those things, it's really exciting. It's a big deal because it's so new and different. There's nothing to get excited about when you do those things all the time."

Ryan considered that for a moment, but Cecily wasn't sure he completely understood what she was saying.

"Yeah," George said. "The little things made her so happy because she didn't have much. I guess you learn to be more grateful when you're poor."

"That's true," Ryan said with a nod.

"Of course, the other side is that poor people might never get the chance to go on vacation. Some people never manage to make it out of their hometown." She paused. "I think about that a lot, too. When I'm driving along a country road and see cows out in the meadow. I think about kids who grew up in a poor city that have never even seen a farm, never mind getting a trip to the beach."

"I wish I could have been around longer," George said wistfully. "I would have done everything I could to show Anna the world, with or without my parents' money."

"So," Cecily prodded gently. "You loved Anna, but you were expected to marry Victoria."

"Right," he said. "Victoria came from a proper family, had the proper connections, the proper looks, and the proper manners."

George spoke the word "proper" as if it burned like acid on his tongue.

"She was a perfectly nice woman. But I didn't love her. After meeting Anna, I didn't know if I ever could love Victoria."

Cecily watched as George's expression changed from wistful to downright tortured.

"It's all my fault," he said, his ghostly voice wavering with emotion. "It's my fault she died."

She and Ryan exchanged pained looks, both helpless to comfort him. How terrible it was to be unable to hug him as he recounted his tragic past.

George hung his head, eyes closed. "By the time I got there, she was already dead."

Cecily held still, waiting for him to continue.

When he lifted his head and turned to look at Cecily, he

said, "You weren't the only one who got hurt from falling down those stairs."

Her blood ran cold.

"My God," Ryan said. "That's how Anna died?"

He nodded slowly, solemnly. She'd had no idea how lucky she had been to walk away with just a few aches and pains.

"No wonder you seemed so freaked out after Cecily fell. I mean, we were all upset, but I had a feeling there was something else going on."

George began pacing in the garden. He spoke quickly as he paced. "It's crazy. It's so crazy ... I always thought it was just an accident. I didn't see it happen ... I didn't know what ..." He stopped walking. "After what happened to you, I'm starting to wonder if Anna was pushed down the stairs."

He glanced at a nearby stone bench. "Why don't you two sit down. Might take a few minutes to explain."

Ryan and Cecily exchanged concerned looks and dutifully sat on the bench.

George stood in front of them, intense pain in his eyes as he spoke.

"The idea of marrying Victoria never bothered me before I met Anna. I knew it was expected of me to marry well, and I was pretty much indifferent to it. She was attractive enough, and I figured that was just what I was supposed to do. I'd never really believed in romantic love, never mind love at first sight." He laughed bitterly. "I remember seeing a performance of *Romeo and Juliet* once, and I found the whole thing ridiculous instead of tragic."

Cecily smiled sadly.

"Everything changed when I met Anna Hawkins. It might not technically have been love at first sight, but it was pretty damned close. But after I got to know her, well, I'd never known I could feel about anyone the way I felt about her. She was so lovely, so kind. So completely and utterly different from anyone I'd ever known in my social circle. She just had a different way of looking at the world."

George gazed off into the distance, lost in thought. Both Ryan and Cecily kept silent, allowing him space to grieve. Birds cried softly in the distance, and Cecily breathed in the scent of the flowers in the garden. Such a peaceful space.

When he was ready, George resumed his tale.

"I knew I wanted to be with her. I wanted her to be my wife, but if I told my parents that, there was a very good chance they would disown me. Cut off my comfortable, pampered existence."

Cecily heard the self-hatred in his voice.

Shaking his head, George said, "I had this stupid idea that I should get her pregnant."

"So your parents would have to accept her," Ryan said. As usual, there was no hint of judgment in his voice. "To avoid the scandal."

"Right. Anna agreed to the idea, but I never should have forced her to make that kind of choice. For all I know, she only went along with it to make me happy. Though, if nothing else, I got to make love to her. Only the one time, but I've cherished that memory for all these years."

"I'm sure you have," Cecily said softly.

"It was stupid and selfish of me. I told myself I was doing it for her. That this way, I could marry her and she could live in the mansion with all the money and the servants and fancy furniture. But the truth was, she never cared about any of that stuff. *I* did. I couldn't give up being rich. I should have just run away with her. Started over from scratch with Anna as my bride."

Glaring toward the Hartley Mansion, he spat out, "I just

had to keep all my material things. My comfortable life."

"Did Anna get pregnant?" Ryan asked.

"I don't know. Not enough time had passed to find out. We certainly didn't have pregnancy tests back then. You simply had to wait and see."

Ryan nodded.

"During the time while we waited, I wanted Anna to come and see the mansion. I was excited to show off the place. I wanted her to see the Orangery, and I knew she'd love to see the harp." George's voice took on a faraway tone. "I thought maybe, once we were married, I could get her harp lessons. She would have loved that."

"I bet she would have," Cecily said.

George blinked. He looked at Cecily and nodded. It was as if he'd forgotten he wasn't alone for a moment.

"Yes. She loved music, and she loved to sing. It was so easy to imagine her playing the harp and singing. She could have sung our child to sleep."

Cecily felt tears forming in her eyes. The poor man had lost so much. Ryan tenderly put his hand on her back, and she loved how he'd noticed her sadness.

"I chose a day for Anna to come to the house when my parents would be away. They had some party to go to. They went to so many damned parties they considered crucial to their precious social standing. Anyway, Anna said she could get to the house around three in the afternoon, and I told her I would see her then. I'd been in town all morning at a business meeting and I got delayed. So Anna got to the house first."

Cecily's muscles tensed. It was awful to hear a story where she knew the ending was horribly tragic, and she was helpless to stop it.

"My God," George said in a pained voice. "When I think

back on how that day was supposed to go. I'd thought I would show Anna all around the house, especially the Music Room. Walk her around the gardens, show her the Orangery. Show off all the Hartley wealth. And then I'd thought we could go upstairs to my bedroom and make love. The slaves and servants would have been in the house of course, but they would likely only gossip amongst themselves. There would have been nothing to gain if they'd tattled to my parents about my having an unmarried woman in the house. I wanted to make love to Anna again. Because I wanted to be with her and because it would double the chance of giving her a child."

Ryan sighed, clearly as affected by this sad tale as Cecily was.

"When I got to the house, all I heard was screaming."

A cold shiver went through Cecily. George painted such a vivid picture that it was easy to visualize the scene.

"Just ... women screaming ... a big commotion. I was confused, trying to figure out why everybody was home instead of at their dumb party. It was raining, and I remembered the party was outdoors. It must have been called off. With all the screaming, I was terrified that something had happened to one of my little sisters. I ran inside."

Cecily and Ryan held still as they waited for George to get to the worst of the story.

"I ran toward the sound of the screams and found Anna dead at the bottom of the stairs."

George stared dully into the distance. Cecily put her hand over her heart, once again inwardly cursing the cruelty of being unable to physically comfort him.

"Jesus, what the hell happened?" Ryan asked.

"They said it was an accident. That's all anybody would tell me. Anna fell down the stairs," George said, shaking his head. "I was so devastated by her death that I never questioned it. Until now."

"If somebody pushed me, then do you think that same person might have pushed Anna?" Cecily said, shivering in fear at the thought. "You think that person is still here in the house?"

"It's a possibility," George said grimly.

"I need you to keep a close watch on the house, George. And on Cecily," Ryan said firmly. "You have the best chance at seeing what's really going on."

George nodded. "Yes. Yes, you're right. I will do everything in my power to keep watch and keep her safe."

"Me too." Ryan's expression was a mixture of anger at this unseen enemy and concern for Cecily's safety.

She couldn't help feeling flattered that both men were so worried about her, and knowing they would look out for her quelled her fears a bit.

"Who do you think it could possibly be?" Cecily asked.

"I hate to say it, but I wouldn't put it past my mother," George said. "She certainly had motive."

"True," Cecily said. "From what you've told us, she wouldn't have approved of Anna."

"Nobody wanted me to marry Victoria more than she did. My mother was obsessed with appearances. But murder? I don't know ... I just don't know."

"Well, everybody knows what an asshole your father was," Ryan said. "Could it have been Oliver Hartley? Was he there that day?"

"Yes. He sure was. You're right. He's a possibility too. It's so strange, because I've never seen any member of my family—or slaves or anyone I knew from back then—as ghosts."

"But you have been in contact with other ghosts around

here, right?" Ryan asked.

"Oh, yes. There are spirits everywhere."

Ryan nodded. Cecily noticed that he didn't shudder. He seemed more intrigued than frightened these days.

"But you said ghosts can disappear—or vanish—for years at a time, right?" she asked.

"Right."

"So the culprit could be absolutely anyone," she said.

"Right," George said again, shoulders slumping. "Oh, and Cecily. You'll never guess on what day all of this happened."

Cecily shook her head. "No idea."

"August 27, 1835."

She gasped out loud.

"Oh damn, the day you died," Ryan exclaimed. Cecily turned to look at him. "It's on his gravestone."

"Yep. Big day for me," George said. Cecily was grateful to see a bit of his dry humor was back.

"You and Anna died on the same day?" Ryan asked.

"Yep again. I guess we were kinda like Romeo and Juliet after all."

"The rainstorm," Cecily said quietly. "You said it was raining and that's why the party got canceled."

George nodded. "Yes. I was in shock after what happened. I just ... I was overcome with shock and grief, and nobody in my family really knew how much I loved Anna. To everybody else, Anna was just some stranger who died in a freak accident right in front of them. I dashed out of there. I couldn't bear to look at Anna's poor broken body anymore ..."

George started to cry. Tearless sobs wracked his body. "I — I got on my horse and rode as hard and fast as I could. As if ... as if I could somehow outrun the pain."

Ryan wrapped his arm around Cecily, who was also weeping. His embrace was warm and comforting.

"And then you were killed by a bolt of lightning," Ryan said gently, saving George from speaking of his own tragic end.

George nodded and then looked at Cecily with tender concern. "I'm sorry, Cecily. I didn't mean to make you cry."

"It's all right," she said, wiping her eyes. "I just hate that you had to go through all of that."

"What's to hate? It's my fault," he said sharply. She understood he was angry at himself and not her.

"How can you think this is all your fault?" she asked.

"Well, of course it's—"

Cecily's watch beeped, cutting him off.

"Oh my God. It's almost time for my tour. The guests might already be here!" She glanced toward the house. "Oh George, I'm so sorry, but—"

"Go, go. You have a job to do," he said with a wave of his hand.

"But—"

"We have an eternity to finish this conversation. Or at least I do."

Cecily nodded.

"We'll talk again soon, okay?" She addressed both men as she spoke.

Though it killed her to have to leave so abruptly, she had no choice.

Her mind and heart reeling, she wondered how she would get through the Hartley tours today. Now she knew so much more about George Hartley than she could share with the tourists.

She would have to keep the most important parts of him close to her heart.

13

George accompanied Ryan to his pickup truck. They walked in silence for a moment before Ryan finally spoke up.

"Thanks for telling us all of that. I know it wasn't easy."

"It wasn't, but in an odd way it made me feel better. It's been a long time since I've talked about what happened. Like I said, nobody in my social circle knew that Anna even existed, not that they would have cared. My mother knew, and all she wanted to do was get rid of her."

"Do you think she did? Do you think she's the one that pushed Anna?"

George shook his head. "I don't know. I just don't know. I suppose it's possible. I wouldn't have thought she was capable of such a thing, no matter how obsessed she was with social standing. But then again, I found out all sorts of terrible things about my father after I was dead."

"That's really rough. I'm sorry, man."

Ryan hoped it did help the guy to talk about things like this. Men weren't known to be great about expressing their feelings. Not now, and definitely not then.

"I saw you in the truck with Cecily last night," George said as they reached the parking lot.

"What?" Ryan was about to open the door of his truck but pulled back and turned to stare at the ghost. He had to squint a bit in the morning sun.

"After the hospital. I couldn't follow you there because I'm not physically able to leave town."

"Really? What happens if you try?"

"I just disappear. Fade out, and wind up back where I started from. Ghosts can never travel far from where they died. At least no ghosts that I know of."

"Fascinating," Ryan said, shaking his head.

"I guess. If you're not the one trapped."

"True."

"Anyway," George said. He sounded annoyed for some reason. "I saw you in the truck with her last night. That was your chance."

"Chance for what?"

"Your chance to kiss her. To make a move. It was the perfect moment, and you blew it."

"What are you talking about?"

"You sayin' I'm wrong?" he snapped. George's jaw was clenched, his steely glare fixed on him. He wasn't merely annoyed. He was pissed. And Ryan had no idea why.

"Umm ... no?"

"You'd been taking care of her all night. You got a chance to play the hero for her by checking around upstairs to look for whoever might be lurking up there, and then you took her to the hospital. At the end of the night, when the crisis had passed, you had the absolutely perfect opportunity to kiss her, and you choked. You *fucking choked*!"

"What's it to you, George?" Now it was Ryan's turn to get mad. Who the hell did this guy think he was anyway? "This is none of your damn business. And why do you think it's okay to skulk around watching everybody when they can't see you?"

"There was a time I might have apologized for overstepping, but not anymore," George said, eyes blazing. "*Nobody* knows better than I do what can happen when you hesitate to do the right thing. You never, ever know when somebody's goddamn time is up."

The raw pain in George's voice managed to sap the anger right out of him. This man knew what he was talking about.

"I can't sit idly by and watch you make the same damn mistake I did."

"I suppose that's fair enough," Ryan said wearily.

"What the hell are you afraid of?"

Ryan was starting to regret his earlier stance on men talking about their feelings. He remembered there was a reason for that. Because it sucked. It felt weird and uncomfortable. "I don't know," he lied.

"Yes, you do. Now spill it."

Ryan groaned. "Because she's so different from me in so many ways. She's so much smarter than I am, and she is the child of billionaires. I mean, do you get that?"

George shot him a wry look.

"Okay, fine. So you get it. Sort of."

His George's expression softened. "You feel out of your element the way I'm sure Anna did."

"Yeah. I guess you could say that."

"Cecily doesn't look down on you the same way I never looked down on Anna. I got caught up in my own desires to stay rich, but I never thought less of her for being poor. In fact, I admired how kind and sweet she was, even though she didn't have much. I can tell Cecily admires you for all your hard work and building your business. And, unlike me,

Cecily is hardly trying to cling to her family's wealth. On the contrary, she's bothered by it. That's why she hid it from you for so long. She may not have completely disavowed her parents' riches, but she clearly has no desire to live that kind of life."

"She has the gift of living simply," Ryan said, recalling the song George had told him about.

"Yes," George said. Ryan saw the relief in his eyes, seeing that he was finally getting through to him. "Anna and I were different in so many ways, but none of that mattered when we were together because we were in love. Are *you* in love?"

"Yes," Ryan answered without hesitation.

George grinned.

Ryan hadn't even realized that he was in love with Cecily until the word "yes" came out of his mouth. But he did love her. He admired her for being so smart and so brave. The way she cared about everyone, living or dead. She never seemed bothered by the differences between them; she seemed to like that he was into heavy metal music, and she certainly never treated him like he was stupid for not being an expert in history. On the contrary, she seemed genuinely impressed that he took such an interest in the subject.

"Then what the hell are you afraid of?"

"I'm afraid she doesn't feel the same way." Sometimes a future with her seemed too much to hope for.

"Only one way to find out," George said matter-of-factly.

"You make it sound like the easiest thing in the world. It's not. It's one of the hardest things to do."

"I know," he said. At last, there was a shred of sympathy in his voice. "But regret is worse. Believe me."

Sighing, Ryan said, "I do believe you."

"What's the worst that could happen? She'll reject you, leaving you heartbroken and humiliated."

"Thank you, Mr. Hartley, for pointing that out. Incredibly helpful," Ryan scoffed.

"The point is, you'll get over it," he said sharply. So much for the man's fleeting sympathy. "But if you don't do it now, before you know it, it could be too late."

"Duly noted. Can I go to work now?"

"You are dismissed, Canuck," George said dryly.

Ryan opened the door to his truck. Pausing, he turned around.

"Thanks, George."

His ghost friend grinned and saluted.

"Now go watch over Cecily."

"I'm on it. Believe me." With that, George headed back toward the mansion.

He had given Ryan a lot to think about.

Fortunately for him, it turned out to be a busy day. Between coming close to wrapping up the reconstruction work on the theater to meet the promised deadline and being called away to deal with a handful of emergency repair calls, there wasn't much time to obsess over the situation with Cecily. However, less time certainly didn't mean *no* time. He'd had some quiet moments walking to and from various sites that had given him more than enough time to ruminate over what he should do.

In his heart of hearts, he knew George was right. Of course he was. All those clichés like "life is short" and "time is promised to no one" were undoubtedly true. There was also the notion that most people tended to regret the things they didn't do more than the things they did. Telling Cecily how he felt about her was hardly a life-and-death situation, and he knew he was being ridiculous about the whole thing. She really did seem to be interested in him, and she certainly had spent a lot of time with him lately.

Putting himself out there might not even be all that much of a risk.

But it sure felt risky to him.

Though he was hardly an expert in human psychology, he knew enough and he was self-aware enough to realize that his parents calling him stupid all his life had really done a number on him. That, combined with possibly having dyslexia, made it particularly difficult for him to be in love with a woman who was so much smarter than he was. Knowing a lot of his insecurity was all in his head didn't do much to quell his fears.

What's the worst that could happen? She'll reject you, leaving you heartbroken and humiliated.

George's words haunted him.

No matter what happened between them, Ryan knew he needed to stay close to Cecily to keep her safe from harm. They still had no idea who or what had pushed her down the stairs, and she wouldn't be okay until they solved that mystery. He felt better knowing that George was around to keep watch over her when he couldn't, but he would be physically unable to help her or to stop another attack if something were to happen.

The cowardly part of Ryan wanted to put off expressing his feelings to her until they were out of the woods when it came to this ghostly threat. He kept thinking about how awkward and humiliating that situation would be if she turned him down.

Ryan groaned out loud, utterly sick of himself.

"You all right, dude?" Charlie asked.

Ryan startled, having completely forgotten the guy was walking next to him as they headed toward the theater construction site. Damn, he was a mess.

"You're a mess, Canuck," his buddy shrewdly observed. "What's your problem?"

"I'm afraid my family's maple syrup empire is collapsing," he cracked. He frequently beat his buddies to the punch when it came to making jokes about his Canadian heritage.

Charlie chuckled. "But seriously, man, what's up with you already?"

"I don't know. I'm just a mess is all."

"Is this about Cecily?"

"What? Who?"

Charlie huffed out an annoyed breath. "Don't play dumb with me. Although in your case, you're not playin'."

"Watch how you talk to yer boss, eh?" Ryan said in his fake Canadian accent. Then, in his real accent, he said, "Ou devrais-je dire … Fait attention de la façon que tu parles à ton patron."

Or should I say, careful how you talk to your boss.

Though he knew Charlie calling him dumb was simply part of how guys busted on each other, Ryan always worried that there was a kernel of truth whenever someone joked about his intelligence. Or lack thereof.

"Pardon me, Mr. Fancy French Man. I'm just sayin' you spent the night with her last night."

"What the hell are you talking about?"

"You took her to the hospital."

"Oh. Right. So?"

"So, you don't sit in the hospital with a woman all night if you're not into her."

"I would, actually. If she needed help."

Charlie rolled his eyes. "Right, right. I forgot I was talking to a real American hero. Didn't come across any carjackers on the way home, did you?"

"We did. And I fought them off with my Canadian superpowers and defeated them with my enchanted hockey stick."

"Bet you'd like to show her *your* enchanted hockey stick."

Ryan burst out laughing. He couldn't help it.

A tour group led by a woman in a fancy Victorian dress walked by them. Now Ryan had to wonder every time he saw people in costume ... was it possible they were dead?

"What's up with you and her anyway?" Charlie asked. "I mean, what's up besides your dick?"

"You're a real poet, you know that?"

"As a matter of fact, I write Shakespearean-like sonnets in my spare time," Charlie said before punching Ryan hard in the shoulder.

"Ow!"

"Stop changing the subject. Are you gonna go for it with her or what?"

"I dunno," he grumbled.

"Wuss."

"Correct."

"Just go for it, asshole. Worst-case scenario, she says no and you go on with your life."

He made it sound so easy, like George had. What Charlie didn't understand was that Ryan wasn't just hot for the woman. He was in love with her. If she rejected him, he couldn't simply "go on with his life."

Of course, the fact that he was in love with her was all the more reason to at least shoot his shot. All this going around and around in his head was making him crazy.

Ryan grumbled out loud again.

"What's the big deal?"

"The big deal is that if she refuses to convert to Canadianism, my family will disown me."

Charlie laughed and shook his head.

"As long as she's not a Maple Leafs fan."

"Now *that* would be the real dealbreaker."

Throughout the rest of the day, Ryan continued his mental waffling back and forth about what to do about his romantic life. All that was clear and consistent was the need to keep Cecily safe. The only way to do that was to find out who in the Hartley Mansion wanted to hurt her.

As he got in his truck, he made the decision to visit the mansion late at night, when no one else—no one living, anyway—was around. Perhaps then he could discover who else was haunting the place.

Shaking his head in annoyance, he wondered how he could possibly think that visiting a haunted house all alone in the middle of the night was less scary than telling a woman how he felt about her.

Ryan headed to the Hartley Mansion at around 11:30pm. Damn, it was creepy here at night. Just walking down the stone path outside in the dark was eerie. He stepped on a tree branch on the way, and the noise nearly made him jump out of his skin. The haunted mansion would be even scarier this late at night. The only thing that scared him more than being here was the idea of the woman he loved getting hurt again. He would gladly face any kind of danger if it helped keep her safe.

Drawing in a deep breath, he unlocked the door and headed inside. Unnerving how quiet the house was at this hour. The air seemed so still. On edge, his hands shook so much as he entered the alarm code that it took him three tries. Damn near letting the alarm go off did nothing to help his already jangled nerves.

Walking through the Great Hall, the creaking of his own footsteps sounded like something from a horror movie.

"George?" he called out. "Are you here?"

No answer.

George could be anywhere. He might be wandering around downtown, or he might have vanished for the night. Ryan figured that's what he would do if he were a ghost. After all, there wasn't much to do or see around here after dark when the tourists had gone home.

He wandered over to Cecily's office and flipped on the light. Seeing the papers on her desk made him smile. She gave herself such a hard time for being lucky enough to have her dream job, but Ryan respected her so much for her historical work. Especially now that he knew she'd had the option of simply being a member of the idle rich. Cecily didn't have to go to college and then grad school and get her PhD, but she had. She'd come from a rich and privileged background, but she still chose to work hard. He loved that about her. He loved lots of things about her.

Ryan flipped the light off and headed back toward the Great Hall. He checked out the dining room and found nothing amiss. Strange to be here when nobody else was around. Sure, he'd done the occasional repair in the building before when he was alone, but he'd never stopped to linger during those times. On the contrary, he was always eager to get the hell out of there as soon as humanly possible.

Gazing around at the room, he carefully eyed up each corner for fear that ... *something* could come walking out of the shadows. That idea freaked him out, so he tried to imagine what the place had looked like in broad daylight all those years ago. Noting the perfectly set table with all the fancy dishes and utensils, he pondered what it must have been like to have dinner with the Hartleys back in the day. He wondered where George had once sat. And then he marveled at the idea that he could simply ask him. Incredible. He pictured the family all seated together, sharing Christmas dinner more than a hundred and fifty years ago.

His and Cecily's shared passion for history was at least one reason to hope for a future with her. She would never expect him to remember all the important dates and details of American history. It was enough for her that he enjoyed exploring the past.

Thinking about Cecily now reminded him of what was at stake for her. She could have gotten seriously hurt. He shuddered just thinking about how poor Anna had died at the bottom of those stairs.

Such a tragic death. Is it possible Anna is haunting the place? Is she still angry about dying so young ... so much so that she would hurt another young woman?

Ryan didn't think so. Not unless dying drastically changed one's personality. From what George had said, Anna was gentle and kind. Which was why he loved her so much.

His next stop after the dining room was the kitchen, one of the many places on the property where the enslaved people had worked. Staring at the stone fireplace, he couldn't begin to imagine how hot it must have gotten in here during the summer. What must it have been like to work all day every day, and for what? Free so-called room and board? He shook his head, thinking about those slave shacks where crowded families were forced to reside. There were no fancy Christmas dinners for those folks, that was for sure.

Could one of the enslaved people have pushed Cecily? After death, it was no longer possible to get revenge on their tormentors who were also dead. However, if there were any formerly enslaved people that remained on the property and they knew Cecily at all from watching her work, they would know she was a fierce defender of them. She worked hard to include their stories on her tours, making it clear exactly how the Hartleys remained so wealthy for so long.

Ryan checked out the Music Room and the parlor on the first floor and then headed upstairs. He visited Oliver Hartley's office, which was filled with fancy wooden furniture and snooty art on the walls. Everyone knew Oliver was no saint in life, so Ryan wouldn't put it past him to be the culprit. But did he have a motive?

Trying to figure out a motive for a ghost accused of murder was beyond bizarre. Ryan's life had certainly gotten far more interesting now that Cecily was a part of it.

He walked around the office, concentrating hard to determine if he could feel any kind of presence. He'd often heard that some people were particularly sensitive to the paranormal. Ryan was fairly sure that he was not one of those people. He'd certainly been clueless as to "Braydyn's" real identity, and George had snuck up behind him more than once and startled him.

If there was anybody in this room with him, he couldn't tell.

Perhaps that was a good thing. If this huge, empty, creaky house was filled with the spirits of people long dead, would he really want to be able to sense all of them?

Ugh.

He walked around upstairs for a while, long enough that his fear began to subside and boredom set in. There were an awful lot of rooms to explore. So, so many bedrooms, and still they'd forced the enslaved people to live in tiny wooden shacks.

What a bunch of assholes.

At least George had learned his lesson, even if he did so after death. Technically, it had been a little before death. Falling in love with Anna had made him question the morality of owning slaves.

Upon wrapping up his tour of the bedrooms, he made a mental note to ask George which one had been his in life.

He paused at the top of the stairs, holding tight to the railing just in case. He shivered as he stared down the depth of the staircase. Wincing, he thought of how much it must have hurt when Cecily was shoved down those stairs.

And Anna had died from such injuries.

Ryan was suddenly angry on Anna's behalf as well as Cecily's. Chances were one person had injured both women, and he would make it his mission to figure out who the hell it was, no matter how long it took.

He let go of the railing and stormed back along the upstairs hallway.

"Are you up here, you bastard? You cowardly son of a bitch? Show yourself and quit hiding, you prick!"

Ryan angrily searched each bedroom all over again, eventually arriving back at the top of the stairs.

And that's when he saw it in the hallway.

Drawing in a sharp gasp, he froze.

There, standing before him, was a full-bodied apparition.

14

———

Cecily arrived at the Hartley Mansion early in the morning and was shocked—and delighted—to find Ryan sitting at the bottom of the Great Hall staircase.

"Hey. What are you doing here so early?"

"I've been here all night," he said.

She studied him and realized he did look rather disheveled.

"What? Why? Are you all right?"

He stood up, towering over her tiny frame. Ryan gazed down at her and smiled wearily.

"Yes, yes, I'm fine. I came here before midnight to have a look around. I figured if I showed up when everything was quiet, I might have a better shot of finding whoever is still skulking around here."

Cecily held her breath, waiting for him to continue. She could tell by his wide-eyed expression that something had happened. That, and he wouldn't have stayed all night if there was nothing to report.

"I saw a ghost. And it was definitely not George."

"Oh wow. What did it look like?"

"It was a woman. An older woman. Maybe sixties or so," he said, shaking his head in disbelief.

"And you're sure it was a ghost and not a real live woman?"

Nodding his head rapidly, he said, "Ohhhh yeah. One hundred percent certain. I saw her appear and then disappear right before my eyes."

Whipping her head around, she asked, "Where? Where in the house?"

"Upstairs. Come on. I'll show you."

With that, Ryan took her hand and led her up the stairs.

"Careful," he said, gripping her hand tightly. "I don't know if she's still here or if she's the one that pushed you or what."

Even though she was frightened by what they might find, she had the presence of mind to be grateful for Ryan's touch. She still didn't understand why he hadn't made any move toward a romantic relationship with her, even though he showed every sign of being interested in her. But she hadn't given up hope, and right now, holding her hand was all she could seem to get out of him. Cecily supposed she should act like the modern woman she was and make the first move, but she still feared that if he truly was into her, he would say so.

Once they reached the landing, Ryan gently pulled her away from the top of the stairs and kept a protective hand on her back. Now she was grateful both for his touch and the safety he provided her. After all, they really had no idea what they were dealing with.

"Here," he said, gesturing toward the hallway.

They both stared at the empty hallway as if they expected the phantom woman to suddenly appear.

"What did she look like?" Cecily asked.

"She had grayish hair, light-colored eyes." Ryan shuddered as he spoke.

"When did you see her?"

"Oh, hours ago," he said, running his fingers through his hair. "I waited around, but she never came back. I just got that one glimpse of her."

Cecily couldn't begin to imagine how terrified he must have been to encounter a ghost in the huge, empty house in the middle of the night. And yet he'd stayed here all night.

He's so brave.

"You must be exhausted," she said.

He shrugged. "Not as much as you might think. I'll probably crash later. Right now, I'm just runnin' on adrenaline."

Ryan chuckled, a deep, throaty sound that tempted her to just kiss him already.

"I can't believe you came here in the middle of the night."

He gazed into her eyes with such intensity that it took her breath away.

"I had to do something to keep you safe," he said. "I'm so worried about you. Being in this mansion all day. I know George is usually around to watch over you, but there's not much he can physically do if something were to happen."

"Oh, that's so sweet of you," she said, overcome with affection for him.

She instinctively threw her arms around him and hugged him tightly. He wrapped her in an embrace, and she heard him let out a soft sigh.

"I just need you to be okay," he said.

Closing her eyes, she relished the feel of his hands tenderly rubbing her back. His touch felt so intimate. Everything felt so right when she was with him, and she couldn't understand why they weren't officially *together* yet, why he was holding back on taking their deep friendship to the next level. It made no sense.

"Thank you for taking such good care of me," she said when he finally released her.

"Of course." He gazed into her eyes.

It was, yet again, another perfect moment for him to kiss her. But she knew by now not to get her hopes up. He'd had plenty of perfect moments that he had let pass right by for whatever his reason might be.

Cecily sighed heavily, not even trying to hide her disappointment. Maybe it was time to let go of her romantic fantasies of Ryan. Perhaps she'd gotten it all wrong. After all, everyone around here knew that Ryan "Canuck" Armstrong was the heroic type. That was just who he was. He looked out for everybody because he was a good guy.

Maybe Cecily was nothing special to him after all.

That very notion stung so badly, it brought tears to her eyes. She turned to walk down the stairs.

Ryan suddenly grabbed her hand.

She held her breath.

"Be careful," he said, gently leading her back to the first floor.

Of course. He was just making sure she didn't fall again. Because he looked out for everybody.

God, she was an idiot.

He'd never had feelings for her beyond friendship. That was the only explanation for why he hadn't made a move. Ryan was a brave man. He'd proved that in a million ways. A guy like that wouldn't be too timid to ask a woman out if he wanted to. Like the old saying went ...

He's just not that into you.

When they got to the bottom of the stairs, Ryan's face was full of concern. "Hey, are you okay?"

Swallowing hard, she nodded. Cecily absolutely had to pull it together.

Trouble was, she wasn't sure how.

She hadn't realized until this very moment how deep her feelings were for Ryan Armstrong. This was so much more than a simple crush.

Oh God, I think I'm in love with this incredible, amazing, wonderful man. And he just wants to be friends.

Cecily couldn't believe how badly she had misread this whole situation. Ryan loved history, he was intrigued by this ghost mystery, and he was a brave knight-in-shining armor type of guy. It was for all those reasons that he'd stuck around this long. His interest in this adventure had nothing to do with her.

"Cecily?" he asked, sounding alarmed.

"Oh ... Y— yes. I'm fine. I just ..."

Fortunately, something else terribly sad had just occurred to her that could explain her expression.

"It's just ..." she said, "when I saw you sitting on the stairs when I came in this morning, it reminded me that's what George used to do. Back when I thought he was Braydyn. He used to say he was coming inside to take advantage of the air conditioning. And he would sit right there all the time."

She gazed sadly at the bottom of the steps. Now her heart truly did ache for George's pain as well as her own.

"Because that's where Anna died," Ryan said softly.

"Yes." Her voice was barely a whisper.

Cecily took a brief moment to gather her thoughts and control her emotions. She would have to deal with her broken heart later. Right now, she could still be in danger from this unknown spirit. That, and now she wanted to help George more than ever. He deserved answers and perhaps some kind of closure when it came to Anna's death.

"Do you think that woman could have killed Anna?"

"It's certainly possible," Ryan said.

"Do you have any idea who she might be?"

He shook his head.

"Wait ... you said she was a woman who looked like she was in her sixties, right?"

"Yeah. That would be my guess."

"Let me think ..." Cecily said.

She stepped toward one of the giant portraits in the Great Hall.

"Do you think it could be her?"

Ryan walked over and studied the painting of a woman in her thirties.

"That's Penelope Hartley, right? George's mother?"

Cecily tried to ignore the twinge of attraction she felt as Ryan spoke. Few other people in the world would recognize Penelope Hartley. Not even some of the people who worked in the Olde Town historical district would know that. Why did Ryan have to be so hot and so smart?

"Right. But this painting was done when she was much younger. She was sixty-four when she died."

They stared at the portrait of Penelope wearing a fancy white dress with a dainty lace bodice. She wore expensive jewelry, including a string of pearls around her neck and several bracelets on her wrist. Cecily had spent a great deal of time over the years imagining what Penelope Hartley must have been like in life.

Wealthy woman. Overbearing mother. Slave owner. And now, perhaps a murderer.

"I just don't know," Ryan said. "It's definitely possible

that it was her. I got such a quick glimpse before she disappeared. I wish I had gotten a better look."

"Yeah. Plus, it must have been quite a shock to see her appear right in front of you."

He laughed that damned sexy chuckle again.

"Oh yeah. There's that, too. I mean, it was slightly less shocking to me now that I've seen George put his arm straight through the arm of a bench, but still ..."

Cecily forced herself to concentrate on the task at hand. Considering all she wanted to do was go into her office and shut the door and cry, it wasn't easy. Why couldn't she have had the sudden realization that she'd been wrong about how Ryan felt about her when she was alone?

She sighed softly.

"You okay?" he asked.

The kindness on his face made the urge to cry even stronger.

"Yeah. Yeah, I'm just thinking."

With Ryan staring at her, she was forced to shove down her feelings. That actually seemed to help her think more clearly.

"I have an idea. Come with me," she said and walked down the hall to her office.

She sat down at her desk, and Ryan took a seat in the chair across from her. She pulled out a folder from her lower desk drawer.

"Okay," she said, flipping the folder open. "In here, there are a bunch of pictures of pictures. By that, I mean none of these are the original drawings, portraits, or photographs. The originals are either in the museum here in town or are owned by private collectors, that sort of thing. These are just copies, so no need to worry about handling them and getting finger oils and such on them."

Ryan nodded, leaning forward eagerly.

No matter what happened between them, right now she was glad to have him here. Not only did she enjoy the presence of her dear friend, he did make her feel safer. Falling down the stairs had been scary enough. The idea that someone had done it on purpose, and that *someone* might still be lurking nearby, was truly terrifying.

She handed Ryan a stack of photographs and studied his expression as he carefully scrutinized each one.

Cecily held her breath when she watched him pick up a reproduction of an old studio portrait, circa 1850 or so, that had been taken with a tintype camera. It was one of the last known photographs of Penelope Hartley.

He stared at the photograph for a moment. And then he put it aside. Cecily had seen no flicker of recognition in his eyes.

So it wasn't Penelope Hartley.

Which left everyone else in the world who had ever lived in this area over the last four hundred years. She worried that maybe they would never solve this mystery. That her life would remain in danger for as long as she worked in this place that she loved so dearly. And that George might never get closure on the tragic events of his life.

Ryan patiently sifted through image after image, with no hint of recognition on his face.

"Nobody in there looks familiar?" she asked.

"No," Ryan said. "I mean, I don't think so. It's really tough to say for sure. I think it's possible that the woman I saw was in there somewhere," he said, gesturing at the tall stack of photos. "For all I know, what I saw-- or who I saw or whatever--could be the older version of somebody younger in those pictures."

She nodded. "Like it could have been one of George's

sisters. Maybe one of them died in the house? If so, George might not have known about it. From what he says, he's kinda dipped in and out of consciousness over the years."

"I guess the next step would be to just talk to George."

"Agreed," she said. "I can ask him to come with me on my lunch break and we can meet you in town."

"Good deal." He stood up. "Until then, stay safe. George should be around here during the day to keep an eye out. He promised me he'd watch over you when I'm not around."

"That's so sweet," she said with a soft smile. "Listen, be careful too. Working construction when you haven't slept all night isn't exactly safe."

"I'll be careful," he said with an annoyingly sexy smile. "Thanks. See you and George at lunch."

"Hellooooo!" came George's voice from the hallway.

"Speak of the devil," Ryan said.

"I am approaching your office!" he announced a few seconds before walking in.

"Why are you announcing your presence?" Ryan asked. "What are you, the President? Shall we sing 'Hail to the Chief,' your honor?"

"I saw your truck in the parking lot."

"So?" Ryan asked.

"So, I knew you were here alone with Cecily. I didn't know what you were up to, so I figured I better make it clear I was here before barging in."

Cecily felt her face get hot. George's words made her incredibly self-conscious, and she worried that both of the men in the room were aware of her feelings for Ryan.

"I don't know what you're talking about," Ryan said through clenched teeth.

George shot him a look of sheer disdain. "No, I'm sure you don't." Then he muttered under his breath. "Idiot.

Cecily was shocked.

"What did you say?" Cecily asked.

"Nothing, nothing," George said. He looked annoyed.

"Well, I better get to work," Ryan said. "See you guys later."

George watched Ryan head off toward the front of the mansion, then turned back to face her once he was out of earshot.

"What was he doing here so early?" he asked.

"He, um, wanted to make sure I was okay."

Cecily didn't want to get into the whole "Ryan saw a ghost last night" until the three of them could meet to talk. "I don't think he likes me working here all by myself."

"Yeah," he said. "I'm not so happy about that either."

"Ryan is eager to figure out who might have hurt me, so he wants the three of us to meet at lunch today to talk about it. Will you come with me to town after the morning tours?"

He grinned. "I'll try to clear my busy schedule."

She smiled back. "Good, good."

After she wrapped up the first tours of the day and she'd changed back into her street clothes, Cecily found it rather pleasant to walk into town with George.

"It's amazing to me that you've been able to pass as Braydyn for so long around here."

He chuckled and shrugged. "It wasn't that hard. People usually aren't suspicious of you unless you give them a reason to be. Around here, plenty of people are dressed just like me. And there's too many employees for anybody to realize I'm not on the payroll."

"I guess that's true. I never thought twice about you. I mean, I never thought to wonder whether or not you were who you said you were."

"Right. And I knew a lot about the history of this place

because I've been around to see it!" He laughed, but she could hear the sadness in his voice.

"Are you tired of being here?"

"Yes. But having you and Ryan around makes it a lot less lonely." George looked at the tourists milling around. People were wandering in and out of historical buildings, some holding bags from their shopping adventures. "I don't mind being Braydyn when I'm here, but it's been nice to be George Hartley again."

"I get that," she said.

Cecily hated the idea that he was sad and lonely, wandering around that empty house all the time.

Or rather, the house they'd thought was empty.

"I see Canuck over there," George said, gesturing. Ryan sat on a bench near the theater.

"Oh good." At first, her heart leapt like it always did when she saw him. Then her earlier realization sent her mood plummeting. She would have to get used to envisioning a future where the two of them were just friends. It wouldn't be easy.

"What's up with you two anyway?" he asked.

"What do you mean?" She was taken aback by his question.

"I think he likes you."

"You do?" she asked, shocked. At this point, she was entirely convinced there was no hope for a romantic relationship with Ryan.

"You don't?" he asked, looking equally surprised.

Cecily had no idea how to answer that question anymore; she only knew she was tired of her heart getting knocked around. She was about to press George for more information, but just then Ryan spotted them. He got up and walked over.

Sighing softly, Cecily shoved down her feelings for the moment. There was no other choice. Right now, the top priority was telling George about seeing a ghost and hoping he didn't get too upset.

"Sitting around not working as usual I see," George teased.

"Oh, that's me all right," Ryan said with a grin.

"Between taking me to the hospital the other night and being up all night last night, I don't know how you're still standing," Cecily said. She couldn't help wondering how the man could be so tired and still look so damned good.

"And why were you up all night last night, young man?" George asked, looking intrigued.

"Yeah, well ... we need to talk about that," Ryan said.

Cecily happened to glance up and see Dr. Adam Gallagher walking toward them. He offered a friendly wave. It was too late to pretend she hadn't seen him. Normally, she wouldn't have minded chatting with him, but she really wanted to talk privately with George and Ryan.

"Well, hello there," Adam said, striding up to the three of them.

He shot a knowing glance first at Cecily and then at Ryan. It seemed like the whole world expected them to be an item already. Why didn't Ryan see it that way?

"Hi," Adam said, nodding toward George. Clearly, he was waiting for an introduction.

"Oh, Adam, this is Braydyn," Cecily said. "Spelled with a 'dyn' at the end."

"I see," Adam said.

Cecily had to suppress a giggle as she could plainly see the judgment on his face. No doubt he was thinking something along the lines of "kids these days," despite being only ten years or so older than Braydyn. The truth, of course, was that Dr. Adam Gallagher was the kid compared to George Hartley.

"He's one of the best reenactors in town," Ryan said with a smirk.

"Is that right?" Adam said, this time with a fairly genuine smile. The man always approved of anyone who was dedicated to the study of history.

"Oh yes," Cecily said. "He's quite authentic."

George snorted, which made it much harder for Cecily not to laugh. Somehow, she managed.

"Nice," he said. "So how are things at the mansion these days? Your research going well?"

"Quite well, thanks. Those documents you gave me have been incredibly helpful."

"Good. I was so psyched to find that image of George Hartley. I know how you've always said you wished you knew what he looked like," Adam said. Clearly, just having seen the image of George Hartley in the pile of documents briefly wasn't enough for him to recognize Braydyn now. After all, there had been dozens of pictures in there with the evidence he'd given her that day.

"That is true," Cecily said with great fondness. "I've always felt a kinship with George. I'm not sure why."

Braydyn/George smiled, and it warmed her heart. She did have tremendous affection for her dear friend and lost soul.

"I will say, though, that some of the spiritual activity has increased since I got that portrait of George. More footsteps, more haunting piano music ..."

Adam scoffed audibly. "Oh, please. Braydyn, you don't believe in that ghost nonsense, do you?"

Ryan had to fake a cough to cover his laughter. Cecily watched George's eyes flicker with amusement.

"No way. What a bunch of bullshit," he said with a dismissive wave of his hand.

"*Thank* you," Adam said with a triumphant grin.

Cecily shook her head and smiled. "Well, I'm sorry to cut this discussion short, but I gotta get on with my lunch break before I get back to work."

"No problem. Nice seeing you Ryan and Cecily. And nice meeting you, Braydyn."

George nodded in his direction, which made Adam put down the hand that he was about to extend for a handshake. Interesting. She supposed George needed all kinds of tricks up his sleeve to avoid touching people.

After Adam walked off, George said, "Okay, *that* was hilarious.

Cecily and Ryan laughed heartily.

"Yes it was," Ryan said. Then he turned to Cecily, who nodded.

"George," she began, "We need to talk ..."

15

─────────

That sounds ominous.

George watched as Ryan and Cecily exchanged looks of concern.

"What's going on?" he asked.

Cecily looked around at all the tourists milling about.

"Not here," she said. "Let's go somewhere else to talk. How about we take a walk down by the river?"

"Okaaaay," George said suspiciously.

Perhaps Cecily had unearthed something new and unsavory about his family during her research. It wouldn't be the first time. That didn't worry George much, since nothing about his family surprised him anymore.

They walked in silence toward the river. As they strolled, George watched the breeze ripple through the leaves of the trees. He was grateful for his gifts of sight and sound, but he missed his sense of smell and the sensation of feeling. He could hardly remember what summer smelled like anymore, and his body ached for the feel of the wind in his hair.

When they reached the banks of the St. Mary's River,

Cecily sat down in a grassy area. Ryan followed suit, so George sat across from the both of them.

"Okay," George said. "Why has a meeting between the living and the dead been called?"

Cecily smiled gently. "The meeting agenda definitely concerns the dead. And not just you."

"Really?"

Ryan nodded. "So, I spent the night at the Hartley Mansion last night. I went there to see if I could find whoever tried to hurt Cecily. And I might have found what I was looking for."

George stared at him. "You did?"

"Yes. I guess you weren't around last night?" Ryan asked.

He shook his head. "No. I wasn't. I'd vanished for the night."

"That's kind of what I figured," Ryan said. "So, I was searching around upstairs, and I saw a woman. A ghost."

George's eyes flew open wide.

"Was it Anna?"

Ryan exchanged a sad look with Cecily.

"No. I'm sorry."

"Are you sure?" he asked. He wasn't ready to lose the flicker of hope that had sparked in his heart that Anna might be near.

"I'm sure," Ryan said, compassion in his voice. "This lady was older. She must have died in her sixties."

"Oh." He should have known it was too much to hope for. Besides, if Anna had remained behind, she would have shown herself to him long ago. "Was it my mother?"

"No," Cecily responded. "That was my first thought too. But I showed Ryan a bunch of pictures to help us figure out who she was. I have lots of pictures of Penelope as an older woman, and he said it wasn't her."

"Who the hell was it?"

"We don't know," answered Ryan and Cecily in unison.

"Do you think whoever it was is the one who pushed Cecily?" George asked.

"I don't know. But I sure as hell would like to find out."

George heard the anger rising in Ryan's voice. This ghostly woman may have been the one who had hurt Cecily, the woman Ryan loved. Could she have caused Anna's death too?

"What did she look like?" he asked.

Ryan paused, thinking. "She appeared and disappeared so fast. It was such a shock to see her. I wish I'd had more time to look. The one thing I can tell you is that she wore one of those big fancy dresses. A lot like the ones Cecily wears sometimes in the winter."

"Victorian era?" Cecily asked.

"Yeah," Ryan said. "Late 1800s I'd say."

She smiled at him, impressed with his knowledge of history. They really would make the perfect couple.

"We were wondering if it could have been one of your sisters?" she asked.

"Maybe," he said. "But none of them died in the house that I know of."

"Well, you died in the house. Or rather, outside the house," Ryan said. "But you roam all over Olde Town. It's not like your spirit is tied to the mansion. So it could be somebody who passed away in town, but not necessarily in the house."

"Right," Cecily said.

"For all we know, it was a reenactor who died in costume," Ryan offered.

George groaned. "I hadn't even thought of that. So it

could be someone who has nothing whatsoever to do with my family."

How he hated getting a tiny bit closer to solving the mystery and then suddenly farther away. It was maddening.

"It's possible," Cecily said. "But I kind of doubt it. I would think if a reenactor died here on the grounds in costume, I would have heard about it by now."

"True," Ryan said.

"Are you okay?" Cecily asked George, looking worried.

"I don't know."

She nodded, patiently waiting for him to continue.

"For so long, I thought Anna's death was nothing more than a terrible accident, but now I'm not so sure. If someone murdered her, I want to know," he said, his voice taking on a hard edge.

"I get that," Ryan said. "And if that same someone tried to hurt Cecily ..."

Though his voice sounded threatening, they all knew there wasn't much they could do to get revenge on a dead perpetrator of violence. Still, they needed to know who or what they were up against.

"I know you weren't there when it happened," Cecily said. "That Anna had already died by the time you got to the house."

He nodded numbly.

"What did your family tell you about what happened?"

George froze, his mind traveling back to that tragic day.

"I know this is traumatic to think about," she said. "But we just want to help."

"I know that," he said softly. "I was so much in shock that it's hard to remember everything that was said. I mean, I heard screaming when I was outside the house. And then when I rushed in, headed toward all the commotion, it was like ... I had ... I had no warning. I ran in and saw Anna lying on the floor ..."

His voice cracked with emotion as he spoke. He was vaguely aware of the sound of Cecily's sniffles. She was so sweet and kind, that dear girl. More than a century had passed since he'd had real friends to talk to about his life. As hard as it was to talk about all of this, he relished not having to be Braydyn around Ryan and Cecily. His friends knew who he was and what he had been through. And they cared. What a gift that was.

"I don't know what I expected to find, but I never dreamed it could be something so tragic. I dropped to my knees beside her body. I remember yelling, screaming over and over, 'What happened? What happened?'"

Cecily put a hand over her mouth, her eyes spilling silent tears. Ryan wrapped his arm around her.

"I didn't even have to touch her to know she was gone. She didn't look bad or frightening. She just looked ... peaceful. It was as if I could feel that her ... her light was gone ..."

He did his best to keep his emotions in check, not wanting to upset Cecily any further. Later, when he was alone and invisible, he could sit at the bottom of the stairs and weep over his lost love. Just as he had done many, many times over the decades that had passed since her death.

"I remember my father saying it was an accident, there's been an accident ..." George said. "Then my mother said something about how they were giving the 'guest' a tour of the house. And they said she slipped and fell down the stairs. They said ... I think they said the stairs were wet from the rain on people's shoes and she fell."

George thought back to that day, trying to remember any little detail of what had been said to him.

"You'd think I would remember more about the worst

moment of my life, but ... My God, it happened so *fast.* So fast ... you just don't realize how suddenly your life can change and how quickly everything can be taken away from you."

His voice took on a hard edge and he shot a sharp, angry look in Ryan's direction.

That stupid bastard could be with the woman he loves right now, but he's too much of a fucking coward.

Ryan still had his hand on Cecily's back, caring for her as a *friend.*

She is your soulmate, you yellow-bellied fool. You should be with her, showering her with attention, and making love to her every chance you get.

George had to fight the urge to yell in Ryan's face. What he wouldn't give to have the ability to physically punch him, literally smack some sense into him.

Deep down, he knew he was inwardly unloading his fury onto Ryan because the person who might have been responsible for Anna's death was long dead.

Long dead ... but perhaps not totally gone.

He managed to keep from verbally attacking Ryan, if only for sweet Cecily's sake. It wasn't her fault that the man who loved her was such a dolt.

"So that's all anyone said? That it was just an accident?" Cecily asked.

George's rage subsided as he turned toward her. Better to talk with her instead of looking at Ryan.

"Yes. I was so utterly shocked and distraught that I just ran out of there. I couldn't bear to look at ..." Cecily nodded in understanding. "So I jumped on my horse and rode away. And then ... It was such a crazy twist of fate. Moments later, lightning struck. And I was dead."

He laughed suddenly. "Dead, and more confused than

ever. When you die suddenly, it takes a while to realize you're dead."

"Fascinating," Ryan said, and George couldn't fault him for his comment. When you're alive, you're super curious about death. How could you not be?

"I wandered around, confused, trying to make any sense of everything that had just happened. I honestly thought I was dreaming. Anna was dead, I was dead; it all seemed utterly impossible. It took a while to realize that nobody could see or hear me."

"My God, that must have been terrifying."

"It was. It sure was," George said. A great deal of time had passed since his death, so it was easier to look back at his accident with some degree of detachment. At the time, though, he had felt as if he was going out of his mind. "I suppose that's why I never questioned that Anna's death was an accident. There was so much confusion with my family and everything that was going on, and it was all such a shock. If I hadn't died right after she did, I would have been in the house to hear what my family was saying. Or, if I hadn't been so shocked by my own death, I could have been there, invisible, to hear what they said to one another about what happened."

"I see what you mean," Cecily said thoughtfully.

George gazed out at the gentle, rippling waves of the St. Mary's River. Such a peaceful spot. The waves and the sun sparkling on the water calmed him. Somehow, it reminded him that the universe was so much bigger and more expansive than anything he had experienced here on earth. He knew there was something beyond this life. Obviously his soul had remained here after death, but so many others had gone on somewhere else. Deep in his heart, he knew Anna was in paradise where she belonged. That thought had always comforted him in his darkest of days.

"After a little time had passed, I accepted that I was dead. I had no choice, really. Then I was able to focus more on what was happening with the living. Turned out my family covered up Anna's death."

"Really?" Ryan asked. "They did?"

George nodded. "They ... They moved her body." Just thinking about what they had done made him feel physically sick to his phantom stomach. "They put her body in a field and made one of their slaves tell everyone in town that he'd come across her body by accident."

Cecily gasped.

"Nobody bothered with an autopsy because nobody gave a damn about some *poor* woman," he said sharply. "All the neighbors assumed she died of natural causes." With a bitter laugh, he added, "Shit happens, right?"

"George," Cecily said gently, "didn't you think that was odd? That they would cover up her death like that?"

"Absolutely not. It wasn't odd in the slightest. Not with my family. The Hartleys couldn't have something as unseemly as a *peasant woman* dying in their house become known among their society friends."

"Ahh, yes," Cecily said with a firm nod. "That tracks for the Hartleys."

George felt such a deep kinship with Cecily in moments like this. He loved that she knew all about his difficult family, and that made him feel less alone. "I can definitely see them covering up an accident. But ... that doesn't mean it *was* an accident."

"Right," Ryan said.

"How much do you know about your family and what

they did after Anna's death? Were you around much?" Cecily asked.

"I was around some. I checked in once in a while to see what people were up to. Mainly, I tried to look after my little sisters. They turned out okay, thank goodness." He paused a moment, needing time to get his emotions under control once again. "I had four little sisters. They had a hard time after I died. I know they missed their big brother."

Cecily wiped yet another tear from her eye as she listened to his sad tale.

"Eventually, they all got married. Caroline and Jane stayed in town. Mabel and Lydia moved away, though. Out of reach from where I can travel as a ghost. I never saw them again."

Cecily drew in a shaky breath. "Mabel died at the age of sixty-two, and Lydia made it to seventy-five. From what I know, they both had happy families. Children and grand-children and all that."

"Thank you," George said, fighting the urge to cry once again.

"You'll see them again," she said. "You know that, right?"

He shrugged. "I don't think I know anything anymore."

"Victoria married," Cecily told him.

George nodded. That much he had known. "Yes. I saw her around town a few times. She married a wealthy landowner, so I guess she was okay after I died."

Cecily's phone beeped. George knew exactly what that meant—a tour was to start in thirty minutes.

"Tour time!" he said.

"Yes," she said, jumping up. At this rate, she would have to run to make it back and still have barely enough time to slip into her costume.

"I'm so sorry, George. I—"

He laughed good-naturedly. "I understand. Go. Go! I'll meet you there soon."

"Do you want a ride back?" Ryan asked her.

"Oh, thank you. I would, but by the time we get back to your truck it would probably be faster for me to just run."

"Okay," he said. "See you later!"

With what could only be described as a longing look from Cecily at Ryan, she dashed off. Once she was out of earshot, he turned to face Ryan.

George wasn't in a hurry to get back to the mansion because he knew she would be safe with the tourists around. He had something to say to Ryan first.

"We need to talk," he said sharply.

"Okaaay," Ryan said, holding out his hands as if to say "so ... *talk*."

"Not here. Not now. You have to get back to work soon. I'll meet you near the theater at 5:30pm. *Sharp.*"

Chuckling, Ryan asked, "Am I in trouble?"

"*Yes,*" George said through clenched teeth.

16

George was clearly mad at him for some reason. Though it was surreal to know that a ghost was angry with him, Ryan was no longer scared of George. He hadn't been for quite some time. Having the spirit annoyed with him was really no different than having an argument with a living friend. And Ryan truly did think of George as a friend.

He wasn't sure why George was pissed off, but he had his theories. He was most likely still mad that Ryan hadn't made a move on Cecily. Part of him understood the man's feelings, but another part of him was tired of hearing it. His love life was none of George's business, and it wasn't fair of him to try to live vicariously through Ryan. Even if he was gonna mess up his life—and to be fair, he probably was—that was his own business.

If it turned out that his situation with Cecily was the issue, he planned to tell George to stay the hell out of it. Enough was enough already.

By the time 5:30 finally came, it had been a long day and Ryan was tired. He hoped to wrap up this conversation with George quickly so he could go home and get some rest.

Fortunately, the man showed up on time, standing on the street outside the theater construction site. Fairly impressive for a dead man with no watch.

"Hello, Braydyn," Ryan said with a wry smile. Though it likely wasn't necessary to use his code name, he figured he might as well be cautious while they were in the historic district.

"Hello," George responded. He didn't smile.

Ryan's anger flared. He'd done the best he could to treat George with dignity and respect. The way Ryan saw it, Cecily had been dragged into his family drama and could have gotten severely hurt. Plus, he'd stayed up all night in the haunted mansion to try to identify the culprit and untangle this whole mess. What possible grudge could George have against him?

"Whatever this is, can we make it quick? I'm tired. I've been working on my feet all day."

George's hard expression softened ever so slightly.

"I know. But this will be worth it. Ultimately, anyway."

"What the hell does that mean?"

Glancing at the work site, George asked, "Are you all done here?"

Wearily, he nodded.

"Good. Follow me."

"Are we going back to the mansion? Because if so, I'd rather drive—"

"No," he said firmly. "Just walk."

"Fine," Ryan muttered, hoping wherever they were going wouldn't be too far away. All he wanted to do was crack open an ice-cold beer in the air-conditioned splendor of his apartment. Though George had regrets about his privileged lifestyle and his family, Ryan couldn't help thinking that the guy had no idea what it was like to work out in the hot sun all day.

They walked in silence, Ryan practically counting the steps they took. When whatever the hell George had planned for him was over, he was gonna have to walk all the way back. George led him toward the St. Mary's River, but at a different spot than where they'd gone during lunch.

Before he knew it, George was leading him toward that creepy-ass church.

"Oh dude. Seriously? I hate this place."

"Why?"

"There's dead bodies in there."

"True. But so what? There's dead bodies out here, too." George gestured at the cemetery located behind the church.

"Is that supposed to make me feel any better?"

"Not really. Suck it up, buttercup. We're going in."

Ryan sighed heavily and trudged toward the front door. At first, he hoped the door would be locked. But then he thought better of it. George would just make him come back later—it was best to get this over with, whatever it was.

He held the door open for George even though he could have easily walked through it. It was still daylight out, but nobody was around. All of the other touristy buildings closed at 5pm, so most of the visitors had left Olde Town for the day.

"Okay. I'm here. What already?" Ryan asked.

"I can't stand to see you dragging your feet when it comes to Cecily. You just don't fucking get it."

Ryan blinked. George rarely used such language. Then again, the guy was old-fashioned and tried not to cuss when Cecily was around.

"You could be with her right now, Ryan. You could make

love to her. You could have been with her a long time ago. I will not sit back and watch you waste your life like I did."

"Look, I'm sorry you had a sad life. Really, truly I am. But this is none of your damn business."

George laughed ruefully. "You know what I wish?"

"I imagine any number of things," Ryan said, not without sympathy. He felt bad for the guy. To a point.

"I wish that when I was alive, I had a true friend to talk some goddamn sense into me before it was too late. I didn't have that. *You do.*"

George proceeded to walk down the aisle toward the altar, leaving Ryan little choice but to follow him.

Eyes darting around the church, Ryan asked, "So what's the deal? You got Cecily and a preacher stashed away somewhere for a shotgun wedding?"

Turning to face him, George said grimly, "This is where they had Anna's funeral." George's words and his agonized expression knocked the wind out of him.

"Oh." He didn't know what else to say.

"Did you go to your own funeral?"

"Yes. This was worse. Much, much worse." Gesturing toward the front row pew, he said, "Sit."

Ryan obeyed like a golden retriever. George walked closer to the altar and turned around as if he were about to address the congregation. Which was accurate, Ryan supposed. Only he was addressing an audience of one.

"I need you to understand—really, truly understand—what it's like to bury the woman you love."

Oh, this isn't going to be pleasant.

But Ryan had to indulge the man.

"She was so young," George said. "A funeral for a young person is often filled with other young people. Friends, family members ... And, in this case, her father."

He paused then, gathering his emotional strength.

"My God, her father. He was ..." George dragged out the next five-syllable word as if it was literally painful to speak. *"Inconsolable."*

Ryan swallowed hard. Anna's father was dead now, too. He hoped they were together at last.

"They ... They had to practically carry him into the church. He was so grief-stricken, he could barely stand on his own. He'd already buried his wife. And now he was burying his child." His voice barely a whisper, George said, "My God, can you imagine?"

"No," Ryan said quietly.

"And it was all my fault."

"George, no." Ryan couldn't bear the thought that George had taken on Anna's tragedy like that. "Of course it wasn't your fault. You didn't—"

"It doesn't matter now," he said sharply.

Ryan understood that now was not the time to argue the point. Perhaps later, along with Cecily, he could talk some sense into his friend. Help ease his centuries-long burden.

"It was strange," George continued. "I was dead too, but I knew Anna was gone in a different way than I was. She was somewhere else. Not stuck here like me. I knew because ... because I couldn't feel her presence anymore."

Despite his best efforts to resist the lesson George was trying to shove down his throat, he found himself imagining a world without Cecily. The Hartley Mansion was *her* place. He couldn't imagine the house without her in it.

The image of Cecily lying at the bottom of the stairs flashed in his mind, and his breath caught in his throat.

She could have died.

He could have run into the mansion and found the love of his life gone. Just like that, in the blink of an eye. Just like

George had. Ryan's friend stood up at the front of the church, lost in a sea of painful memories. He could hardly wrap his mind around what George had been through. The way he'd arrived at his home to the sounds of screaming. How he'd rushed into the house, only to find—

I cannot even imagine ...

"To think," George said, "Anna and I could have held our wedding here. But instead, this church held her coffin. For all I know, there were two bodies in there. She might have been pregnant with our—" His voice cracked, and it took a moment for him to go on.

"I think about that sometimes. How if I hadn't been so goddamned stupid, we might have had children and even grandchildren. How many generations did I fuck up because I didn't want to give up my family's riches?"

Ryan wanted to argue with him. Tell him he was crazy to think that he was to blame for all of this, but he knew George didn't want to hear it. Not right now, anyway. Even after all the time that had passed, George needed to stand here and grieve.

"Gene, her father, was in no condition to speak. I know that if I'd been alive, I wouldn't have been able to get through it either. Anna's Aunt Elizabeth spoke instead. She did a lovely job. I had never met the woman, but it was clear she knew Anna well. Her aunt talked about how the smallest things would make Anna happy."

Simple Gifts.

"She spoke of how Anna loved baking cookies for other people, even more than she loved eating them herself. How true that was," George said fondly.

Ryan watched George as he relived his memories of Anna, perhaps remembering her hands as they lovingly prepared cookies for him, knowing he had a sweet tooth.

She would have taken good care of him. She would have loved him dearly. Ryan was sure of it.

"Her aunt talked about how much Anna loved sitting on the front porch of the farmhouse, just watching the sunset. Then, in the mornings she would prepare breakfast for herself and her father. She would make coffee and scrambled eggs. And she loved ... sh-she— lov-loved— or- ora- oranges ..."

It was all too much. Collapsing to his knees, George sobbed uncontrollably.

Keening.

The pure, unadulterated wailing of sheer *grief.* George's pain was so raw and so deep that Anna Hawkins might as well have died yesterday.

Rocking back and forth on his knees, George repeated, "I'm sorry, I'm sorry, I'm sorry ..."

Ryan's eyes welled up with tears just like Cecily's did when anyone around her was upset.

Cecily.

Images of Cecily Rosewood filled his brain. Her version of sitting on the porch watching the sunset was the way her eyes lit up when she discovered something new in her research. Like Anna's fondness for oranges, Cecily couldn't get enough of the coffee and the molasses cookies from Stonehouse Bakery. Ryan closed his eyes and thought about how he felt when he was with her. Whether they were sitting in the hospital waiting room watching silly sitcoms or sitting by the river and talking, *everything was wonderful with her.*

Dear God, he really was stupid.

And not in the way his parents always called him dumb, or the way the smart girls made him feel like an idiot. He was stupid as hell not to tell Cecily how he felt about her. Maybe she would reject him.

But maybe she wouldn't.

Either way, he knew his only regret would be to do nothing.

Ryan opened his eyes to find George slowly getting to his feet, having thoroughly exhausted himself by reliving the trauma of his past. And his friend had done it all to help him.

He would never be able to find the words to thank George. Truly, the only way to repay him was to do what he should have done long ago.

Tell Cecily that he was in love with her.

He watched George helplessly, wishing like hell there was something he could do to comfort his friend.

Slowly, he walked over to where Ryan sat in the pew, his face still wracked with grief.

"Is it possible that woman you saw might be involved in Anna's death?"

His heart ached seeing how the appearance of that random ghost woman had dredged up even more pain for him.

"I don't know. I just don't know."

George nodded wearily. Then his expression hardened.

"If she was, then Cecily could be in great danger. And you will never, ever forgive yourself if something happens to her and you never got a chance to tell her how you felt about her."

A lump formed in Ryan's throat, and he nodded. George was right. No question about that.

Wordlessly, George walked back down the aisle, so Ryan jumped up to follow him. His heart was heavy, clearly envisioning both Anna's coffin and a happy, newly married couple traveling down this same church aisle.

Frightening how thin the line was between life and death.

George stalked through the cemetery behind the church, and Ryan had to jog to keep up. Suddenly, George whirled around, eyes blazing.

"Stop wasting your life, Ryan. Quit squandering your chances because sooner or later, we all end up here." He gestured at a tombstone before storming off.

Ryan was about to follow him, but George vanished into thin air.

He sighed heavily, wrung out by emotion as he stared out toward the river. Then he glanced down at the grave in front of him.

Anna Hawkins.

Beloved daughter.

Departed this life August 27, 1835.

Ryan read the lines over and over again before sitting down in front of the grave. Closing his eyes, he said a silent prayer in memory of a woman he never knew but who had meant so much to so many.

17

George was waiting at the Hartley Mansion when Cecily arrived. That wasn't unusual, as he was almost always around in the morning these days to keep watch over her until the tourists arrived for their tour. With that mystery ghost woman still potentially skulking around the house, she was grateful for his watchful presence. Lately, he'd taken to doing rounds in the morning, searching the place.

"Good morning, George," she said when she spotted him in the parlor.

"Good morning." His brow furrowed.

"Are you doing okay?"

"I'm fine," he said unconvincingly. "Have you heard from Ryan lately?"

"No. Why? Is something wrong?"

What if Ryan had come back to the house last night for more ghost busting and had gotten hurt? Her imagination quickly ran wild.

"No. Everything's fine. I just ... wondered if he said

anything more about, you know, seeing that ghost. Or anybody else around here for that matter."

"Oh." She shook her head. "No, he hasn't said anything to me since we all talked down by the river."

"I see," George said, pursing his lips tightly. He seemed angry.

"Everything okay with you? I mean, all things considered."

"Yes, I'm fine," he said with a smile. "Don't worry about me. Just a lot on my mind."

"Of course. Let me know if I can do anything."

He nodded. "I will."

George headed upstairs.

Cecily settled in the chair in her office to get some writing done on her book when her phone pinged with a notification. It was from Ryan.

Ryan: *Can you meet me in the garden behind Hartley after work? It's important.*

Cecily: *Sure. Is something wrong?*

Ryan: *No no. All good.*

Cecily: *Glad to know it.*

She stared at her phone, intrigued. Maybe Ryan had uncovered some new information about that woman. Or perhaps he had seen another ghost? She almost texted back to ask if he wanted George to join them but then thought better of it. Though she had given up on her dreams of any romantic future with Ryan, she still loved him. She couldn't help that, and she wasn't about to pass up any chance to be alone with him.

Cecily decided not to tell George about Ryan's texts. If he wanted to meet with only her, there could be a reason. If he had uncovered something new, it was possible it could upset George. In that case, as they had with the woman ghost situation, they could meet up again and tell him together.

Throughout the day, she tried to quell her excitement about being alone with Ryan, but it was tough. If she wanted to keep the man in her life, she would have to figure out how to be just friends with the guy despite being in love with him. That wouldn't be easy.

At last, the time arrived. George was nowhere to be seen, which didn't mean he wasn't around. Either way, she was grateful not to have to explain why she was heading out to the garden instead of toward her car after the workday ended.

Cecily was surprised to find Ryan already sitting on a garden bench. He must have gotten off work early today. As always, her heart skipped a beat when she saw him.

I'm not sure I can ever be just friends with this man.

But that was a worry for another day. Right now, she needed to find out what he had to say after she'd been wondering about it since this morning.

"Hi," Ryan said, looking her directly in the eye.

Cecily took a seat beside him.

"Is everything okay?" she asked.

"I guess we'll find out," was his response.

Now she was nervous. She didn't understand what he meant. Holding her breath, she waited for him to speak.

But he didn't say a word.

Instead, he reached over and ran his fingers through her hair. He had never touched her so intimately before. Ryan gazed into her eyes for a moment, giving her a little time to slowly comprehend what was happening. It was all too much to hope for ... she worried this was too good to be true. After all, she'd gotten her hopes up so many times before.

Ryan dipped his head down to kiss her.

Cecily positively melted into his arms, as if kissing him was the most natural thing in the world. His mouth explored hers as her whole being responded to his passion.

He lifted his lips and kept his eyes locked on hers.

"Wh-what was that for?" she asked, recovering from the shock of his closeness. She reveled in his intoxicating scent of masculine cologne and the sweat from a hard day's work.

"That was because I'm in love with you, Dr. Cecily Rosewood," he said, still stroking her hair.

Cecily gasped.

That was the last thing she'd expected him to say.

Ryan drew in a shaky breath, let go of her hair, and sat back on the bench.

"I don't know what you're gonna say to that," he continued. "I have no idea how you're going to respond, but all I know is that I will never regret telling you how I feel."

Her heart pounded and her body quivered from head to toe. "Well ... how's this for a response," she said. With that, she leaned close to him and stroked his hair the same way he had done for her. She was sure to gaze deeply into his eyes as she said, "I love you too, Ryan Armstrong."

He let out a sharp breath of relief and surprise. "You do?"

"Yes," she said with a smile.

"That was the scariest thing I've ever done," he confessed.

"Even scarier than ghost hunting at the Hartley Mansion after midnight?"

"Yes."

Cecily laughed. She found it quite charming that he'd admitted his fears to her. The warm summer breeze gently cooled her face, and the smell of the garden flowers over-whelmed her.

"Well, thank you for being so brave."

"I've wanted to ask you out properly for a long time, but I just never had the guts to do it. I'm sorry it took so long."

She tenderly kissed his lips, still relishing the physical closeness between them.

"Better late … than … never," she said between sweet kisses. "To be fair, I could have done it. I'm supposed to be a modern woman, after all. I guess I was scared too."

"I thought you were out of my league," they said in perfect unison. And then they laughed in perfect tandem.

"And what do you mean, I'm out of your league?" Cecily asked. "Was it the whole being the child of billionaires thing?"

"Well, that and you're so damn much smarter than me."

She rolled her eyes. "Oh, I am not."

"Sure you are."

"I am *not*. I'm more educated than you, and that is not the same thing as being smarter. My billionaire parents paid for me to get my PhD."

"But you had to work for it."

"I had the privilege of working for it because I didn't have to get a real job to support myself."

Ryan shrugged, clearly not believing her.

"You are so much smarter than you give yourself credit for," she said. She meant every word and wished she could make him believe it.

He shrugged again, and she sighed.

"I don't know how to say this without sounding arro-gant," she said.

"You can tell me anything. I won't judge you."

"I know," she said with a smile. "Okay well, the truth is, I wouldn't be so attracted to you if you *weren't* smart. I understand people are born with different abilities and various degrees of intelligence and all that. And I guess you could say I have a 'type' or whatever. I'm just not really attracted to people who aren't smart." She winced as she spoke. "Does that make sense?"

Ryan nodded thoughtfully. "Yeah, it does, actually."

"You don't have to be well-read or formally educated to be smart. You just don't," she said firmly. "I think one of the many reasons you're so sexy is your intelligence. Your natural curiosity and your interest in history."

"Ya think I'm sexy?" he asked.

"Oh, yeah," she said in a sultry voice. "I've been hot for you for a long time."

"Is that so?" Ryan asked, his mouth forming an incredibly sexy grin.

"Hell, yeah," she said, making him laugh. "And not just for your intelligence. I love watching you work, when you're all sexy and sweaty and looking all muscular." Cecily squeezed his bicep for effect. "I used to try to watch you working without you catching me."

"I never caught you," he said with a chuckle. "Believe me. Never occurred to me that you were into me."

"And that's another thing that I find sexy." She stroked his throat seductively. "That deep, manly laugh of yours."

Ryan gazed at her with an expression of sheer wonder. Clearly, he'd had no idea how into him she was. And had been for so long. Cecily delighted in finally being free to tell him everything she adored about him. And the list was long.

"And you're so brave, Ryan."

He chuckled again and shook his head. Her body tingled at the sound of his laugh.

"I mean it. So you took a while to make a move on me.

You also rescued that woman and her kids from a carjacking *and* you braved a haunted mansion for me."

He nodded. "Yeah. I guess. But I don't get how you could ever think *I* was out of *your* league."

"Are you kidding? You're like the sexy hot jock type who was super popular in high school. Guys like you go for pretty cheerleaders, not nerds like me."

Ryan's expression softened at the hurt in her voice. Nobody liked feeling excluded. Not even if you were born rich.

"I did date some cheerleaders in high school," he said. "Believe me, they're not all they're cracked up to be. I mean, I'm sure some of them were fine, but ... I don't know. Turned out they weren't my type after all."

Cecily smiled. His words did make her feel better.

"And I hate to say it, but in my high school, the nerdy girls were meaner than the popular cheerleaders."

"Really?"

"Well, I never had a cheerleader call me stupid."

"Oh, that's awful," Cecily said, getting angry on his behalf.

"Enough about other girls," Ryan said, gazing into her eyes. "Let's talk about you. When you start spouting off all those facts about Olde Town and the Hartleys? I think that's the sexiest thing in the world."

"How is that possible?"

He laughed again. "It's true."

She searched his face and found that he was truly sincere. So often she felt like an outsider, being so obsessed with history, and now she'd found a wonderful guy who loved that about her.

Ryan dipped his head down and kissed her again. Now that the sweet shock of his profession of love had worn off a bit, Cecily was able to lose herself in the deliciousness of his touch. Truly living in the moment, she relished the sheer pleasure of his lips on hers. Ryan kissed down her neck as she moaned with delight. For far too long she had craved his touch, and she could hardly believe she was now free to express her devotion to him.

Panting heavily, wetness pooled between her legs. She found herself wishing they could dash inside the house, find the nearest bedroom, and make passionate love. Life was short, and they had wasted enough time.

"Do you think it's too soon for us to be, you know, *intimate*?"

Ryan sat back abruptly and looked at her. For a moment, she was afraid she had shocked him with her proposal.

"Hell no, it's not too soon. Not for me at least." Ryan searched her face as if making sure she was serious.

"Me neither," she said, still slightly out of breath even though he wasn't touching her. "Your place or mine?"

As wonderful as having sex in the mansion would have been, she didn't want to risk her job over it. That, and for all she knew, random ghosts could be watching.

His blue eyes filled with hunger, he said, "Whichever's closer."

They jumped up from the bench and headed toward his truck. Once inside, they couldn't resist devouring each other's mouths, finding it impossible to keep their hands off each other.

It was *heavenly*.

"You know," Cecily said, arching her back while Ryan kissed down her chest, nuzzling her skin above the opening of her blouse. "The sooner we get going ..."

With a deep, sexy, throaty chuckle, he said, "I know, I know. You're right."

He gunned the engine, and they were on their way. Fortunately, Cecily's apartment wasn't too far from Olde Town, and traffic was mercifully light. She spent the ride there in breathless anticipation, constantly sneaking looks at Ryan's impressive hard-on. Though she worried the bulge in his tight jeans might be uncomfortable, she found the sight of it alluring.

At last, they made it to her place. Once inside, Ryan took a polite look around.

"Nice place you got he—"

"I'll give you the grand tour later," she said.

"Works for me," Ryan said before scooping her up into his arms. She squeezed his biceps and enjoyed watching his eyes sparkle with pride. She loved building up his confidence, making sure he knew just how sexy and smart she found him. Cecily wanted to love him so hard, physically and emotionally, that he would forget any other person in his life that ever made him feel like he wasn't good enough.

He practically threw her down on the bed.

"Sorry. Didn't mean to be that rough," he said.

"You don't hear me complaining," she said seductively. She was rather petite and Ryan was huge, but she had a feeling he would be just the right amount of rough and tender in bed.

Cecily grabbed him and unbuttoned his shirt. Ryan kissed her while he undid her blouse at the same time. As far as she was concerned, they could not get naked fast enough. He fumbled with the belt buckle of her jean shorts, groaning in frustration as it took far too long to get it unstuck. He finally snapped it off, tossing it on the floor behind him. After sliding off her shorts, he kissed down her belly before pulling her panties off.

Relieved of their clothes, he resumed kissing down her

body just as he'd done in the truck. Only this time, there wasn't a blouse in the way. She cried out with need as he sucked on her hard nipples.

"Oh damn," he muttered. "There's condoms in the truck I think."

Mumbling, he pulled away from her. She grabbed his shoulders, pulling him back down on top of her where he belonged.

"No need. Pill."

"*Sweet,*" he said, turning his attention back to her breasts.

He rubbed his rock-hard cock between her legs; the pleasurable sensation made her see stars.

Without even penetrating her or touching her most sensitive spot directly, he had her so aroused by his touch that every sensation was heightened.

"I can't wait anymore, baby," he moaned.

"Then don't," she said through panted breaths.

Ryan rammed his cock into her, and her eyes rolled back in her head as she cried out his name. Digging her fingernails into her back, she did her best to live in the moment. She had been fantasizing about this man for months, and she reveled in the fact that Ryan Armstrong, the hunky, muscular construction guy she adored, was *making love to her*. So many times she had touched herself, imagining he was on top of her.

And now he actually is on top of me.

"Oh God, Cecily," Ryan repeated in that voice that was so familiar to her after all this time of desiring him. Hearing her name in his voice sent her heart soaring. Ryan Armstrong was making love to her. And he was *in love* with her.

The desperate sounds of his deep, throaty grunts and

groans told her he was getting close. Showing remarkable restraint, he pulled out so he could take care of her.

Good thing, because she was ready to explode with need. Lucky for him, and for her, it wouldn't take much to get her there.

He dipped his head between her legs and stroked her with his tongue. Cecily threw her head back and arched her back. The deeply pleasurable sensations of his swirling tongue were so intense that she couldn't even scream at first. That was, until she came.

She let out a deep, primal cry of pure ecstasy and the relief of long pent-up sexual frustration as her new lover gave her the most earth-shattering orgasm of her life.

Cecily was so lost in her own sexual relief that she barely noticed when Ryan re-entered her. When she caught her breath, she once again reminded herself to relish every touch. Her own needs sated, she could savor the sweetness of Ryan's closeness. She watched as the man she loved thrust in and out of her, his eyes closed as he neared his own climax. Breathing in the scent of sweat and manly cologne and essential *Ryan-ness,* she was overcome with emotion. Tears sprang to her eyes.

Ryan let out a deep, sexy groan as he reached orgasm. He collapsed on top of her, and she ran her fingers through his sweaty hair. When he finally lifted his head, his eyes flew open wide at the sight of her tears.

"Oh my God, are you okay?" he asked, clearly terrified that he'd done something wrong.

"I'm fine," she said with a soft smile. "I just love you, that's all."

"Oh," he said, letting out a breath of relief. "Cool."

She laughed.

"Sorry. I mean I love you too," he said.

Cecily laughed again as she gazed into his eyes. He was so adorable.

Ryan lay down on the pillow next to her. They let out a deep, happy sigh at the same time, which made them both laugh.

"It is wild how in sync we are," Cecily said. "In every possible way." They were certainly in sync in the bedroom.

"You're right. We're gonna be one of those perfect, happy couples that makes everyone puke."

She burst out laughing. "You are so right. I look forward to making people puke."

"Me too."

They lay in bed lazily for a while and eventually got up. Ryan ordered pizza for dinner, extra pepperoni just the way she liked it, and Cecily marveled again at how in sync they really were. After all, they had been friends for a while. All it took was for one of them *finally* to admit they wanted more than just friendship. Being a couple felt so natural, it was as if they'd been dating for years.

Since she had a spare toothbrush in her cabinet and Ryan was a man of few needs, he spent the night. They made love again before going to sleep, holding each other.

The next morning, they were delayed going into work.

Cecily had been sitting in her living room chair, putting on her shoes and getting ready to leave, when Ryan wandered over to kiss her. Before they knew it, they were naked with her legs flung over his shoulders and him pounding into her like his life depended on it.

"I am a stupid, stupid man," he muttered between thrusts.

"What?" she asked, barely able to form a thought let alone words. Ryan's thrusting rhythm was just so *perfect.*

"If I wasn't so stupid, we could have been doing this a

long time ago," he said, his heavy breathing driving her wild.

"Okay, just this one time I'll admit you were stupid," she panted.

Ryan chuckled, which only made her hotter. She let him know with a moan of desire. He slipped his fingers between her legs to maximize her pleasure.

"Well ... at least we're making ... up ... for lost ... time." Then she threw her head back and cried out as she reached orgasm.

He finished shortly after.

With him still inside her and her legs still on his shoulders, she said, "Okay, we really have to get to work now."

Ryan kissed her and said, "I know."

He gently disentangled her body from his and helped her stand up. She saw him grin when he noticed she was a little wobbly.

"Definitely making up for lost time," she said, gazing up into his eyes.

On the truck ride back to work they had more time to talk, which was lovely. As she gazed out the windshield at the cloudless blue sky, she felt positively giddy. After pining for Ryan for so long, everything had finally come together. And so quickly! They professed their feelings and made passionate love. Multiple times. She could hardly wrap her head around it all.

"George will be happy about this. About us," Ryan said.

"You think so?"

"Believe me, I *know* so. He knows I'm in love with you, and he's been after me for a long time to tell you."

"You're kidding!" she said.

"Nope. He's taken a personal interest because of his past. You know he carries so much guilt about Anna, about not running away with her and marrying her when he had the chance. He saw me making the same mistake and was doing everything he could to stop me."

"Wow, I had no idea."

"I didn't want to say anything to you last night. Spoil the mood and all. But George kinda went to extremes the other day to show me just how dumb I was being."

"What do you mean?"

"After work, he took me over to that creepy church I hate. And then he told me all about what it was like to attend Anna's funeral there." Ryan gripped the steering wheel, his face grim.

"It was ... bad," he told her.

"That poor man." She pictured George in the church, helplessly watching Anna's memorial service.

"He told me what it was like to watch her father have to bury his child." He paused as he spoke, his expression darkening. She could see how affected he had been by this experience. "Then he told me how one of Anna's relatives got up to speak. God, Cecily, he completely broke down. I've never seen him like that before. He could barely talk. He dropped to his knees and just *wept*."

Cecily's heart dropped in her chest as she listened to the tragic tale.

"Anna might as well have died yesterday. That's how raw his grief was," Ryan said, shaking his head at the memory. With a glance over at Cecily, he said, "And he put himself through all of that for me. For *us*. That's how much he wanted us to be together."

"That's amazing. Oh, that dear man." She had the sudden urge to rush to George's side. To comfort him. To thank him.

"Did you ever imagine that *George Hartley* would be the one to help you find love?" Ryan asked incredulously.

"Right? This is all so wild."

"Quite a story to tell our grandchildren." With a bit of hesitation, he asked, "Or is it too soon for me to say stuff like that?"

"It *should* be too soon. But somehow, it's not."

"Yeah," he said with a grin.

It was so easy to envision a future with Ryan Armstrong. In fact, it was already impossible to imagine her life without him.

No doubt that was how George had felt about Anna.

"I wish there was some way to help George," she said.

"I was just thinking the same thing." He glanced over at Cecily in wonder. They were in sync again. "I can't stand how he blames himself for Anna's death." He banged his hand on the steering wheel for emphasis. "Whether or not anybody pushed her, it still wasn't George's fault."

"I agree." Then she thought of something else. "Huh."

"What?"

"I just remembered George asking me if I'd heard from you yesterday. That was before you texted me. He seemed annoyed when I said no. Now I know why."

"Yup," Ryan said with a smile. "I hope us being together helps him. Maybe he'll feel like he's atoned for something. Even though he has nothing to atone for."

"Maybe. Wouldn't it be amazing if we could somehow help him to cross over? Get him out of here after all this time?"

"Yeah, it sure would. Then he could finally be with Anna," he said softly.

She sighed out loud. Ryan was hot *and* romantic.

"You're so dreamy."

He laughed. "If you say so."

They arrived at the parking lot of the Hartley Mansion, and Cecily got out of the truck. She walked around to the driver's side for a proper goodbye. On her toes, she strained to reach his lips for a kiss.

"Thanks for the ride. And, you know, everything else."

He grinned. "You're welcome."

She thought for a moment, and then asked, "Will you say something in French for me?"

"Je t'aime beaucoup, ma belle," he said in a sensual voice that made her tingle all over. "It means—"

She put a finger on his lips. "Believe me, it doesn't matter."

That made him laugh, which made her laugh.

"Wanna meet for lunch?" she asked.

"I'd love it."

She nodded, smiling at him one more time before going inside the mansion.

Cecily could feel him watching her as she walked away.

It made her feel cherished and loved.

18

George was sitting on the steps of the Great Hall when Cecily came in. He often sat there, near where Anna had fallen. He would close his eyes and try to feel her presence. All these years he had hoped and prayed for a sign from her. Something to tell him that she still existed somewhere. But he never got anything. If it weren't for his own ghostly existence, he would have stopped believing in life after death altogether.

Cecily smiled at him when she arrived, and he marveled at how nice it was to be visible to her all the time. He could be in the house and sit on the stairs any time he wished without having to pretend to be Braydyn the Reenactor. Befriending both she and Ryan had been such a blessing for him.

"Good morning, Cecily."

"Good morning," she said. "I'm here early as usual, so I have time to talk with you for a bit if you'd like."

"That would be nice. Would you do me a favor?"

"Of course."

"Would you turn on your music in your office like you do when you're working?"

"Sure. Anything you'd like to hear in particular?"

"I really like the classical piano music you play sometimes."

"You are a man of fine tastes."

He sighed. "Comes from my fancy upbringing, I suppose."

She laughed. "Yeah, I guess it does. I mean, my parents weren't all that big on classical music, but they did take me to a symphony once. That's where I got my love for that kind of music."

Cecily went into her office, and soon lovely classical music began to play. She turned up the volume a bit higher than normal so they could hear it throughout the house.

"Thanks," he said when she returned.

"We can sit in the Music Room if you like."

"Good idea."

They went to the luxurious Music Room where she took a seat on the couch and he sat behind the piano. The walls were painted a light blue that was similar to the dining room, and the windows featured dainty lace curtains. Unfortunately, a painting of old Oliver Hartley hung prominently over the fireplace.

Cecily watched George as he mimed playing the piano along with the music coming from her office.

"Do you miss playing?" she asked.

"Very much."

He paused to listen to the beautiful melody flowing through the air.

"Anna loved listening to music. If we'd married, I would have played the piano for her all the time. And the harp," he said, glancing over at the other instrument in the room.

"She loved the harp. I would have arranged for her to take lessons so she could play any time she wished."

After allowing him a few moments of quiet reflection, Cecily spoke up softly. "Ryan told me he loved me last night."

Whipping his head around to face her, he asked, "He did?"

She nodded.

"What did you say?"

"I told him I loved him too."

George's face broke into a grin.

"That's fantastic. I'm so happy for you both!"

And he was. He truly was thrilled for his dear friends. They were both lovely and good-hearted people who deserved happiness.

"He told me what you did for him. For us. I know that couldn't have been easy. Thank you."

"Well, it certainly wasn't the first time I've been back in that church over the years. I go there often. I go inside, and I visit her grave out back."

"And it's still so hard," Cecily said sadly. "Even after all these years."

"Yes. I mean, I have good days and bad days. Sometimes I'm more or less okay, but then other things send me spiraling back down in the pit of grief."

"And yet you put yourself through that for Ryan," she said, her pretty eyes filled with concern for him.

"Yeah well, he can be a stubborn bastard. Somebody had to knock some sense into him."

Cecily laughed.

"Don't take that to mean I forced him to say something he didn't feel. Trust me, the man is head over heels in love with you. He just had to get the nerve to say it."

"I understand."

"You two belong together, you know."

"Yes, I know," she said with a gentle smile.

It soothed his soul a little to see her so happy, and he looked forward to seeing Ryan, too. He wanted to see the look on his face now that he had landed the girl of his dreams.

George's gaze landed back on the harp.

"Are you thinking about Anna?"

"I'm always thinking about Anna."

Cecily nodded. "Tell me about her."

He was surprised but quite pleased by the request.

"She was spirited. She laughed easily. That was one of my favorite things about her. We had so much fun together. It's hard to imagine laughing with Victoria. After I met Anna, it was damned near impossible to picture myself as Victoria's husband. It just ... It just no longer made any sense."

"I can understand that."

"Anna was passionate about lots of things. She loved animals and music. And oranges," he said with a laugh. "And she was passionate about justice. Anna wanted everything to be fair, and it infuriated her when things weren't just. Makes me wonder how she would feel about being the victim of murder."

"Well, I guess she can't be that upset about it, or she'd still be here. Like you."

"I suppose."

"I really wonder if it's your guilt over her death that keeps you here. Even though you are not, in any way shape or form, responsible for what happened to her, you feel terribly guilty about it. Maybe if you could resolve that, you could cross over."

George shrugged wearily. "I don't know. Maybe."

"Ryan and I want to help you cross over so you can be with Anna."

"Is that so?" George said with an amused smirk. He'd long ago given up on moving on from this place, but it was sweet that they wanted to try.

Gazing around the room, George said, "You know what I hate?"

"I imagine any number of things," she said.

"That's so funny."

"What?"

"Ryan used that same turn of phrase the other day."

Cecily laughed. "Yeah, we tend to talk and think a lot alike. Ryan says we're gonna be such a cute couple that we'll make people puke."

George laughed heartily. "I love that. Yes, yes you sure will."

"So what do you hate?"

"I hate that nobody really knows who Anna was. Bad enough that my family covered up her untimely death, but since she wasn't rich and powerful, nobody remembers her. My funeral was a giant spectacle. Everybody rallied around my famous family and supported them after the tragedy of my death. Anna's demise was just as tragic, but nobody made a big deal about it. Only her family and friends. And now, around here with all the tours and such, people talk about my family and other famous historical figures, but not about simple, wonderful people like her."

"Yeah, you're right. I wish I had a picture of her. Better yet, a portrait to hang in the Great Hall."

"Oh, that would have been wonderful," George said wistfully.

"I bet she was beautiful."

"Yes, yes she was. She had light blond hair and blue eyes. Anna looked so sweet in her bonnet and simple farm dress," he said, picturing her so clearly even after all these years. "One of those women who was beautiful but didn't know it. Such things weren't important to her. Victoria could not have been more different. She really leaned into the whole dainty female act."

"A woman should be 'kept like a jewel in a case,'" Cecily said.

"Exactly." What a pleasure it always was to sit and talk with Cecily, with her extensive knowledge of 1800s America. How comforting it was to speak with someone who understood him. "Victoria was all about that. Loved to be treated like a delicate flower. Anna had no need for that kind of thing. She was my equal. And she was my friend."

Cecily nodded. She was always fine with sitting in silence when she felt that was what he needed.

Sighing and looking at his surroundings, he said, "That's the thing about her. She didn't need all of this. Sure, she would have enjoyed the piano and the harp and the Orangery, but she didn't need any of those things to be happy. Sitting and watching the sunset. Lovingly preparing food for other people. Laughing at the silliest things in life. Being with the people she loved. Those were the only things she needed to have a good life. And I took all of that away from her."

"George, you did no such thing. Deep down, you must know that, right?"

Cecily sounded so insistent, and it would have been wonderful if he could believe her. But he didn't.

"You only wanted the best for Anna. That's why you wanted to marry her and live here in the Hartley Mansion."

"Or maybe I was the one who wanted to live here. Maybe

I couldn't bring myself to live on a poor farm," he said bitterly. He sure as hell knew better now. None of the superficial trappings of wealth mattered one damned bit. Too little too late, as the saying went.

"I love this house," Cecily said. "It's beautiful. And especially for the 1800s it was the height of luxury. Sixteen bedrooms, a fancy parlor, your father's exquisite upstairs office, the Music Room, the Great Hall, a glamorous dining room, and all of it overlooking a garden and lush, rolling hills. Who wouldn't want to live here? And with the woman you loved by your side? That would be paradise. Do you really think you're a bad person for wanting that?"

She made a lot of sense. Not enough sense for him to forgive himself, but it was harder to argue with her when she laid out the bare facts like that.

"Your intentions were good, George. If you'd willingly sacrificed Anna's life just for riches, well *then* you would be a monster. And there are plenty of monsters out there in the world. There always have been and there always will be. But that's not you. You could not possibly have foreseen what happened to Anna. If you had any kind of inkling whatsoever that she could be in danger, you never would have told her to come here."

Once again, it was tough to argue with that. Of course he would never have brought her here if he'd thought there was any chance of harm coming to her.

"I miss it sometimes," she said softly.

"Miss what?"

"Living in a big house. The one I grew up in had its own library that I adored. The place had huge windows overlooking acres of lush, green property. We had this little stream out back where you could hear the trickling water at night." She let out a sigh. "I live in a two-bedroom apartment now. It's small, and it's noisy. The traffic is loud, especially when I'm trying to sleep. When you walk through the hallway, you can smell a mix of what all your neighbors are cooking."

George nodded as he listened.

"For the most part, I try to be grateful for what I have. So many people are homeless and hungry, suffer abuse and neglect. I am so incredibly lucky in my life. But I admit, I miss my old life sometimes. Does that make me a bad person?"

He knew the question was meant to be rhetorical. She was making a point, after all. But there was a tinge of sadness and worry in her voice. She seemed to be genuinely asking *does that make me a bad person?*

"Of course not," he said.

Cecily smiled sadly, clearly unconvinced.

"Wealth is what you grew up with," he said. "That was all you knew."

"Exactly," she said firmly. "It would have been awfully hard for you to walk away from your childhood home and from everything you'd ever known. Just as you'd had servants—as well as enslaved people—I grew up with housekeepers and gardeners and cooks and the like. At first, I didn't know how to take care of myself. And I bet you didn't either."

"I sure didn't. Especially not as a man during those days. I knew my father's business of course, but nothing about actually taking care of a home."

"It would have been really hard for you to just leave your home and your family and start completely over. And yet, I know you would have done that in a heartbeat if you'd had any clue what the future held if you stayed. You could not possibly have known the outcome, so maybe give yourself a damn break already?"

George laughed, and Cecily looked relieved to see him smile.

"I mean, what's the plan here? You beat yourself up for eternity, which will change nothing?"

He sighed. "I have no plan." George looked around the room, his gaze landing on the harp.

"You realize that if you figure this all out, you'll probably go join her where she is."

"Do you really think so?"

"I'm hardly an expert on the afterlife," she said. "Sometimes it's hard to know what to believe. But I do know it's worth a try. If there's any way you and Anna can be together, you and me and Ryan are gonna find it."

For the first time in ages, George felt the tiniest glimmer of hope.

And it was wonderful.

Cecily's watch beeped with the usual "it's almost time for a tour" warning.

"You have to get ready," he said. "Thanks for talking with me. It always makes me feel better."

"I'm so glad," she said. Her eyes narrowed.

"What's cooking in that brain of yours, little lady?"

"I was thinking that it might be fun to have Braydyn join me on the tour. What do you think?"

He considered for a moment.

Then he grinned.

When tour time came, George and Cecily greeted the visitors together in the Great Hall. Today's tour consisted of a couple in their late forties, accompanied by two girls around the age of sixteen or so. George figured the two teenagers were friends rather than sisters, judging by the way they joked around together. They might be fraternal twins, but it was more likely one of those family vacations where the parents allowed their child to bring a friend along. There were also two older ladies; George wondered if perhaps they were sisters. Either that, or they were a couple. So much had changed over the years since his death, and he found it fascinating that gay couples could appear openly in public now. He was happy for them. Gay people had existed back in his time of course. He was certain that at least one of his schoolmates was gay. The man wound up marrying a woman, but George had known he was unhappy. It was a sad but not uncommon tale back in his day.

"Good morning, everyone, and welcome to the Hartley Mansion," Cecily said. George watched her eyes as she discreetly checked to see that each guest had a badge, ensuring that they'd paid for admission. "I hope everyone is enjoying their trip to Olde Town."

Various nods and murmurs all around.

"This here is Braydyn, one of our reenactors here at Olde Town."

George bowed politely. That was his go-to greeting, lest people get any ideas about trying to shake his hand. That wouldn't go down so well for anyone involved.

Cecily briefly went over the ground rules about staying on the carpeted path and not touching anything, and then the tour was underway. As they stood in the Great Hall, she went over the nearly four-hundred-year history of the Hartleys living on these grounds. She also mentioned the indentured servants and slaves, which made George happy. For many years, tour discussions only mentioned the rich and fancy folk. He was grateful that these days the whole story was told.

Next, they moved on to the dining room.

"Oooh, this is really pretty," said one of the teen girls. She looked around the lovely room with large windows overlooking the lush garden. As always, the table was set with fancy glassware and china.

"This room was definitely a favorite of George Hartley," Cecily said, smiling over at Braydyn. "They say he loved food and had quite a sweet tooth."

"The Hartleys were certainly accustomed to the finer things in life," George said. "Especially food."

Cecily nodded at him, encouraging him to take an active part in the tour.

"They would have dined on dishes like beef or chicken with potatoes. The meat might be garnished with jellies or jams and would be served with corn, peas, cabbage, or maybe beets."

Polite nods from the guests as they scanned the room and listened. George found talking to the guests highly entertaining. Though he often strolled the grounds of Olde Town posing as an employee and answering the occasional query, he had never had the opportunity to actually give a tour. The people listened to him, just as Ryan and Cecily always listened to him. It made him feel human again.

"Salad didn't come around until much later," Cecily added. She looked at George, and he understood she was giving her blessing for him to chime in any time he pleased. Though she adored talking about history, she was not an attention hog. From what he had observed, she just wanted her guests to be entertained, and she wanted them to learn a little something while having fun.

"Right. They might have had lettuce or dandelion greens seasoned with sugar and vinegar," he said.

"Ugh," said the other teen girl, wrinkling her nose.

"It's actually not bad," George said.

"You've tried it?" she asked.

"Yes," he said with amusement. The teen girl shrugged and smiled. Many times the teenagers on the tours were surly, clearly wanting to be anywhere else but here. George was pleased to see these young ladies seemed to be having a good time.

"Of course, as Cecily mentioned earlier, these meals were prepared by the slaves," he said. "You'll notice right over there is a door where they came and went. Though the Hartleys owned many slaves, they preferred to keep them more or less hidden. Seen and not heard."

"Like a dirty little secret," said one of the older women, a bit of an edge in her voice.

"Correct," George said with a nod.

The woman smiled slightly at him. She, too, seemed pleased that he and Cecily were being straightforward about the horrors of slavery.

Cecily glanced at him, waiting to see if he had anything else to add in this room. He shrugged and she nodded.

"Okay then, let's move on over to the Music Room," she said, leading the way.

Once they arrived, the guests seemed excited by the beauty of the room.

"Oooh, look at this!" exclaimed one of the teenagers as she eyed the antique upright instrument. "I play piano."

"So do I," said the older woman who had spoken in the dining room. The lady with her smiled proudly and wrapped an arm around her.

Ah, so they are a couple.

Their happiness made him wonder how long they had been together. For the millionth time, he thought about what it might have been like to grow old with Anna. So many lost years.

"Oh wow, look at this harp," remarked the woman who was probably the mother of one of the teen girls.

"Isn't that lovely?" Cecily said. "Sometimes we have a guest harpist come in and play for us. It's so beautiful."

Cecily admired the harp with reverence. Funny how Cecily had grown up wealthy but still had great appreciation and wonder for the finer things in life. She never seemed to take anything for granted.

They provided the guests with more information about the Music Room, and Braydyn told them all about how George Hartley used to play the piano. With that, they moved the tour upstairs to see the bedrooms.

While everyone milled around on the second floor, someone asked the inevitable question.

"Has anyone ever died in this house?" asked one of the teens.

Cecily glanced at George, who smiled. He never minded the question, no matter how many times it came up. He'd heard it asked in every old building in Olde Town. People always wanted to know if places were haunted.

And the answer was a resounding yes.

George didn't answer, though, so Cecily took the reins.

"Yes, it was quite common for people to die in their own homes in the past. It's only in recent times that people die in hospitals, nursing homes, or hospice care facilities. We do know that Oliver Hartley passed away here, probably in his own bedroom." Cecily nodded toward one of the bedrooms they'd already visited. "Penelope Hartley might have died here too, but I don't have any specific record of that to be sure."

Cecily paused and then went on.

"There was a tragic death that occurred here as well," she said.

That got everyone's attention. All eyes were on her as she spoke.

"A beautiful young woman named Anna Hawkins died here on August 27, 1835. George's family wanted him to marry a wealthy woman named Victoria, but he fell in love with Anna instead."

She watched George carefully as if to gauge his reaction. He nodded, encouraging her to go on.

"Anna was visiting the mansion one day when it was raining outside. The stairs leading down to the Great Hall may have been wet from people walking in from the rain. They say she slipped and fell, but there was also the possibility that she was pushed by someone."

"Wow," said one of the teen girls.

Cecily walked to the hallway window and gazed out. Turning back to face her audience, she continued her story. Her voice was a tad shaky as she spoke.

"George wasn't home when it happened. He had been planning to meet Anna here, but she got here early. When he arrived, he found her lifeless body at the bottom of the stairs. He was so distraught that he raced out of the building and jumped on his horse. Moments later, he was dead."

Gasps came up from the rapt tour group. Cecily knew how to tell a story, that was for sure.

"Did the horse buck him off?" asked one of the teens.

She shook her head. "No, he was struck by lightning."

"Oh damn," said the girl. "That's really sad."

"Yes," Cecily said somberly.

"Well, at least George and Anna died at the same time so they could be together," the girl said.

"Like Romeo and Juliet," added one of the older ladies.

"I suppose so," Cecily said with a rueful glance at George.

They headed back down the stairs, and George watched to make sure Cecily gripped the handrail as she walked. He also kept a careful watch on the guests lest any naughty ghosts who might have remained here got any bad ideas.

Once they reached the Great Hall, several of the guests eyed the bottom of the steps with interest. Again, he understood their natural curiosity about death. He was also grateful that Anna's story had finally been told. Thanks to Cecily, Anna's life was no longer lost to history.

Cecily wrapped up the tour by asking if anyone had any questions. No one did. She thanked them all for coming and encouraged them to take their time to enjoy the gardens out back and see the Orangery before they left. Everyone politely thanked George and Cecily before going on their way.

"I think that went pretty well," Cecily said with a smile.

"Yes, I think it did. Thank you for including me."

"You are welcome to join me any time," she said. "After all, it's your house."

He laughed. "I suppose."

George and Cecily conducted another tour before lunchtime, and that was a success as well. He enjoyed spending this time with her.

"I'm meeting Ryan for lunch in town. Want to walk over there with me?"

"I'd love it," he said. Being with Cecily was such a pleasant reprieve from his crushing loneliness. He just hoped he wasn't getting in her way by hanging around all the time. This was her job, after all, and he didn't wish to intrude.

"Thank you for telling Anna's story," he said as they walked in the sunshine toward the main part of town.

"I'm happy to do it, believe me. I'm trying to figure out how to incorporate her into my book on the Hartleys."

"What do you mean?"

"Well, I have a primary source for my information," she said, gesturing at him. "But it's not like I can explain that to anyone."

"Ah, a good point."

"Maybe if I do some more digging, I can find some concrete information on her. Then again, I am known as the expert on the Hartleys. It's my area of expertise, and it's not exactly a hot topic in historical research. I'm not writing about the founding fathers or anything, so it's unlikely that anyone would challenge my work."

"True."

He watched her eyes light up when she caught sight of Ryan. He was such a good guy, and she obviously loved him. George hoped with all his heart that the two of them would have the future that he and Anna never shared. He hoped they would marry and have children and grandchildren and still go on historical tours together like that adorable older lesbian couple from this morning.

Wiping his dirty hands on his pants, Ryan headed toward them.

George eyed him suspiciously.

"What?" Ryan asked.

"You're wearing the same clothes you were wearing yesterday."

"Oh." He glanced at Cecily, who giggled. "Guilty."

"Interesting ..." George said. "And just what were you two up to last night?"

"Ah ... making up for lost time," Ryan said, attempting to be a gentleman with the delicate subject.

"We certainly did," Cecily said. George raised an

eyebrow at her, and she held up three fingers and mouthed "Three times."

"Now *that* is impressive!" George said, looking at Ryan. "I would high-five you if I had the physical ability."

Cecily laughed, but she also blushed. George took it as a sign that she did not wish to discuss her sex life any further, and he would respect that.

"Now go enjoy your lunch together," George said. "I'm sure you're starving."

Ryan nodded. "Thanks, George," he said. George knew he was really thanking him for helping him with Cecily.

"You're very welcome," he said, his heart filled with joy for his dear friends.

19

R yan and Cecily were seated at the same table at the Cedar Tavern where they sat together the last time. Everything felt different, though. Now they were officially together, and he didn't have to hide his feelings anymore. And he had George Hartley to thank for it.

Sitting across from him, Cecily drew in a deep breath and smiled. Ryan could practically read her mind. She was probably thinking about how much she loved this place, what with its old-timey smells of hickory-smoked meats and its colonial atmosphere. Hopefully she was also thinking about how happy she was to be here with him.

After putting in their food and drink orders, they settled into a comfortable conversation. Ryan regretted the time he'd wasted by not speaking up sooner, but it was better late than never. They were together now, and that was all that mattered.

"How's your day so far?" he asked her.

"It's been really good," she said, sipping her soda. "George and I had a nice talk this morning in the Music

Room. He opened up a bit more about Anna. And you're so right, Ryan. He's still grieving as if she died yesterday."

"Poor guy," Ryan said. He would never forget the image of George on his knees, sobbing in the throes of deep grief.

"I really think it's his guilt over her death that has kept him trapped all these years," she said.

George's words from that day in the church were also permanently burned into his memory.

I'm sorry, I'm sorry, I'm sorry ...

Sighing, Cecily said, "George is not optimistic about ever getting out of this place, but I'm determined to help him."

Ryan grinned at her, feeling proud. He knew she worried about being a spoiled rich girl, but she was anything but. Now she was a champion of the downtrodden, even if they happened to be dead.

"I just don't know how to help him understand that none of this is his fault," Cecily said, grabbing a piece of bread from the basket in front of them. She paused as she spread butter on it, then said, "My God, he would never put Anna in harm's way on purpose. He must know that, right?"

"He has so many regrets. So many what ifs. That's why he jumped on my ass for being so stupid when it came to you," he said.

She smiled softly. "You're not stupid."

"I was either stupid or a coward. Not sure which is worse."

Cecily reached over and took his hand. "You're human. How about we go with that?"

Ryan glanced to his right. "Remember how we said we're gonna be so cute together that we'd make people puke?"

"Yeah?"

"I think we've got our first victim."

Cecily followed his gaze and saw Adam Gallagher sitting

at his usual table. He was watching the couple curiously. She turned back to face Ryan and laughed.

"Nice," she said, squeezing his hand. She held onto him for a little longer than necessary for effect before letting go.

"I always thought maybe you two would hook up," Ryan said, hating how jealous he sounded. He had no intention of being a controlling, possessive boyfriend. He would just have to deal with his insecurities, and there were many. Dr. Adam Gallagher was super smart, which tied directly into his worst fear about his relationship with Cecily. He believed her when she reassured him that she found him to be intelligent, but still. As she'd just said, he was only human.

Cecily shrugged. "I don't know. I mean, I can see how on paper we would make sense as a couple. We're both scholars and all, but I never really thought of him that way."

"Well, don't start thinking about it now," Ryan said with a nervous laugh.

"Why on earth would I when I have you?"

Her sweet gaze reassured him. Both because he believed her words, and she seemed to know that he needed reassuring. She didn't judge him for it, either. She understood.

"Adam's had a steady girlfriend for as long as I've known him, so it wasn't worth thinking about. Besides, I was too busy watching you flex your construction-working muscles."

Cecily gazed at his biceps, and he resisted the urge to flex them for her. He didn't want to be *that* guy. Still, he appreciated her appreciation of him. The desire in her eyes helped his confidence immensely.

Their food arrived, and they took their time to enjoy it. Ryan was immensely grateful for the warmth and comfort of being in the company of his lover and his best friend.

After they'd finished eating, Adam Gallagher stopped by their table.

"Well, hello, you two," he said, eyeing them both with interest.

"Hi, Adam, how are you?" Cecily asked, greeting him with a smile.

Ryan studied her face and found only an expression of amusement and friendship. If she thought Dr. Gallagher was attractive, she certainly hid it well.

"It's going great. How are *you* doing?" he asked. Clearly it was a loaded question. Cecily rolled her eyes, which made Ryan laugh.

Turning to Ryan, he said, "You know, Olde Town has strict rules against employee fraternization."

Cecily drew in an audible breath, but Ryan rolled up a napkin and tossed it at the "good professor."

"Oh, they do not," Ryan said. "Besides, I'm a contractor, not an employee, so stick it."

Ryan stuck out his tongue and Adam laughed.

"Fair enough, fair enough," he said, looking back and forth from Cecily to Ryan. "Well, good for you both. You make a cute couple."

"We know," Ryan said confidently.

Adam laughed again. "Welp, see you around, kids."

He went off to pay his bill.

"It's fun being out and, you know, official with you," Cecily said, gazing fondly at him.

"It is. Although ..."

"What?"

"Just ... I don't know what my guys are gonna say when they find out, so be prepared for that."

"Duly noted," she said.

They each paid their bills. Cecily didn't make a ton of

money at her job, and Ryan knew she wasn't crazy about being dependent on her parents' money. He knew she still used some of her trust fund to make ends meet, but she didn't like paying for a lot of extras with money she hadn't felt she'd earned. A complicated situation, but an understandable one.

Once they got outside the restaurant, Ryan thought of something that could possibly help George.

"I keep going over the whole ... situation," he began. He glanced around at the crowded streets, taking care to avoid talking about ghosts and alleged murders too loudly.

"I'm listening."

Lowering his voice, he said, "What if we could somehow confront the woman I saw and see if we can get some answers? If this lady died in the 1880s in or around the Hartley Mansion, she must have been alive in 1835 when this all went down. Maybe she can help somehow. Maybe she pushed Anna, who knows? Either way, if George had somebody to blame for her death, maybe he could let go of some of that awful guilt he's still holding onto."

"Oooh, I really like that. I think that might actually work!" Cecily's eyes lit up with excitement.

"Trick is, how the hell do you nail down a *ghost* to confront them?" he asked a bit too loudly. He glanced around. Luckily, nobody was paying any attention to them.

"There's only one thing I can think of," Cecily said.

"And that is?"

"Go back to the Hartley Mansion really late at night. I mean, that's the only time she's appeared."

"You're right," Ryan said. "That just might work."

They walked back to the theater construction site before going their separate ways.

"I'll talk to George and see what he says. You up for it tonight if he is?"

"Sure," Ryan said. "If there's anything I've learned from George Hartley, it's that there's no time like the present to get stuff done."

Cecily nodded and then stood on her tiptoes to kiss him goodbye.

That's when the hoots and hollers and whistles from the construction site started.

Chuckling, Ryan mumbled in her ear, "Sorry."

He felt her chest shake with laughter.

20

───────

"Maybe this was a bad idea," George said to Cecily and Ryan when they came back to the Hartley Mansion at nearly midnight. They met up in the Great Hall, and George seemed agitated.

"Why do you say that?" Cecily asked.

His brow furrowed with worry. "It's ridiculous to have you both here at this ungodly hour," he said, his chest moving in a sigh without breath. "You guys work all day here, and you have to get some rest. And you have each other now. This is such a waste of time for you both."

"It is not a waste of time," Cecily insisted. "Helping you is really important to us both."

"Exactly," Ryan said. "You've been through enough. God knows you've suffered all these years, stuck here in the house. Us being here for one night is nothing."

"I don't deserve you guys," George said somberly.

"Of course you do. And you deserve to be with Anna."

At the mention of his beloved, his eyes perked up ever so slightly. Though it was almost imperceptible, it was there. A spark of hope. Cecily realized that keeping his focus on Anna was the key to helping him.

"So what exactly is the plan here?" George asked.

Scratching his chin, Ryan said, "Well, it all depends on whether this lady ghost shows up. If she does, hopefully we can get some answers. Most importantly, we might be able to find out once and for all what happened the day Anna died."

"Then maybe you can finally let go of the guilt that's keeping you earthbound," Cecily said. "And if that happens, you can finally move on to heaven and be with Anna forever."

"Maybe," George said uncertainly. He looked so tired. Cecily knew that as a spirit he didn't get physically tired anymore. This was more of a beaten-down, deeply emotional type of weariness. She couldn't fathom what it must be like to feel that way for so long. Thank goodness he had the option of vanishing when he needed a break from consciousness. No doubt that had helped him stay sane all these years.

"Let's go upstairs," Ryan said, and Cecily was grateful that he was taking charge to get things started. She'd been unsure of what to do. Going upstairs where the ghost had last been spotted made sense.

Of course that was also where she had been when Cecily got shoved down the stairs.

George walked up ahead of them; Ryan held Cecily's hand tightly in his. Even if the ghostly woman had vengeful ideas in her head, her spiritual form should be no match for Ryan's physical, living body strength. For so long, ever since she'd heard of his bravery in the carjacking, she had admired his strength. How wonderful it was to have him as her protector.

The three reached the top of the staircase and paused in the upstairs hallway.

George turned to face Cecily. "Are you okay?"

"Yes. I'm fine. Don't worry."

"I know this is kind of scary. I feel terrible for dragging you two into this mess. And I feel even worse about you getting hurt, Cecily."

"You didn't drag us into anything," Ryan reassured him. "We butted into your business."

George smiled weakly.

"You didn't hurt Cecily or Anna. But someone did," he said, his voice taking on a hard edge. "And I want answers."

"I understand," George said.

It *was* rather creepy wandering around this place at night. Cecily marveled at how different the mansion was now compared to daylight hours. The three of them stayed together as they searched each and every bedroom, which took quite some time. And they found nothing.

"What do we do now?" Cecily asked.

Ryan thought for a moment. "I don't know. I guess the best thing is to go downstairs and get comfortable. This could be a while."

"If it happens at all," Cecily said sadly.

"I really don't want you two stuck here all night," George said, shaking his head.

"You're worth it," she said, and Ryan nodded.

"Thank you," he said quietly. "You both mean more to me than you will ever know."

Once they got back downstairs, they performed a cursory search of the rooms on the first floor.

Still nothing. They stood together in the Great Hall, pondering their next move.

"Where will you be the most comfortable?" George asked.

Ryan glanced at Cecily, deferring to her.

"How about the Music Room?" she asked.

"Sounds good," Ryan said.

"I'll go turn on some music in my office," she said. "Be right back."

She left to turn on some classical tunes while Ryan and George walked over to the Music Room.

I hope this works.

The adrenaline of searching through a haunted house in the middle of the night had worn off, and now she was plain tired. She wished she had thought to bring some coffee for her and Ryan.

When she arrived in the Music Room, she found Ryan sitting on the couch and George at the piano. Cecily took a seat next to Ryan, and he wrapped his arm around her. She let out a soft sigh. She felt so safe with him. George smiled over at the two of them.

"This house really is beautiful," Ryan said, scanning the room. "No wonder you wanted Anna to come and live with you here once you got married. You know that doesn't make you a bad person, right?"

George eyed him wryly. "That's what Cecily said."

"Well, my better half is right."

He chuckled and said, "I suppose."

They sat without talking for a while, listening to the soft piano music coming from Cecily's office. She rested her head on Ryan's shoulder and even dozed off for a while. Maybe Ryan did too. She woke up to find George wandering around the room, seemingly lost in thought.

Yawning, she asked, "Did I miss anything?"

George shook his head.

"What time is it?"

"Almost 5am," Ryan answered.

Cecily sighed softly. Though she wasn't about to give up on helping George, she did wonder how many sleepless nights it might take to do it.

"I don't know, guys," George said, sounding tired and frustrated. "Maybe we should call it a ni—"

He froze suddenly, staring at the doorway of the Music Room. Ryan and Cecily whipped their heads around, following his gaze.

There was nothing there.

"It's you," George whispered.

Cecily sat up. "What? Where?"

"Victoria is standing in the doorway."

Cecily and Ryan looked at the empty space again then back at each other. She shook her head, and he shrugged.

"She's choosing to be invisible to the living, but I can see her." To the apparition, he said, "Show yourself. *Please*."

Ryan pulled Cecily close as if to protect her from the potential, if invisible threat.

Slowly, the image of an older woman materialized.

Cecily gasped. She stared at Victoria, more fascinated than afraid. The woman was dressed in the height of fashion for the time of her death in 1883. She sported a tightly laced corset over her bodice, and her skirt was adorned with fancy embroidery and trims. A deep shade of dark blue, the dress clearly had several layers. Cecily felt like she had traveled back in time for a moment.

"That's her," Ryan said. "She's the one I saw." He held Cecily tighter, his steely gaze fixed on the apparition.

The woman narrowed her eyes in Cecily and Ryan's direction.

"It's okay," Cecily whispered to Ryan, encouraging him

to loosen his grip so she could stand up. She felt rather vulnerable in her current seated position. He let her go, and they both stood, facing Victoria.

"You two are relentless," she said. "Just leave me be."

"Did you push Cecily down the stairs?" Ryan asked.

She smirked.

Cecily's blood ran cold. In that moment, she knew ... simply *knew* that Victoria had not only pushed her down the stairs but that she had killed Anna.

"Oh, calm down. I'm not going to harm your girlfriend again," she said. "It's too much work and effort anyway."

"So you admit you pushed me?" Cecily asked. Ryan put his arm around her waist, wanting to protect her without restricting her too much. She appreciated that.

"Yes. I sure did," Victoria said, anything but remorseful.

"Did you push Anna?" George asked, getting straight to the heart of the matter.

They held their breath for the answer.

Those who still had breath, anyway.

"What do you think?" she asked.

"I think you did." George's expression was a mix of shock and horror.

Victoria shrugged. "So what if I did?"

George stalked over to her. His voice shook as he spoke. "Enough with the stupid games. I want to hear you say it."

"Fine," she said with a smug grin. "I pushed Anna Hawkins down the damned stairs. And I would do it again."

Cecily gasped loudly, and Ryan muttered obscenities at the wretched dead woman.

"Why? Why?" George cried out.

"Because I was mad," the prim lady said matter-of-factly.

"Because ... you were mad ..." he said as if trying to process her words.

"That whore was only after your money. You know that, right?" she hissed.

Cecily scoffed out loud at that. Victoria whipped her head around to glare at her. Ryan tightened his protective grip.

"No, I think *you* were after his money," Cecily said angrily.

"Well of course I was. It was my *right!*"

"How do you figure that?" Ryan asked.

"Because we were supposed to get married. George was going to be *my* husband, and this would be *my* house."

"I— I hadn't even proposed to you yet," George said. "Our parents wanted us to wed because it made sense for their business interests."

"Right," she said coldly. "It made sense for everybody. What was so bad about that?"

George looked at Cecily and Ryan. He shook his head as if to say *how do I even begin.* Cecily understood exactly what he was feeling. George loved Anna dearly, just as she loved Ryan dearly. It was plainly obvious what was wrong with a marriage based strictly on a business arrangement. Even back in the 1830s people typically married for love. Gone were the days when you married for more practical purposes. Except when one's parents pushed for it, she supposed.

"I— I ..." George faltered, utterly overwhelmed with the knowledge he'd just received from Victoria.

After all these years, he now knew that Victoria had murdered his precious Anna.

"You killed her ... you really killed her," George said in a dazed voice.

"For what it's worth, I didn't really *mean* to kill her. Like I said, I was just mad."

"She was just mad," Ryan said through clenched teeth.

"Your mother had warned me all about the slut you were seeing on the side. She told me that's why you were dragging your feet when it came to proposing to me," Victoria said bitterly. "And then lo and behold, we all arrive at the house to find one of the slaves had let her in. She was standing at the front door like she already owned the place. So I offered to give her a complete tour of the mansion, including the upstairs."

"Dear God," George moaned.

Cecily's heart ached for him, being forced to hear the details of Anna's tragic death.

"I was angry and made a rash decision. Pushed her when nobody else was looking. Then the chowderheaded woman had to go and die," she said with a shrug.

Perhaps Victoria hadn't intended to kill her, but she certainly wasn't sorry.

I pushed Anna Hawkins down the damned stairs. And I would do it again.

The woman was plain evil.

"I was supposed to be the next Mrs. Hartley, not some pathetic farm girl."

An agonized groan escaped from George's throat.

"Why the hell did you hurt Cecily?" Ryan asked.

Victoria shot Cecily a look of fury. How odd it felt to be hated by someone she had never even met.

"I came back after vanishing for all these years and saw *her*"—Victoria waved dismissively in Cecily's direction —"cozying up to George."

"So you were 'just mad,' I suppose," Ryan snapped.

Shrugging, she simply said, "Yeah. Look, I committed murder. My ticket to hell is already punched, so what did I have to lose by pushing that other girl down the stairs?" With that, she shot Cecily a look of disdain.

"Jesus," George muttered.

"I'm a victim too, all right?" Victoria said, fixing her burning glare on George. "I was robbed of my destiny. Once that girl was dead, I figured everything was gonna be fine. We would get married, and that would be that. Then you had to go and get yourself killed."

Cecily stared at this woman, unable to comprehend what she was hearing. Both Anna and George had died tragically, and somehow she felt she was the wounded party.

"I'd say things worked out pretty well for you, lady," Cecily said, gesturing at Victoria's fancy clothes. "You clearly married rich."

"Please," she said bitterly. "My husband owned a few properties here and there. That was nothing compared to the Hartley fortune."

George stared at Victoria's clothing, indicative of a woman who had been quite well off.

"So you married rich, but not rich enough for your liking," he said in a pained voice. "You enjoyed a long and comfortable life, while Anna died so young."

She scoffed in his face. "Am I supposed to care?"

His phantom hands shook with rage. "You-you-you got to get married and have children ... and grow old ... and Anna ... An-Anna ..." George sputtered, so overcome with fury and heartbreak that he could hardly form the words to express his emotion. "Anna ne-never even got a chance to—"

"Is there a point to this? Because you're boring me, George. And considering my existence, that's really saying something," she said with a laugh.

Victoria's utter indifference to Anna's tragic death was so

much worse than her bitter hatred. Cecily couldn't imagine accidentally killing someone and simply not caring. She knew Victoria's attitude must be torturing George. She had no remorse, and there would be no comeuppance for her crimes. Not in this life, anyway.

"Look, she's dead. I'm dead. You're dead. Who cares anymore? What do you want me to say? I'm sorry?"

"Yes!" George roared.

Victoria startled at his response at first, then she laughed. Not just laughed—she cackled like a Disney villain.

"Nope, can't do it," she said flippantly. "I'm not sorry. That harlot had it coming. At least with her dead I didn't have to suffer the societal humiliation of being thrown over for a simpleton like her. Nobody ever found out you wanted her over me. With her dead I was able to go on and live a great life."

She did a little dance to show off her fancy clothes, which weren't good enough for her just moments ago. Now she acted like she'd won the lottery of life.

"I still remember what she looked like, lying all broken at the bottom of the stairs," Victoria said, her face sinister as she twisted the knife in George's heart. "Those pretty blue eyes closed forever, her blond hair all splayed out—"

"Stop!" George cried out, his expression one of sheer grief and agony.

"Okay, I'm done here," she said with a shrug. "Bye!"

With that, she disappeared.

George, Ryan, and Cecily stood, stunned by everything that had just transpired. Cecily's adrenaline had her heart pumping, and her whole being was filled with rage and despair. She couldn't begin to fathom what George was feeling. He no longer had physical hormones like adrenaline in his system, but she knew his emotions were quite real all the same.

He stood there for a moment. Motionless. Not speaking.

Slowly, he walked out of the room.

Cecily and Ryan exchanged worried looks and followed George. He walked through the back door of the Great Hall and out toward the garden. Cecily tried the door, but it was locked.

"Dammit," she said. She had a key, but not on her right now. She and Ryan ran to the front door and quickly raced around the back of the building.

Day was breaking. The sun was peeking through the clouds. The sky was colorful and lovely, but it was hard to be inspired by nature's beauty right now. Not when their hearts were so heavy and everything seemed so cruelly unfair.

Ryan and Cecily rushed to where George stood in the middle of the garden, but then Cecily put a hand on Ryan's back, stopping well short of him. Ryan stopped running too. They both wanted to be respectful of George's space during such a vulnerable time.

George visibly shook. Cecily felt utterly helpless as she witnessed her dear friend's pain. In the early morning silence, they heard his soft weeping.

"Oh God," she whispered. Ryan nodded grimly.

Sobbing openly now, George dropped to his knees in the midst of the garden.

Then, lifting his face toward the sky, he cried out one word that seemed to be ripped from the core of his very soul.

"*Why?*"

Cecily said softly, "I think we managed to make it worse."

21

―――――

Ryan rolled over in bed and wrapped his arms around Cecily, who sighed with contentment. The two of them had been inseparable since the day he finally told her he loved her. He could hardly remember what it felt like to sleep alone anymore.

Good thing it was a Saturday and they could sleep a bit after pulling that all-nighter at the Hartley Mansion. After snuggling together in the warmth of Ryan's bed for a while, Cecily turned around to face him.

"I guess I better get up," she said. She kissed him and then added, "Sorry about my morning breath."

He watched her get up and head toward the shower. Still lying in bed, he put his hands behind his head and took a moment to reflect on how lucky he was. Having Cecily here seemed so right. So natural. How easy it was to imagine his future with her.

Ryan hoped George was okay. He knew his friend had felt exactly the same way about Anna as he did about Cecily. He had planned to marry Anna and have a wonderful life with her. To have that happy future taken away in the blink of an eye was unthinkable. No wonder he still grieved for her after all these years.

He tried once again to figure out what he and Cecily could possibly do to help George. After last night, he feared Cecily was right and they had only made things worse.

By the time he heard her turn off the water, he still had come up with nothing. Reluctantly, he heaved himself out of bed.

Both showered and dressed, they figured it was too late for breakfast. Instead, they decided to head toward Olde Town to pick up lunch. First, though, they stopped by the mansion to check on George. Cecily unlocked the front door and they stepped inside.

"George?" she called out.

Silence.

She sighed.

Cecily walked into the dining room to search while Ryan headed upstairs. He was looking for Victoria as well as George. For all he knew, she had come back this morning to torture that poor man further. Shaking his head, he replayed in his mind all the terrible things she'd said last night. The wretched woman clearly had no remorse whatsoever for what she had done.

Much like that terrible day at the church, Ryan knew he would never forget the sight and sound of George in the garden at daybreak, crying out to a God that had seemingly abandoned him.

Why?

Why indeed. Ryan sure as hell had no answers for him.

Cecily was waiting for him in the Great Hall when he went back downstairs.

"He's not here," she said sadly.

"Maybe he just needs some time alone. We'll check back again later, okay?"

She nodded, and they headed off to get some lunch.

Since it was such a gorgeous day with a perfect breeze, Cecily suggested they get some takeout food and sit by the river. It was perfect, right down to the fact that they both ranked Chinese food as their favorite meal.

Their hunger—for food, anyway—finally sated, Ryan gazed at Cecily. The soft wind blew through her pretty brown hair, and she looked like an angel in the sunlight.

Cecily smiled at him, and he knew the look they shared meant the same thing.

I love you so much.

"I feel like this is something Anna would have loved, ya know?" Ryan said. "Just sitting by the water and eating lunch."

"You're so right. Like George always said, she loved the simple things. It's funny," Cecily said, gazing out at the water. "I never knew Anna, but I feel like for the rest of my life, when I see a pretty sunset I'll think of her and how much she loved watching the sunset from her porch."

"I love that, Cecily. Thank you." Ryan and Cecily turned to find George standing in the grass.

"Didn't mean to eavesdrop," he said. "And I didn't mean to sneak up on you. But that was so lovely, what you both said about her." George's voice wavered. "It's good to hear people talk about her all these years later. I don't want her to ever be forgotten."

"She won't be," Ryan said. "Not with us around."

"Join us," Cecily said, patting the ground.

"Oh, I don't want to intrude."

"You're not intruding," she said. "The only reason we came to Olde Town today was to check on you."

George sat on the ground between Ryan and Cecily.

"I know," he said sadly. "I was in the house this morning when you were there."

"You were?" Ryan asked, surprised.

He nodded. "Yes. I'm sorry. I just ... I wasn't ready to talk yet."

"I can understand that," Ryan said, and Cecily nodded her agreement.

George hung his head.

"I want to apologize for my outburst before," he said, sounding embarrassed.

"You have nothing to apologize for," Cecily exclaimed. "Are you kidding me?"

He lifted his head. "It's so stupid, I was so stupid."

"I don't follow," Ryan said. Cecily was right. He had nothing to be sorry for.

"Don't you see? That's exactly what I did last time! After Anna ... I ran out of the house, not thinking. Letting my emotions get completely out of control. Flipped out, jumped on my horse, rode out into a thunderstorm and got myself killed."

Ryan and Cecily exchanged a look of shared disbelief. It was so strange that George thought of it that way.

"My God, George," Cecily said softly. "You had just found out that the woman you loved was *dead*. Do you really think you overreacted?"

George blinked. He seemed surprised by her words. Ryan figured he'd spent so long blaming himself for everything that had happened, it was odd for him to hear another point of view. A perfectly rational point of view.

"I don't know what I would have done if that had been Cecily," Ryan said. "I just ... It's too horrible to even think about."

"B-but to just run away like that," George sputtered.

"She was already gone, George," Cecily said softly, sounding as if she were on the verge of tears. "What else could you possibly have done?"

He thought for a moment and then nodded hesitantly. "I guess."

"And why would you have wanted to stay in that room?" Ryan said. "Seeing her like that must have been incredibly traumatic. I ... I wouldn't have been able to bear it either."

George looked at Ryan and then at Cecily as if he were picturing the scenario in his head. Ryan knew George wouldn't have expected him to behave rationally if Cecily had been the one tragically killed.

Cecily shot a worried look at Ryan.

"We really hoped that finding out the truth would help, but I'm worried we might have made you feel worse," she said.

Ryan nodded grimly.

George's expression hardened. He certainly seemed to feel worse. Now it wasn't just guilt he had to contend with, but rage. Rage at a murderer with zero remorse. Worst of all, Victoria was *dead.* There was nothing anyone could do to exact any sort of revenge on her. She could disappear at will for God's sake.

"I cannot believe how badly I misjudged Victoria. All this time ... I thought she was this demure lady, this gentle woman who wasn't capable of harming anyone. Now I see she was a scheming social climber, worse than my mother or anyone else I knew in life."

George paused for a moment, and then added, "I don't know what to do."

"What do you mean?" Cecily asked.

"She killed her," he said dully, his eyes taking on a look of utter defeat. "And she doesn't even care."

"I know," she said with a sigh. "I was hoping that if we had someone to blame that maybe it would help you let go of some of your guilt over what happened. But now ..."

Cecily looked defeated now too.

"I keep thinking about when she said something like her ticket to hell was already punched," Ryan said. "Kind of makes me feel like she's staying around here on purpose to avoid punishment."

"Maybe," George said with a weary shrug.

Ryan realized George's rage had turned to depression. It was hard to tell what was worse.

"Strange," Ryan continued. "I mean, there's plenty of murderers and rapists in the world, and you don't see a lot of them still hanging around here. Like your father, George. He was a rapist, but he's not a ghost. I guess he crossed over and then maybe God sorted him out, one way or another."

George turned toward Ryan, listening intently to what he was saying.

Too bad Ryan wasn't exactly sure what he was saying. He went on anyway, trying to figure it out as he went.

"So maybe one day Victoria will move on to wherever, and God will sort her out."

"What's your point?"

Good question.

"Umm well, since there isn't anything *we* can do to get back at Victoria, we just have to trust that when she meets her maker, she'll get what she deserves."

"I guess," George said, sounding unconvinced. After reflecting for a moment, he said harshly, "That's not good enough."

Ryan and Cecily sat quietly, allowing George the time

and space to gather his thoughts. The sound of the rippling river was so peaceful, and a soft breeze cooled them. The ones that could still feel, that was.

A little time passed, then George spoke slowly and deliberately. "I am not okay with simply sitting back and waiting for 'God to sort it out.' That ugly, horrible, and sadistic woman literally got away with murder. All she wanted was money and power and a position in high society, and she got it. Sure, maybe she wasn't as prominent as she would have been as Mrs. Hartley, but she lived a life in luxury and comfort. All Anna wanted was to *live*."

George's ghostly hands quaked with rage as he spoke.

"I want her to suffer too," he said, his eyes blazing. "Victoria deserves that. She deserves to know what it's like to be poor and desolate. She deserves to live as a desperate nobody, in a low position in society where she actually has to *work*. She deserves to live with the agony and grief and anguish that I suffered all these years."

Ryan nodded. Listening. Understanding.

"But she never will, will she? I saw her around here now and again when she was alive. Everybody thought she was great!" George said, his voice rising. "She had servants at home, and I'm sure she treated them like garbage because it made her feel powerful. But all her friends and neighbors thought she was a *fucking pillar of the community!*"

The pain and anger in George's voice was pure and raw and terrible.

"And all along, she was a ruthless killer! She murdered the sweetest, kindest, most beautiful angel that ever walked the earth." A tearless sob wrenched from George's throat, while Cecily silently cried her own wet tears.

"And nobody remembered Anna even existed," George said, still shaking with grief and anger. "But everybody knew and loved Victoria for the rest of her days. Nobody ever found out who she really was. Why is there never any *justice* in this world?"

Ryan wrapped his arm around Cecily, comforting her as best he could while wishing he knew what he could do to comfort George.

And that was when the idea came to him.

He knew what he could do.

But it wouldn't be easy.

Ryan tenderly wiped away Cecily's tears with the back of his hand, she smiled gratefully at him. Then he pulled away from her so he could address George.

"You have to let go of your anger at Victoria before you can move on," he said.

George glared at him and shook his head.

Ryan understood. He *absolutely* understood. "How do you forgive someone who isn't sorry for anything they've done?" he asked.

George still seemed furious, but he was listening. There was hope.

"Victoria isn't sorry, and she never will be. Not as long as she still roams the earth as a ghost. And you're right, she got away with terrible things in life. She never got punished. And that is not okay and never will be."

George nodded sharply.

"Not gonna lie, George," he went on. "That seems to happen an awful lot in this life. Sometimes the bad guy gets thrown in jail, but all too often, the bad guy wins."

"Yes," George said, his expression softening. He seemed to appreciate that Ryan had no intention of bullshitting him or offering weak-ass platitudes. Sometimes life just sucked.

"It's incredibly difficult to forgive someone who isn't sorry. Victoria was so awful last night. I cannot imagine how hard that was for you to hear, George. But I'm really hoping this is one of those deals where it has to get worse before it gets better."

George shrugged grimly.

"But I think maybe the worst might be over," Ryan said. With a nervous glance at Cecily, he continued. "I know what it's like to forgive people who aren't sorry for anything they've done. People that got away with wrongdoing. And people that, given the chance, would do it again."

Cecily gazed at him with concern. George leaned in to listen.

"Cecily, you know some of this already but ... not the extent of it, I guess."

"It's okay," she said gently, nodding to encourage him to continue. The look in her eyes told him he was safe with her and he always would be. He wasn't familiar with that feeling, but he could sure as hell get used to it.

"When I was growing up, my parents always called me stupid and a fucking disappointment," he said, tired just thinking about it. "I always struggled in school, especially with reading. Cecily thinks I might have some kind of learning disability, I don't know."

George nodded kindly.

"They were embarrassed by me and had no problem telling me that on a daily basis. They gave up on me ever being smart enough to be a doctor or a lawyer, so they pinned all my hopes on me being a superstar athlete. I liked hockey, so they wanted me to make it to the NHL. Never mind that I had no interest in playing hockey professionally. I just liked watching the Montreal Canadiens and was a huge fan, and I liked playing on the side for fun. That's it."

Looking at George, Ryan said, "My parents were a lot like Victoria, I think. And your family. Very concerned about status. Keeping up with the Joneses, or the Tremblays ... whatever the Quebecois version might be."

Cecily laughed softly, and Ryan felt the love and support emanating from her.

"My mom wanted me to be popular in school, which I kinda was, I guess. She wanted me to be more successful than her friends' kids, but that was never gonna happen, believe me. So fuckin' hypocritical, my parents are. They both worked normal jobs. My mom was an administrative assistant, and my dad worked on cars. Nothing wrong with ordinary jobs, but why were they allowed to be normal yet they expected me to set the world on fire and become rich and famous?"

"Because they wanted to live vicariously through you," Cecily said.

"Bingo," Ryan said, pointing at her. "And isn't that exactly what Victoria was doing? All she wanted was to marry rich. What the hell did she ever accomplish on her own in life?"

"Nothing," George said bitterly. "Unless you count murder as an accomplishment."

"Right. She never accomplished anything *good* in her life, and she's still a bitter old bitch in the afterlife," Ryan said. That made George laugh, which gave Ryan hope. "She was basically a kept woman who leeched off her rich husband her whole life."

"Kept like a jewel in a case," said both Cecily and George at the same time, then they laughed. It was cute.

"When we were out in public, my mom and dad were the perfect parents, believe me. Everybody thought they were wonderful."

George nodded slowly, clearly understanding the parallels between their two experiences. It felt good to have someone else get how it felt to be trapped in a situation like that.

"They said the cruelest, most sadistic things to me behind closed doors," Ryan said, struggling to get through the worst of his tale. "My favorite was when they said they wished I had never been born."

"Dear God," Cecily said mournfully.

"It makes me ..." Ryan's voice shook as he spoke. "It makes me scared I won't be a good dad to my own kids."

"Oh, Ryan." Cecily put a hand on his shoulder.

"You guys will be amazing parents," George said confidently.

"Actually, we haven't talked about having kids or anything yet," Ryan said a bit awkwardly.

"Talk about it now," George said bluntly. "Do you want kids?"

Ryan and Cecily looked at each other and said "Yes" in unison.

All three of them laughed.

"But not yet," Cecily amended quickly.

"Right," Ryan said with a chuckle. "So the point is, George, to this day, nobody really knows the truth about my parents. To this day, up in Canada, *I'm* the bad guy. As far as my extended family is concerned, I'm the evil son who won't visit his parents on the holidays. And when I'm around any of those family members, I feel like I'm going crazy."

"Gaslighting. Isn't that what they call it these days?" George asked.

"Yes. Exactly! That's exactly what it is. My parents are terrible and abusive. Always have been. And they got away with it. Everybody in town and everybody at their church, they all think they are pillars of the community, just like

Victoria. There's been no justice, George, and there never will be. Not in this life. I've had to live with that."

"How?" George asked.

"It took a long time. I'm still angry. But as angry as I am and as angry as I always will be, I will not let those bastards control me anymore," he said defiantly.

"That's amazing," George said.

With a hesitant look at Cecily, Ryan said, "I— I've been to therapy. Like, a lot over the years."

She smiled and nodded approvingly.

"It was tough. So much garbage to wade through. My therapist helped me work through a lot of it. But as Cecily can attest, I still have issues I struggle with. Deep down, some days I worry that I really am stupid like my parents said. That's why—well, that's why I was scared to ask Dr. Rosewood out. She's so damn smart," he said with a laugh.

George didn't laugh. "That's rough. No wonder you took so long to tell her how you felt. Now I feel bad for pushing you."

"Don't. I needed pushing. And now I'm pushing you."

"I get that," he said, and Ryan knew that he truly did.

"You were really honest about what you were going through that day in the church, so I'm trying to do the same for you. I've been there, George. My situation might not be as tragic as yours, but I get it. And dude? That need for vengeance? It will eat you up inside, I swear. Some battles are worth fighting for, but you gotta know which ones you can win. I knew I would never win with my parents. They had the upper hand. They brainwashed my whole family, and that's why I left the whole damned country and started over."

"Well, I'm glad you did," Cecily said.

"Me too," George agreed.

Ryan smiled and then gazed fondly at George. "I know it sucks, but you can't win this battle with Victoria. At this point, it really is in God's hands now. Only He can mete out any kind of justice in this case. The way I see it, you've spent more than a hundred years feeling guilty about something that was never your fault. Don't spend another hundred years being angry with Victoria."

"That bitch isn't worth it," Cecily said angrily, surprising Ryan and George. She wasn't wrong. Then softly, she said, "But Anna is worth letting go of your guilt and your rage for. Forgive Victoria and let go of the hold she has on you. And forgive yourself. You and Anna deserve to be together."

"There's one more thing," Ryan said quietly. "When I still lived in Canada, one day Mom left her phone on the table after we had just finished lunch at a restaurant. I don't know why I even bothered to go out with her since she texts the whole time while we're eating. Anyway, I realized she left her phone on the table, and I grabbed it so I could run after her before she drove off. I just happened to see the most recent text message she had sent to my father about me. Seven words. Seven words that my mother wrote to my dad that are burned in my brain forever."

Cecily and George waited to hear the words that were so hard for him to say. He'd only ever said them out loud to his therapist before.

"Sometimes I wish he would just die."

Cecily gasped.

"I'm sure she meant those words," Ryan said. "Knowing her, she would have loved to play the grieving mother. People would feel bad for her, and she would get to act all brave while having a real excuse for why I was never around. I forgave her, George. I had to. I could never move on with my life if I hadn't. I forgave her for me and not for her. My philosophy is you forgive, but you never forget. You forgive and then you move on. I think forgiving is the key to you moving on. Think about it, okay?"

"I will," he said. And Ryan was pretty sure he meant it. "Thank you."

George looked at the two of them. "Go back to your lunch date. We'll talk again soon."

"Okay," Cecily said with a sweet smile.

George walked away, heading down toward the river. Cecily turned toward Ryan.

"That was so brave of you to share all of that. Thank you," she said, wrapping her arms around him. He closed his eyes, reveling in her warmth and love.

Yes. He was safe with her.

She was the warm, loving home he'd never had. And someday, together, they would expand their family.

22

———————

As George strolled along the river, he pondered Ryan's words. He deeply appreciated his friend for sharing the truth about his painful past with him, but he hated that Ryan had endured all that trauma with his family. Ryan was a good man, and he deserved so much better.

He couldn't imagine how hard it must have been for him to pick up and leave his own country and start all over here. His parents were the stupid ones. Any normal mother and father would be proud of the young man Ryan had become, what with starting his own successful business. And no doubt they would miss out on knowing their grandchildren.

Very stupid parents.

It's their loss.

Gazing out at the St. Mary's River, he thought over everything Cecily and Ryan had told him. Cecily wanted him to stop blaming himself for Anna's death, and Ryan wanted him to forgive Victoria.

Forgive, but not forget.

He understood Ryan's plan and the reasons behind it. He

knew he could never move on as long as he clung to resentment for Victoria. Ryan had every reason to resent his parents, and no doubt he still did, but somehow, he didn't dwell on it. He didn't wallow in it day in and day out because he had a life to live. And now that he was with Cecily, he had a life to build with her. Drowning himself in anger and bitterness over his parents' abuse would accomplish nothing and would only hold him back. George was certain of that.

But how could he possibly forgive that evil, smug woman who killed his precious Anna?

Because that's what Anna would want.

The thought came to him unbidden. For all he knew, it had come from Anna herself. Perhaps it was a message from her.

An unusual sense of calm swept over him as he looked out over the soft ripples of the river. Regardless of where the thought had originated, he knew it was true. Anna would want him to forgive. She'd always had a strong sense of justice, but that was usually out of concern for other people and not for herself. In life, she'd had weak moments when she was angry with God for taking away her mother. She was only human, of course. But she was able to let go of her anger so she could move on with her life.

The life she never got to live.

Whenever anger and thoughts of vengeance bubbled up again, he was able to quell them a bit. Ryan was right. Nothing could be done to get revenge on Victoria. Nothing could be done to her at all anymore, so what good would it do to hate her forever?

"I forgive you, Victoria," he said out loud. He wasn't sure he really meant those words, and he certainly didn't feel them. But it was a start.

At least if he crossed over now, Victoria wouldn't be there. That thought made him laugh.

George took his time walking along the river until he made it back to the Hartley Mansion. Once inside, he sat on the bottom step as he so often did.

"Help me, Anna," he whispered. "I'm so tired. For so long I wanted to punish myself for your death. And then I wanted to punish Victoria and make her suffer. Now I just want you. I want to be with you."

He closed his eyes and concentrated, trying to feel Anna's presence.

He felt nothing.

23

———————

Cecily and Ryan arrived at the Hartley Mansion a little after noon the next day. She sighed sadly when she saw George sitting at the bottom of the steps.

"Have you been sitting there all day?" Cecily asked him.

"And all night," he said wearily.

It had been such an intense few days that Cecily was a little surprised he hadn't vanished for at least a few hours to give himself a break from everything. Cecily was quite grateful for being able to sleep in this morning. For sure she needed an emotional break, and this was nowhere near as hard on her as it was for George. And probably for Ryan, too, for that matter. She was incredibly proud of him for baring his soul like he did, but she knew it couldn't have been easy.

"Why are you two here on a Sunday afternoon?" George asked.

"Checking on you," she said. "I thought we'd have lunch with you."

He furrowed his brow.

Ryan held up the bags of takeout food he'd brought. "Shall we go to the fancy dining room?"

"Might as well," George said.

Cecily and Ryan sat next to one another and George sat across from them.

"Do you miss food?" Ryan asked as he unpacked the sandwiches he had bought from a local shop.

"So, so much." George gazed longingly at their food. "I don't get hungry anymore, but yes, I miss it. I enjoyed food so much in life. It was something to look forward to every day, you know? Several times a day it was something fun to do. Enjoy your food and share a meal with friends or family. It is nice to share this with you, even though I can't eat. So thank you."

"It's our pleasure," Cecily said, feeling slightly guilty about eating in front of him but glad he was enjoying the company.

George looked around at the dining room. "I was really spoiled in life. We had so many delicious meals in here when I was alive."

"I'm sure you did," she said. Many times she had imagined the Hartley family seated around the table, sharing an elegant meal. How incredible it was that she could sit here with George Hartley! She still couldn't believe it.

"Anna and I could have had a wonderful life here," George said. "But I wonder ..."

"What?" Ryan asked curiously as he munched on his potato chips.

"Would we have kept the slaves?"

"Oh wow. That's a good question," Cecily said.

"I mean, please don't get me wrong," George said quickly. "Knowing what I know now, there's no way I would have slaves. It's unthinkable. But then? Right before I died, I'd just started questioning it."

Ryan and Cecily nodded in understanding. Understanding as best they could, anyway. In their lifetime, the idea of holding slaves had always been unthinkable.

"What do you think Anna would have done?"

George smiled like he always did when anyone mentioned her.

"That's a good question. I think she would have had a hard enough time getting used to having paid servants take care of her. I can't imagine she would be okay with having slaves here."

He glanced toward the doorway the enslaved men and woman used to come through to serve the meals they had prepared.

"Living here would have been quite an adjustment," he said. "She certainly wasn't used to all this space."

"You loved each other. You would have been happy anywhere." Ryan took a bite of his sandwich.

Cecily smiled at him. She loved how he always got straight to the heart of the matter. Of course he was right. She knew she would be happy with him anywhere. Some of the most fun times she'd had with him were sitting at his tiny kitchen table and eating dinner together.

The simple things were truly the most important.

George was quiet for a moment.

"What are you thinking about?" Cecily asked, knowing the answer. Anna. It was always Anna.

"I never got to dance with her, you know? As in formally dance with her."

"Like an old-fashioned waltz?" she asked.

"Yes," he said, his eyes lighting up. "As you know, we held fancy parties in the Great Hall. I would have loved to take her to one of those." George's eyes took on a faraway look. "Get her all dressed up in a pretty gown and show her off to everyone."

For once, he didn't look utterly despondent when speaking about Anna. There was a sparkle of joy in his eyes, and Cecily was quite heartened to see it. Perhaps he was feeling more optimistic about seeing her again.

"Dance with Cecily, Ryan," he said suddenly. "Promise me you will."

Ryan smiled. "I will, George. I promise. On my honor."

George nodded and smiled. "Good man."

After Ryan and Cecily finished eating and painstakingly cleaned up after themselves so as to leave no trace that they'd been in the dining room, they all retired to the parlor to talk.

"You don't have to stay here with me," George said.

"You say that like it's a chore for us to be with you," Cecily said. "We're friends, you know."

"Yes, I know. But both of you work here. It's not right that you've been hanging around here all weekend. You deserve a break."

"It's okay," Ryan said. "Really. There's been so much going on lately, with Victoria showing up and making everybody miserable, that we just want you to be okay. And Cecily's right. We're all friends here, and we enjoy talking with you." He laughed and then added, "I don't think she'll ever get over the fact that she actually got to meet the real George Hartley."

George laughed. "That's sweet."

They sat and chatted like old friends for quite some time, and it was lovely. Cecily picked his brain for details about his family for her book, and he seemed to enjoy telling her about his life. They weren't talking about the sad stuff for once. Rather, they chatted about his earlier family life with his sisters. Since both Ryan and Cecily were fascinated by history, there was never a dull moment.

Before they knew it, the sun was beginning to set outside.

"I can't believe I've kept you here all day," George exclaimed.

"Are you kidding?" Cecily said. "Talking to you is like free entertainment. And a free history lesson."

He smiled. "Still. You guys have got to be hungry by now. You ate lunch a long time ago."

"Yeah," Cecily said. "I am getting hungry, but I also don't feel like getting up. Doesn't get more comfortable than this."

Ryan had his arm wrapped around her, and she felt warm and safe and happy.

"The simple things in life," George said with a smile, gazing at his friends.

They sat in contented silence for a few moments, neither Cecily nor Ryan wanting to get up.

And that's when they heard it.

The sound of harp music.

The two stared at George, and he put his hands out to show his innocence. "Don't look at me."

They had forgotten to put music on to listen to while they talked. And there was nobody else in the house, that they were aware of anyway.

Then came the sound of a woman's voice singing like an angel.

"'Tis a gift to be simple ... 'tis the gift to be free ... 'tis the gift to come down where you ought to be ..."

George froze as he listened.

"And when we find ourselves in the place just right ... 'twill be in the valley of love and delight ..."

Cecily watched as his ghostly body began to shake.

"When true simplicity is gained ... to bow and to bend we shan't be ashamed ... to turn, turn will be our delight ... 'til by turning, turning we come 'round right."

George's eyes opened wide as he stared at Ryan and Cecily.

"It's her, isn't it?" Cecily asked, her voice barely a whisper.

In a state of shock, George slowly nodded.

24

———

*I*t's her.

Not only would George have known that voice anywhere, in any time, in any universe, now he could *feel* her presence. She was merely feet away, in the Music Room.

His ghostly body shook, unsteady, and he feared he would be unable to stand up and go to her. But then he was filled with a sensation of deep and utter peace and love, as if his entire being was made of light. Slowly, and as if not of his own volition, his head turned toward the door of the parlor.

Then he stood and walked or perhaps floated toward the Music Room.

George let out a deep, primal cry when he reached the doorway. There she was, seated at the harp, appearing just as he'd always remembered her. Anna wore a simple but lovely cotton farm dress, and her blue eyes sparkled even brighter than they had in life. He could smell the sweet fragrance of molasses cookies and oranges, the first scents he had experienced in over a century. He was utterly over-whelmed by the sheer essence of Anna Hawkins.

The room was bright as daylight, or even more so, but the light didn't hurt his eyes. Instead, he was surrounded by it.

Anna smiled at him.

"It's time, George," she said with a lovely delicate laugh. "It's finally time for you to come home with me."

He was dimly aware of the sound of someone sobbing in the room with them. It was Cecily.

George was still too stunned to move any closer, so Anna came to him. She enveloped him in her warm, loving, and purely angelic arms. He, too, began to sob, real tears that soaked the front of the outfit he'd worn since 1835.

"It's all right, darling. It's all right now," she said in her sweet, soothing voice.

He wept openly, as if releasing all the pain and terror and grief and desolation he'd carried all these many years.

"You're coming home now," Anna said.

"An-Anna ... Anna ... I'm sorry, I'm sorry, I'm so—"

"I know you are," she said, tenderly wiping his tears. "You needn't be, but I know you are. It wasn't your fault, my dear George. None of this was your fault. But you had to figure that out before you could come join me. Your friends were right. It was your strong and terrible emotions that kept you trapped here."

"My friends," George said, suddenly remembering that Ryan and Cecily were here.

He turned to see Cecily crying happy tears, Ryan smiling and rubbing her shoulders as he watched the glorious reunion. George rejoiced that they were here to witness the fruits of all their hard work.

Turning to face Anna, George said, "I'm sorry I made such a mess of things."

"Don't be sorry, my dear love," Anna said, gazing affectionately into his eyes.

George could hardly believe this was happening. Anna was here. With him. It was everything he'd dreamed of for as long as he could remember.

"I love you, Anna," he said, voice shaking.

"And I love you too. Forever and always," she said, stroking his hair.

How wild it was to feel that, to feel anything! All his senses were so heightened now.

"And I want you to know," Anna continued, "I have always, *always* been here with you. Just because you couldn't feel my presence doesn't mean I wasn't here."

"You were?" How many times had he closed his eyes, concentrated, meditated, and done all he could to feel any kind of sign from her? "Then why ..."

She smiled sadly. "Living people and those who have died but haven't crossed over have lots of filters to keep out heavenly things while they are here. You need them to get through life, to fulfill your purpose on earth so you won't be distracted by all the wonderful joys of what comes beyond this life. Some people's filters are not strong, so they can sense spirits, that kind of thing. And, perhaps somewhat unfairly, deep feelings like guilt and grief can keep you blocked from feeling anything spiritual."

George nodded, trying to understand.

"Once we get to where we are going, you will understand everything much more," Anna said, her eyes lighting up with love and excitement.

"Am I really going with you? Now?"

After all this time, he was afraid to hope. This might be too good to be true.

"Oh yes. You certainly are. And nothing can separate us anymore."

George let out a choked sob of relief.

"But first," she said softly, "you'll want to take a moment to say goodbye."

Anna gazed over at Ryan and Cecily, and George could actually feel Anna's love for them radiating from her spiritual form.

Squeezing George's arm, she told him, "You can touch them now."

George gasped, and Anna laughed with joy at his delight. She nodded, encouraging him to go to them.

He turned and rushed toward Ryan and Cecily, and they shared a warm, loving, and deeply enthusiastic hug. Cecily and George were both crying. Ryan was tearing up, despite his best efforts to fight it.

"Cecily ... Ry-Ryan. I can't thank you enough for ... I don't even have the words for ..."

Laughing, Cecily wiped her tears. "I know, I know. I do have the words, George. I love you. I'll never forget you."

"I love you too. Both of you," George said. Ryan wiped a tear and nodded. Then he grabbed George and pulled him in for one last hug.

"Love you too, buddy," Ryan said.

"I'll miss you so much," Cecily said. "But we'll all be together again someday. Right?"

She addressed the question to Anna, who nodded and smiled serenely.

"It is certain," she said.

"Go," Cecily said. "Be with her. You've waited long enough."

George smiled and turned toward his love. Anna spread out her arms, and then a big, bright portal opened up before them. Anna took George's hand and they stepped, together, into the great beyond.

25

It had been a few weeks since George had crossed over. Cecily missed him greatly but was overjoyed for his happiness. He and Anna deserved their happy ending, and she considered it her great honor to have borne witness to it.

Both Cecily's and Ryan's apartment leases were up soon, and they'd recently been looking for a bigger apartment where they could live together. It was funny how quickly they had fallen into step with each other after all that time of being too afraid to share their feelings. Now, it was as if they'd always been together. And always would be. Cecily was excited to spend the rest of her life with her soulmate, and she vowed never to take a moment for granted. George had taught her so much about life and love and regret, and she wanted to make him proud.

With George safely tucked away in heaven, they no longer spent much time in Olde Town when they weren't working. Instead, they went on lots of fun day trips that often included some type of historical element. How fun it was to nerd out with her boyfriend!

Tonight, they had plans to dine at a fancy restaurant in the next town over that they'd both been excited to try. The place had been highly recommended by friends, and it had been on their to-do list for a while.

After work at a construction site outside of Olde Town, Ryan planned to go home and get cleaned up for their dinner date. He'd asked her to meet at the Hartley Mansion, and then they could ride together from there to save time.

She saw Ryan's truck parked in the parking lot when she pulled her car into the lot. She was surprised he hadn't just waited in the truck for her to arrive. Maybe he'd gotten there earlier than expected and was waiting in the mansion instead of out in the summer heat.

Cecily walked down the path toward the Hartley Mansion, the soft breeze rippling through her hair. She felt like one of the Hartleys of old, clad in her delicate pink dress with a floral print. It was as if she was headed to a fancy soiree thrown by Penelope herself.

The door to the mansion was unlocked, so she headed inside.

"Ryan?"

"In the Great Hall," he called back.

Okayyy, she thought, wondering why he seemed determined to make her go out of her way to track him down. Soon enough, the reason became apparent.

She gasped when she caught sight of the Great Hall. The place was entirely lit with candles—*real* candles, not the fake electric light ones they normally used in the house. It looked just like it must have all those years ago when the Hartley family threw those elegant parties. As she so often did in this house, she felt as if she had stepped back in time. It was magical.

Ryan was decked out in a suit and tie, looking unbelievably dapper. Though she'd known he was going to dress up for dinner tonight, this was the first time she'd ever seen him dressed up all fancy. He was so handsome that it literally took her breath away.

"What's all this?" she asked.

"I promised George I would dance with you," Ryan said with a grin.

"So you did," Cecily recalled, breathless. She couldn't believe how lucky she was to have Ryan Armstrong in her life. This was like a moment out of a fairytale.

"Now I warn you, I don't really know how to waltz, but I learned what I could from YouTube. I'll fake it the best I can." Ryan walked over to a small speaker he had brought with him. He cued up a recording of a waltz and offered his hand to her.

Tears in her eyes, she took his arm. She felt like an old-fashioned lady being courted by a handsome suitor.

Ryan was surprisingly light on his feet, and Cecily was deeply touched to see how hard he must have worked on the dance. She envisioned him practicing in his kitchen, dancing alone or perhaps with a mop. The thought made her smile.

Together they waltzed throughout the Great Hall the same way countless others had done before them over the last several hundred years.

"This is for George and Anna," Ryan murmured in her ear. "And for us."

"Yes," she said. "George taught us not to take one moment for granted. And I'm grateful for that."

Ryan gazed into her eyes and said, "Me too."

When the waltz ended, she said, "That was so lovely."

"And so are you," Ryan said. "Dr. Cecily Rosewood, will you marry me?"

She gasped, astonished. Perhaps she shouldn't have been, but she was. Her heart was instantly bursting with joy. She could so easily imagine walking down the aisle with Ryan Armstrong. This was all happening so fast, and yet it wasn't too soon. Not for them. They'd only been together for a short while, but there was no question in her mind that she wanted to spend the rest of her life with this man. She could practically hear George yelling in her ear to say yes already. She nearly laughed at that thought.

Instead, she cried as Ryan got down on one knee and pulled out a ring from his pocket.

Through tears, she managed to say the all-important word.

"Yes!"

Ryan slipped the ring on her finger and stood up to kiss her. As she stared at the beautiful vintage-looking ring on her finger, she could feel Ryan watching her.

"It's so beautiful," she said, admiring the sapphire-encrusted gold ring. Cecily tore her gaze from her sparkly ring to look into his eyes. "I love you so much."

"I love you too," Ryan said. He offered his arm again so they could dance their first dance as an engaged couple.

Just then, there came a loud pounding on the front door.

Cecily's eyes went wide.

"What the hell?" Ryan asked.

She shook her head, having no clue who that could possibly be here on a Saturday night. Glancing at the candles, she worried it was someone from the Park Service. Needless to say, lit candles were prohibited in these old buildings for obvious reasons. But who could possibly know they were here?

The pounding stopped and then started up again.

"I'll check it out," Ryan said. "You stay here."

Cecily appreciated that Ryan wanted to protect her, but no way would she let him face whatever this was alone. She quietly followed him as he rushed to the door.

There was no peephole to look through, so he had no choice but to simply open the door. He did so cautiously.

There, on the doorstep, stood Dr. Adam Gallagher.

Ryan put his hand on his chest. "God, Adam, you scared the hell out of me."

"Sorry. Sorry! I'm really really sorry!" Adam spoke quickly, nervously. "I didn't mean to interrupt ... um, whatever this is ..."

Adam glanced at Cecily's dress and Ryan's fancy outfit. She expected him to make some crack about Ryan "cleaning up nice" or something like that. But he didn't. He seemed really freaked out about something.

"I— I saw your truck in the lot and thought you might be here," he said, his voice sounding shaky. Cecily had never seen Adam look afraid before. It was unnerving. "And thank God you are!"

"What's going on, man?" Ryan asked, clearly as bewildered as she was.

"I— I saw ... a *ghost*."

❧

Thanks so much for reading!

If you enjoy historical/paranormal/ghost romances like this one, be sure to check out my Gettysburg Ghost Series and my Williamsburg Ghost Series!

. . .

IF YOU JOIN my email list, I will send you any one of my books for **FREE**. It can be a ghost romance book or any other book of mine. Your choice! Visit lindafausnet.com to sign up!

Heartfelt thanks to you for reading!